Dear Reader:

Thank you for purchasing this book, a Strebor Books title that I believe will engage, entertain, and excite you as a reader. *Larger Than Lyfe* by Cynthia Thornton is a fictional account of Keshari Mitchell, a young lady determined to obtain fortune and fame at any cost... and there is always a cost. Love can make you do un-imaginable things and the right words can convince you to toss aside your beliefs, ethics, and morals to please another. Such is the case with Keshari. Once she realizes that she is in way over her head, she attempts to alter the parameters of a game that she never should have agreed to play in the first place. Droves of women are behind bars today after realizing that the stakes of love were way too high.

Cynthia Thornton has a wonderful literary career ahead of her and I am proud to present *Larger Than Lyfe* to my dedicated supporters.

Thanks for supporting all of the Strebor Books authors. You can contact me directly at zane@eroticanoir.com and find me on Twitter @planetzane, and on Facebook at www.facebook.com/AuthorZane.

Blessings,

Zane

Zane
Publisher
Strebor Books
www.simonandschuster.com

ZANE PRESENTS

LARGER
than
LYFE

CYNTHIA DIANE THORNTON

SBI

STREBOR BOOKS

NEW YORK LONDON TORONTO SYDNEY

U.

Thornton

SBI
Strebor Books
P.O. Box 6505
Largo, MD 20792
http://www.streborbooks.com

This book is a work of fiction. Names, characters, places and incidents are products of the author's imagination or are used fictitiously. Any resemblance to actual events or locales or persons, living or dead, is entirely coincidental.

© 2010 by Cynthia Diane Thornton

ISBN 978-1-59309-320-4
ISBN 978-1-4391-9846-9 (e-book)
LCCN 2010940491

First Strebor Books trade paperback edition February 2010

Cover design: www.mariondesigns.com
Cover photograph: © Keith Saunders/Marion Designs

10 9 8 7 6 5 4 3 2 1

Manufactured in the United States of America

For information regarding special discounts for bulk purchases, please contact Simon & Schuster Special Sales at 1-866-506-1949 or business@simonandschuster.com

The Simon & Schuster Speakers Bureau can bring authors to your live event. For more information or to book an event, contact the Simon & Schuster Speakers Bureau at 1-866-248-3049 or visit our website at www.simonspeakers.com.

7.99
2/14/13
SB

13899363

JG

FOR JASON AND DEVAN—
I love you infinitely, eternally, my 6'2" babies.
—Mommie

FOREWORD

The following fictional account is ENTERTAIN-MENT, no different than the erotic novel or the lyrical braggadocio of the hip-hop star. The closer that I came to completion of the entire publishing process for this novel, *Larger Than Lyfe*, the larger the moral implications of it all became for me. I did not want readers to believe that I was attempting to glamorize drug trafficking nor the gangster's lifestyle; hence, this foreword.

My primary goal for this novel, from the very beginning, was ENTERTAINMENT. My mission is to provide to readers with what so many of us LOVE…the gangster's story…because there are millions of us who are absolutely mesmerized by the danger, the intricate schemes, the unbelievable sums of money, the power, the corruption, the sex, and the bloodshed that are always associated with gangsters.

In every major city in America and in a few, not-so-major cities as well, a gangster's story exists. The gangster's story and his (or her) organized criminal affiliations and activities are as much a part of the fabric of this country as the dead presidents depicted on the currency that we exchange. Two, relatively new genres in the publishing industry called "street lit" and "true crime" were created to feed the fascination of those of us who love the gangster's story and a whole smorgasbord of authors in these two genres relish in feeding us what we love, from Nikki Turner's *Riding Dirty on I-95* to Mario Puzo's classic, *The Godfather*, to Teri Woods's series, *True to the Game*.

Scarface, *The Godfather*, *The Sopranos*, *GoodFellas*, *Belly*, *American Gangster*, *State Property*, and *Casino* are all well-known and highly successful films. The film industry has probably been the most successful at providing us with vivid, mostly fictionalized depictions of the gangster's story.

A multibillion-dollar, money-making enterprise has been created using every available form of media, from music to books to movies to video games, to feed the overwhelming fascination that so many of us have for the gangster story. We all know that what these people do is unbelievably, heinously wrong, but, just like watching the aftermath of a horrific car crash, we cannot seem to stop watching, reading and wanting to know more, as much as we can about what gangsters do, how they live, who they are.

Once I've fully engaged my readers' attention with sex, humor, drama, danger and luxe lifestyles and landscapes transpiring in the lives of some of America's rich, famous and infamous, my mission is always to drop some knowledge, to educate, to give readers mental "food" to turn over in their minds. My desire is to provide readers with some truth, facts, provocative topics for more serious and substantive discussions and debates and, quite possibly, progressive action once they've finished reading my book. For example: some of the most ruthless and most intriguing gangsters of all are members of our own government, past and current. Powerful figures who are connected, well-connected, and very well-connected in American politics have closely protected their own dirty, little secrets of direct involvement in organized crime— from the Iran-Contra scandal to Halliburton to the alleged affiliations of "Camelot's" patriarch, Joe Kennedy, to what is taking place in the Middle Eastern areas of Iraq and Afghanistan right now. There is enough material throughout the history of the United States and American government that exposes ruthless, deceptive, and completely illegal financial schemes and enterprises committed by powerful political figures or powerful men with powerful political connections to make blockbuster, gangster page-turners for years to come. You see, real gangsters do more than run drug rings, racketeering and prostitution operations in the seedy underbellies of major cities. Real gangsters have the power to affect the policies that directly affect YOU and ME.

Enjoy *Larger Than Lyfe*. There is definitely more to come.

PROLOGUE

Misha had given Keshari all of the fucking space that she intended to give to her. Enough was e-goddamned-nough. Misha knew that Keshari had been going through a lot over the past few weeks. Nix that. The past year had been a long one for Keshari. Keshari had some major, life-altering decisions to make. She had a mountain of demands to shoulder from one day to the next and it was a wonder that she hadn't burnt out or collapsed from stress and exhaustion a long time ago. She kept so much bottled up inside herself. Misha was closer to Keshari and knew her better than anybody else, but even she often glimpsed that solemn, distant look in her best friend's eyes and said to herself, "She's right here in front of me, yet she's so, so damned far away...like she's all alone in the world. I wonder what she's thinking about because I know she'll never tell me."

The last time that the two of them spoke, Keshari had told Misha that she was going to take a bit of time to herself to try and get her head together. She started working from home. She was taking very few, if any, calls. She wasn't accepting any visitors either. For the past week, Misha had called Keshari's house more times than she could count and, although Keshari's damned housekeeper could barely speak English, she could definitely crank out that "Mees Mitchell es unavailable," and then promptly hang up.

That morning, however, Misha had firmly decided to bypass the futile phone calls. She was going straight to Keshari's house and she was NOT leaving until she saw Keshari, made sure that her best friend was okay, and gave her a piece of her mind. If Keshari dedicated more time to her personal needs on a regular basis instead of putting everything she had into work, Misha planned to tell Keshari, she wouldn't be all holed up in that big ass house like she was Howard fucking Hughes! She knew that there was so much more to Keshari's situation than a constantly gargantuan workload, but she didn't even know how to begin to touch upon those things. So Misha would do what she had always done with Keshari. She would scold Keshari in the way that best girlfriends often did, in the trademark fashion that only Misha could do; she would act as if Keshari's situation was almost a normal one, with a solution as simple as Keshari "taking personal time for herself, chilling out, and getting some rest." Then she would end her admonishments by letting Keshari know that she loved her and that she would always be there for her in whatever way that she needed her to be…for ANYTHING. Keshari would come through her current situation just as she had courageously, miraculously come through so much else.

Misha got dressed and was preparing to leave when a messenger rang her doorbell. Misha quickly signed for the envelope the messenger held on his clipboard and ripped it open. It was a letter from Keshari. Misha read it as quickly as she could while juggling files from her office, invitation samples for an upcoming party that she was throwing, her purse, sunglasses, BlackBerry, and keys.

"WHAT THE FUCK?!" Misha exclaimed, realizing what was being conveyed in Keshari's letter to her.

Everything she held went all over the floor as she went racing frantically out to her car.

♪ 🎧 ♪

Mars was in his office when his secretary came to the door escorting a messenger delivering a package that could only be signed for by Mars Buchanan himself. Mars opened the messenger envelope and instantly recognized the pink parchment stationery inside. He closed the door to his office and sat down to carefully read Keshari's communication to him in privacy. He hadn't seen her in weeks, not since their break-up, and he had to admit to himself that he really, really missed her.

"Shit!" Mars exclaimed in shock, dropping the letter to the floor.

He told his secretary to cancel his schedule for the day, saying quickly that he had an emergency, as he went running for the elevator. A moment later, his Mercedes was speeding at 100 miles per hour up the 405 freeway to Keshari's Palos Verdes home.

♪ 🎧 ♪

Mars arrived at Paradiso Drive to a scene of utter chaos. Emergency vehicles were everywhere and emergency workers contended with television news crews arriving on the scene. Mars could barely get through the pandemonium as he pulled up outside the gates at Keshari's home. A reporter recognized him and rushed over to the car.

"Get the FUCK away from me!" Mars yelled, rolling up his window.

Sam Perkins, head of Keshari's security team, opened the gates and Mars's car sped inside.

"Sam, what's going on?" Mars asked anxiously, hopping out of the car.

Sam Perkins bowed his head and Mars took off running up the drive.

Misha was standing on the lawn, emitting the most chilling scream that Mars had ever heard, as a pair of police officers attempted to calm her. Mars went to her and she collapsed in his arms. Cold, frozen fear took hold of his heart.

"What's happened, Misha? Come on. What's happened?" Mars asked, hugging Misha and attempting to console her.

"She's...she's...she's...dead!" Misha garbled through her hysterical sobbing. "She's GONE!"

– 1 –

A caravan of black, customized Suburbans coasted swiftly up Alameda Street, across Broadway, and into Long Beach's deserted industrial section near the waterfront. It was almost 2 a.m. and virtually all of the shipping and manufacturing facilities in the area were closed down for the night, scheduled to reopen for their daily business around 6 a.m.

The caravan of expensive SUVs pulled onto the graveled lot of a white brick warehouse at the darkened end of Third Street. The driver in the first truck pressed the buzzer at the warehouse entrance. The warehouse's tall, steel doors rolled open. The caravan of trucks pulled smoothly inside. The doors rolled shut again behind them.

Four armed men, with the kind of muscular bulk acquired during lengthy stints in state and federal prison systems, hopped out of the front and rear vehicles and checked the warehouse's perimeter. After confirmation that the warehouse was secure, one of the men gave a signal to the middle truck's driver. The driver hopped out and held open the Suburban's rear door and out stepped Keshari Mitchell, tall, brown, exotic-looking, clad in black leather Chanel, with a long, sleek, braided ponytail and striking, almond-shaped green eyes. She strode with refined confidence over to the center of the warehouse where her business associates awaited her, her bodyguards watching everything around them as if they were protecting the President.

"Ms. Mitchell," Javier Sandovar said graciously, taking Keshari's hand, "so good to see you again. Why don't we get right down to business?"

Mario Jimenez and Oso Suarez, two of the bulky, tattooed men who'd accompanied Javier Sandovar, whipped five, large utility cases onto the table and clicked them open. Inside each of the utility cases were fifteen kilograms of 80 percent pure, Colombian cocaine. With smooth precision, Oso Suarez cut a small slit in one of the large, plastic packages of white powder. With the blade of his knife, he scooped out a small amount of the powder and dropped it into a tiny test tube. He added solution with a dropper to confirm that the product he'd brought was exactly what Keshari had come to buy. The mixture of the solution and white powder turned a bright blue.

"Very nice," Keshari said, removing a gold, Cartier cigar holder and lighter from her clutch. She clipped the cigar's end and lit it, exhaling a pungent cloud of the expensive, Cuban cigar smoke into the air. Javier smiled at her and nodded, pleased with her approval.

"Two million?" Keshari asked.

"Two million," Javier answered.

Keshari nodded to one of the bodyguards, who pulled two large duffle bags from the rear of the middle Suburban and brought them over to the table, unzipping them to display crisp, new hundred-dollar bills bound together in ten thousand-dollar stacks. Oso Suarez carefully went through each of the duffle bags to confirm that all of the money was there. He nodded to Javier.

"Very good, then," Javier said. "We'll see each other again in one month. The offshore accounts will be in place. Payment is expected upon confirmation of completion of each delivery."

"Of course." Keshari smiled, Javier kissing her on both cheeks.

"By the way, we have been following Mr. Tresvant's upcoming trial," Javier said. "Tell him that we send our regards and support. It is all most unfortunate. My family hopes that his current situation will not interfere in any way with our business relationship. Murder charges against powerful, Black men tend to draw federal attention."

"I assure you, Javier, and I ask that you pass my assurances on to the rest of your family. All bases are covered. We look forward to Richard's exoneration on all charges and a very prosperous future between our two organizations."

"Let us hope so." Javier smiled.

Keshari strode over to her waiting car and slid inside

while her bodyguards kept a watchful eye on Keshari's business associates and the product that their organization had just purchased. Two of them loaded the cases of cocaine into the front and middle SUVs. The warehouse doors rolled open. Keshari's bodyguards all loaded into the three trucks. A moment later, the caravan of black automobiles disappeared back into the early morning darkness.

-2-

Phinnaeus Bernard III was a prominent corporate attorney in Los Angeles legal circles, but, unbeknown to most, he was becoming as dirty as it gets.

It was nearly 11 p.m. in the underground parking garage at 300 South Grand when security guards, making their final round before the next shift took over, discovered Phinnaeus Bernard's silver Mercedes sedan, not in his reserved space, but at the bottom level of the high-rise office building's parking structure with the driver's side door ajar.

Sirens. Police arrived at the scene to find Phinnaeus Bernard inside his car with his brains and blood splattered all over the car's interior. He'd been murdered execution-style, a bullet to the head and two bullets to the chest, apparently with a gun that had a silencer since there'd been no reports of gunfire. Phinnaeus's BlackBerry was beside him on the passenger seat with a partial phone number entered as if he had been in the process of making a call. In the car's trunk, detectives found a large file case, Phinnaeus's laptop, and his briefcase. A substantial quantity of cocaine was in the file case and one hundred-thousand dollars cash was inside the briefcase, along with client documents and legal pads of notes related to an upcoming trial.

Phinnaeus Bernard III had been an astute litigator who had established an illustrious career defending and winning cases for multimillion-dollar, corporate clients who, more often than not, had some questionable corporate ethics; and Phinnaeus Bernard had died, leaving behind an extremely messy set of questions and incriminating evidence against himself that was bound to be one of the greatest scandals that his prestigious law firm had ever seen.

-3-

Keshari could remember the events surrounding the very first man that she'd murdered as if they had happened only moments ago. It was the first and last time that she'd ever used cocaine. She'd had to. She wouldn't have been able to do what she did if she hadn't.

Ricky had said that the man, her target, was a threat to the organization and that his termination was required and overdue. "This is a test," Ricky had told her, "and if you want all the way into this, you MUST pass this test."

That night, Keshari saw death with her own eyes... for the second time in her life. The blood splattered and she'd been so close that it went all over her. She could smell the thick, metallic smell of gunfire after pulling the trigger, and the smell still lingered so potent in her nostrils and memory despite all the years that had passed. She snapped her mind out of it. She hated when the hit that she'd personally carried out, the first of three murders that she'd committed with her own hands, popped into her mind out of nowhere and dominated her thoughts.

Keshari parked her Range Rover in the public parking

structure at Vignes Street, crossed over to Men's Central Jail, and went inside. She stored her purse in one of the lockers in the lobby. She was subjected to metal detectors by sheriff's officers. She was required to show identification and sign in. Then she was escorted to the visitation room to await the inmate she'd come to see.

She looked around her at the fluorescent-lighted, windowless surroundings with its metal tables bolted to the floor. Televisions were bolted high up on the wall on either end of the large room. Although she'd never seen any of the cell blocks, Keshari could imagine the suffocating frustration of the inmates locked away in this place. She had no criminal record, not even a misdemeanor offense, and she had Richard Tresvant, largely, to thank for that, but, in her line of work, she knew that she had been pressing the full extent of her luck for a long time and, eventually, that luck would run out.

Richard "Ricky" Tresvant was escorted into the visitation room from the segregated housing unit. Ricky was thirty-eight years old, six feet three inches tall, with long, lean, muscular legs and enviable six-pack abs rippling underneath his orange, inmate-issue uniform. His intense, brown eyes sparkled with extreme intelligence, charisma and danger, even after weeks of confinement in a jail cell. He was equal parts "sex symbol" and "menace to society" and it was this mesmerizing combination of attributes that had attracted Keshari to him when she was only fifteen years old. A whole host of factors kept her locked under his Svengali-like spell fifteen years later.

Ricky was preparing to go to trial for a high-profile murder that he was adamant he did not commit. His "dream team" of attorneys was working around the clock and calling in favors everywhere to ensure that he was exonerated once the trial commenced.

Keshari rose from the table at the rear of the room as Richard approached. She smiled and kissed his lips before the two of them sat down. The sheriff's officer who'd escorted Ricky to the visitation room joined the other officers at the room's control station. Keshari and Ricky were left in virtual privacy. Keshari smiled at him reassuringly. As powerful as he was and as effortless as it usually was for him to separate himself from his emotions, the fact that there was a large possibility that he would spend the rest of his life behind bars must have been starting to weigh on him mentally.

"How are you?" Keshari asked.

"How do you think I'm doing, Keshari? I'm about to go crazy in this shithole. Every day that I wake up here is like a fuckin' nightmare that keeps rewinding. When I find out who set me up…"

Ricky's eyes darkened. Keshari reached across the table and stroked his face, unable to squeeze his hands because they were cuffed behind him.

♪ 🎧 ♪

Richard Tresvant had painstakingly schooled Keshari to become the woman she now was. From the tenets of fashion, fine jewelry, cars, real estate, food and wine, art, architecture, right down to how to fire a gun, Ricky Tresvant could confidently claim responsibility. No matter how the world perceived him and the dangerous path he'd chosen in life, Ricky was clearly a genius. While he hadn't spent a day in school beyond high school, he was constantly reading, "constantly expanding his intellectual repertoire," he said, and getting very rich through high-stakes criminal activity that he rolled into completely legal enterprises.

Ricky had put Keshari through college at UCLA, where she studied economics and accounting and graduated summa cum laude. Then Ricky pushed Keshari to continue her studies and acquire her MBA from the Wharton School of Business in Philadelphia. All the while, she was flying back and forth from Philly to Los Angeles, earning her stripes in Ricky's operations, The Consortium.

"My organization will come to the table educated enough to make dirty money clean," Ricky had told her. "We'll show the world that crime really does pay. We'll know and be able to play corporate America's game better than they do and we'll build a billion-dollar empire without getting locked up in the process."

Richard Tresvant had seen something very special in Keshari Mitchell many years before, before she was even a woman, before she was capable of seeing anything special within herself; and he'd capitalized on and exploited all of her extraordinary qualities in more ways than one. Theirs was a very complex relationship. Love, business, control, and fear were intricately intertwined.

♫ 🎧 ♫

"Bloomberg will be here in an hour. The assistant district attorney and the polygraphist appointed by the D.A.'s office are also coming. The D.A. wasn't satisfied with the results of the lie detector test from the polygraphist I hired. For whatever reason, even though I hired a very highly qualified polygraphist with indisputable credentials, this asshole believes that the results were rigged…that I may have paid or coerced my polygraphist into rigging the results. I should sue this minimum wage-earning motherfucker for slander. "

"How much longer is it now before the start of the trial?" Keshari asked.

"Three more weeks. The D.A. has been pushing to move forward with the trial immediately. He's feeling confident of a win, but Bloomberg secured a continuance for further development of my defense case. The legal team is viewing the situation from a lot of different angles. They're telling me that there is a chance I may have to take a plea bargain. I am NOT going to jail for something that I didn't do!"

He broke off again. Fury over his predicament had him close to the edge of completely losing control.

It was just too difficult for Keshari to understand how Ricky could continue to vehemently deny his guilt when his fingerprints were at the crime scene as well as on the murder weapon. True enough, the results of the first polygraph test he'd taken had gone solidly in his favor, but Ricky was a master of manipulation. What if he'd tricked the polygraph test?

Ricky calmed down and promptly changed the subject.

"How'd everything go the other night?" he asked, referring to the transaction in which Keshari had purchased seventy-five keys of cocaine from their new, Mexican supplier.

"For the most part, everything went smoothly," Keshari answered.

"What do you mean 'for the most part'?"

"The Mexicans are very apprehensive about your current charges and the trial."

"I hope you assured them that they have nothing to worry about."

"I did," Keshari responded, "but I'm left to wonder if you're not being too cavalier about this situation. Despite your very powerful and well-placed allies, this is not your run-of-the-mill murder charge. This case is receiving a tremendous amount of media coverage. The Mexicans could issue hits on all of us to ensure that their interests are protected."

"Do you think that I would sit here and allow years of

work and millions of dollars of my money to be jeopardized without taking preemptive measures to safeguard against situations like this? You know me much better than that, Keshari. You're overreacting."

"You're under-reacting. Federal authorities could indict all of us any day now while this spotlight is all over you, or all of us could be murdered without a moment's notice; and I think that this murder charge has you too overwhelmed to see that that's a greater probability for us now than it has ever been."

"That is the nature of this business, Keshari. Now…I need liquidation of this product that's scheduled to arrive within one month after its delivery," Ricky said, dismissing Keshari's concerns. "Winning this trial is not going to come cheaply. Oh, by the way, I've been doing some reading on waterfront condominium developments down in Florida. Miami Beach. Get with Strauss and do some shopping. I want to fly down and get my feet wet as soon as this trial is over. I'll pick up a few units, get the contractor and my interior design people in to upgrade the amenities, and then I'll flip 'em for twice the purchase price. I may even eventually join the roster as a developer myself."

Keshari stared at Ricky incredulously as if he had lost his arrogant mind. He vacillated from barely controlled fury over what he claimed was a trumped-up murder charge to cool over-confidence about its outcome. She couldn't keep doing this.

"R, there's something that I've been needing to talk

to you about and I can't continue to put it off. It's the main reason I came today."

"What?" Ricky asked, noticing that Keshari was growing increasingly tense.

She stared down at the huge, Tahitian black pearl on her right hand with its spray of flawless, pave diamonds that cascaded over the pearl and around the band. It had been a gift from Ricky. She hesitated before continuing.

"R, I've been doing some thinking…a whole lot of thinking…and…I…I don't want to do this anymore."

"You don't want to do what?" Ricky questioned.

"THIS…The Consortium…I don't want to do it anymore."

Ricky tilted his head to one side as if looking at Keshari from a different angle might make her look like she had not taken complete leave of her good sense.

"Are you out of your fucking mind?!" he snapped venomously, loud enough to draw the sheriff's officers' attention. The officers looked ready to head in their direction to assess the situation.

Ricky lowered his voice to an angry whisper.

"You mean to tell me that, with all the shit that I have raining down on me right now, you are going to come in here with some shit like this?! I'm in here facing a first-degree murder charge. This is not some corporation where you can just submit your resignation when you no longer like the company's politics. You are in this for the duration."

Keshari was silent. Ricky glared at her furiously, like he might attempt to physically attack her. Then he just as quickly calmed himself. His mind ticked away in calculation.

"You remember when you put me on? My mother had just passed. I didn't give a damn about anyone or anything…not even myself. You were there for me. I didn't have anybody except for you and Misha. You understood me. You taught me everything I know. Everything you did seemed so exciting to me back then and I wanted to be a part of it. My life and my mind are in a different place now and I have got to get out of this business."

"Let me tell you something," Ricky said. "With the exception of your mother's passing, I don't give a fuck about any of that shit you're talking about now. I groomed you to take the position you now hold in this organization. You are the most powerful woman in the United States. I made you that and this is the repayment I get?! When loyalty and commitment are lost at the top of this organization or any other, it trickles all the way down. I love you and you better always know that, but I will off you and anybody else who seriously jeopardizes my business."

"So, you're threatening me now?" Keshari asked.

"You know me far better than that, Keshari," Ricky responded. "I don't issue threats."

"You know what?" Keshari said. "This was patently bad timing to bring up this subject…just like you said.

After the trial, when all of this has calmed down, we can sit and discuss it again and come to an amicable compromise."

"There will NEVER be a right time to broach this subject again, Keshari. This is a blood in-blood out commitment that you made. Now, I don't know what happened between your meeting with Machaca the other night and you coming here today, but what I do know is that I've got eighty million dollars worth of work arriving in three weeks and you had BETTER get your head back in this business well before that time."

Ricky shook his head in disbelief.

"You are second in command in this organization. Surely, you have not gone and forgotten just how very deeply that ties you into this game. Your first obligation will ALWAYS be to me and to the business affairs of The Consortium. Do you understand me?"

Keshari didn't answer him. She glared at him angrily, wanting to just get up, walk out, and take her chances with whatever happened after that.

"I go to trial in three weeks and, at the same time, we are scheduled for delivery," Ricky said. "This is not the time for you to decide to grow some kind of a moral compass, get all self-righteous and careless, and make a foolish mistake where my money is concerned."

Ricky got up from the table.

"You'd better handle my shit, Key! Then take yourself over to Raffinity or Cartier, pick yourself out something nice, charge it to my account, and forget this little discussion that you initiated today…for your own good. The only way that you'll terminate your obligations to The Consortium is in a body bag."

Ricky signaled the sheriff's officer and was escorted out to a holding room to await the arrival of his attorney and the D.A.

4

Keshari arrived at her Century City offices following her visit with Ricky and told her assistant to hold all of her calls. She definitely needed some time to regroup after what she'd just done.

Shutting herself away in her huge, plush inner sanctum, Keshari sat at her desk and stared pensively out her thirtieth-story window at the expanse of Century City and the surrounding West Los Angeles area. She shook her head and laughed to herself at the irony of it all. Richard Tresvant had killed people and had ordered people killed without losing a night's sleep...and would probably attempt to kill her, whether she liked facing that reality or not, but if she had it to do all over again, she would have told Ricky the very same thing that she'd just told him that day. She wanted OUT...out of The Consortium, out of the life, out of the game.

♫ 🎧 ♫

The *SOURCE* magazine did a cover story on Keshari Mitchell at the beginning of her career, titled "The Greatest of All Time?" In a black, pinstriped Armani suit and red Everlast boxing gloves, the new kid on the block in the music industry was stunning.

Five years later, Keshari Mitchell was thirty years old and Larger Than Lyfe Entertainment, which she founded, was a $300 million entertainment company…no longer merely a record label…specializing in hip-hop and boasting representation of a steadily building list of certified platinum artists. Young, beautiful, gifted and Black, Keshari had appeared on the scene out of nowhere and, in a very short time, had become an indomitable force. Her goal from the very beginning was to take the art form of hip-hop that she loved so much and turn it into a mega financial enterprise that was owned and controlled by the very same people who wrote, produced, performed, originated, and developed it—Black folks; and she built from the ground up the first major record label in history solely owned and controlled by an African-American WOMAN.

Most record labels are owned by stockholders and controlled by a board of directors. Keshari Mitchell was the "stockholder" and "board of directors" for Larger Than Lyfe Entertainment. Not since Berry Gordy and Motown had anyone done what Keshari Mitchell did. When Larger Than Lyfe Entertainment's debut artist's CD hit record stores, the entire music industry could only stand back and watch in collective daze and amazement as Keshari Mitchell and her very appropriately named record label made their meteoric rise to the top. Within weeks, her debut artist's CD, Rasheed the Refugee's *Land of the Lost*, was certified platinum. Weeks later, the label's second hip-hop artist, T.E.N., dropped his album and immediately went platinum. The woman had the Midas touch.

Keshari was a perfectionist and a workaholic who went from twelve- to fourteen- to eighteen-hour days in her never-ending quest to be the best in the business. Contract negotiations, album release deadlines, artist promotion, concert tour schedules, and meetings with a host of attorneys and accountants to discuss, allocate, and grow more legal money than she'd ever anticipated dealing with over an entire lifetime were only the beginning of her rigorous day-to-day activities. Publishing rights, ownership issues, artist management, music production, public relations, flights back and forth to cities all over the country for business meetings as many as ten times in a single month, all while sheltering her intensely private personal life from the vulture-like scrutiny of the media were whole other feats onto themselves. But Keshari was not averse to the challenge of such immense responsibility. Larger Than Lyfe had been a huge dream for her for as long as she could remember and she couldn't think of a better feeling than going to work every day and seeing the tangible results of her dream. She was what success stories were all about. She was a little girl from South Central Los Angeles who'd become the New Millennium version of the "American Dream."

For a moment, Keshari's contemplative, green eyes

took in and savored the magnificent, 180-degree view that her office's ceiling-to-floor windows afforded her. The mazes of glass and concrete buildings surrounding her and the Downtown Los Angeles skyline in the distance were marvels that never ceased to amaze her. Millions and millions of dollars exchanged hands daily, hourly, in all of these tall buildings and she was a part of it all. The next moment, Keshari's gaze grew grave. For the past few weeks, she had been closely examining EVERY-THING about her life and wanting to extricate herself from the worst parts of it. When her mind drifted in this way, her thoughts always turned to her mother and she was consumed by the intense mix of emotions she always felt when she thought of her—love, hate, and wondering what her life might be like if her mother was still alive.

She knew that her mother would be immensely proud of her for her tremendous success with her record label. She also knew that it would break her mother's heart to know of her daughter's involvement in the very criminal enterprises that destroyed so many lives and so many communities. She must be spinning in her grave right now, Keshari thought, at some of the things that Keshari had done and had played a part in as a member of The Consortium.

Keshari's whole life was about to change. Something at the very core of her told her that. She was the only woman who Richard Tresvant had probably ever trusted and, with her visit to him that day and the revelation that she'd made, she had betrayed him. Despite his current troubles, Ricky was not going to just dismiss that and there was no way for Keshari to know what nor when the repercussions would be.

Most gangsters who decided to walk away from the game wound up dead. They were risk factors…very large and very expensive risk factors. Keshari knew this and she was going to have to rely on the entire history of her relationship with Ricky to walk away from the game herself in one piece.

The mechanical buzz of her intercom broke the silence, interrupting her thoughts. Keshari spun around to face the small console on the corner of her glass and chrome desk.

"Andre is here," Terrence Henderson, her executive assistant, announced.

"Thanks, T," Keshari answered. "Send him in."

The intercom clicked off and she was left again in silence. She checked her makeup in the Tiffany compact lying on her desk, touched up her already flawless lips, and then ran a hand through her tousled, shoulder-length curls. She took a deep breath and put her mind fully into the mode of record label executive in preparation for her meeting.

-5-

"We'll hold auditions in ten major U.S. cities. Selection of the cities is based upon nationwide record sales from our quarterly reports from SoundScan. Here's the current quarterly report. The audition cities will be as follows: Los Angeles, New York, Atlanta, Miami, Chicago, Memphis, Detroit, Houston, Philadelphia, and Washington, D.C. I've already compiled a potential list of audition venues for each of the ten cities. My team will move to lock down the venues as soon as we receive the green light on this project.

"We'll conduct auditions in the first city for two days, break, and then hit the next city, selecting ten semi-finalists in each city, hyping the project with a huge media blitz as we go, our camera crew covering the highlights of the auditions. Then we'll return to L.A. for a mega-event, televised, grand finale competition of all of our semi-finalists.

"TV viewers nationwide will have the opportunity to participate by voting for their favorite performers to determine the ten finalists. An all-star panel of judges will critique and, ultimately, select the grand prize winner. One grand prize winner will receive a one million-dollar recording contract with Larger Than Lyfe Entertainment. Plus, we'll have the option to sign any or all of the remaining finalists. This will be the new artist recruitment campaign of the millennium!"

♪ 🎧 ♪

Andre DeJesus was director of promotions at Larger Than Lyfe Entertainment. As director of promotions, Andre was responsible for the creation, management and structuring of budgets for such LTL projects as concert tours, national and local promotional contests, new artist publicity campaigns, and many other special projects designed to bring consumer, industry, and media attention to LTL artists and the LTL label. Everything from billboards to listening parties typically had the involvement of Andre and his team, often in conjunction with LTL's public relations executives, legal counsel and the A & R department. Andre had requested a one-on-one meeting with Keshari that day to present her with the details for his latest brainstorm, a nation-wide talent search.

"Key, this talent search project is going to launch LTL to a whole new height in the stratosphere. No other record label in the history of the music business has ever done anything like this. You've said since LTL's inception that you wanted to eventually delve into the R & B and jazz genres. This talent search could be the launch pad for you to do exactly that."

"Yeah, I think you might be onto something," Keshari mused.

She drummed her fingers on the table while she turned the idea over in her mind a few times. She smiled and Andre knew that he almost had her.

"I'm fully prepared to pitch the project to Stanley Schuller over at MTV. The goal, taking our timeline into consideration, is to secure us a spot for broadcast next fall. MTV will easily hit our targeted demographic."

"If I do this, I want to do it with Cassandra Harrington. She has a new network, VIBE Network."

"You know the risks involved in doing a project of this caliber with a substantially smaller, relatively un-known network. Even with corporate sponsorship, this is out of her league."

"We're talking about Cassandra Harrington here, Andre. She's the most powerful African-American in radio…and she's diversified into television. This would be a phenomenal opportunity for collaboration between two of the most powerful, Black businesswomen in the country. You and I both are abundantly aware of the history of a very precarious friendship between MTV and hip-hop, particularly TRUE hip-hop. From its earli-est phase up to this very day, MTV has shown consistent reluctance to broadcast our music and, if I proceed with a project of this magnitude, I intend to send a message. We're going to keep this one BLACK and I want to do it with Cassandra Harrington. Now, let's get back to the budget for this thing. How much are you talking?"

"Page fifteen," Andre said, directing Keshari to the professionally prepared binders that he'd arranged to have assembled for their meeting.

Keshari put on her reading glasses and scanned the lengthy list of meticulously organized itemizations until she reached the bottom line on the fifteenth page.

"Twenty million dollars, Andre? Fuck, most movie budgets are not this large."

Andre chuckled. "Remember, this is a year-long promotional and recruitment project. That kind of undertaking does not come with a small price tag."

"Yeah, and since this record label's doors opened, we've never put this much money into a single project. I'm not going to hop in with both feet without looking at things from every angle."

"Of course, this project can be done cheaper, Keshari. You know that and I know it. There are numerous areas where we could cut corners and narrow the budget… possibly by as much as five million, but it would not be a true reflection of Larger Than Lyfe Entertainment's image. As far as the public and the music industry are concerned, we are the top of the food chain and we've got a reputation to uphold. Now, if it's any consolation to you, I submitted the budget for this project to accounting for a prelim review. The findings of that review are on page thirty. Accounting appears to believe that I did a very satisfactory job. I didn't leave a stone unturned. From airfares to advertising to venue rentals, all of it has been calculated into the budget. I put months of work and rework into this before ever bringing it to you."

Keshari flipped through the binder and skimmed accounting's notations.

"I'm gonna review all of this for a couple of days. Are you prepared to go to press release?"

"You bet," Andre answered.

"You haven't told anyone else about this project, have you?"

"Come on. You know me better than that. Of course not. I'm as concerned about the risk of a leak on a project this major as you are."

She reached over to the console and buzzed her assistant.

"T, what's my schedule look like this Saturday?"

"The first half of your day is clear," Terrence said. "Anything else?"

"No, thanks."

She tapped the console off again.

"I want you to come up to the house on Saturday. Nine o'clock. I'll have made a firm decision by then. In the meantime, I want you to fine-tune the details of the proposal to get ready to pitch to Alton Harrington over at VIBE Network. He's Cassandra Harrington's son and the chairman of the network."

"Sounds like you've already made a firm decision," Andre said, smiling confidently.

"I really like your idea. I know where we can take it… particularly with this enormous budget…and I know what it will mean overall to this record label. But I need to be sure of what I'm getting into, so don't go popping that bottle of champagne just yet." Keshari smiled back at him.

She looked down at her watch. The two had been in discussion for almost two hours.

"Shit! I've got to get out of here. Is there anything else that we need to cover?"

"We can certainly cover anything that I missed on Saturday. I'll see you at Rasheed's party tonight," Andre said.

Keshari tapped the console on her desk and rang the garage. "Mario, bring my car around. I'm on my way down."

—6—

Misha Tierney keyed in the access code at the entrance to Keshari's home. The gate sealing off the mansion's entrance slid open, Misha waved to the two guards at the security office, then her silver BMW convertible cruised smoothly up the winding drive to the front of Keshari's $9 million, Mediterranean-style home. The house sat high atop the cliffs of Palos Verdes, obscured from the view of passersby in front and wide open in back to a spectacular view of the Pacific Ocean and boats sailing to Catalina Island in the distance.

Misha grabbed a garment bag and makeup case from her trunk and went into the house. Keshari sat on the floor in the large, glass-domed solarium, engaged in discussion with her record label's accounting department over the speakerphone. A slew of papers were scattered around her and her open briefcase. She waved to Misha as Misha bounded up the staircase at the end of the foyer. "Marcus Garvey" and "Hannibal," Keshari's two purebred Rottweilers, were at her heels.

♪ 🎧 ♪

Keshari and Misha Tierney had been the very best of friends for more than fifteen years. They'd grown up together, living in houses right next door to each other in the Leimert Park section of Los Angeles. Keshari was an only child and Misha became the sister she'd always wanted. The two girls were inseparable from the day they'd met when they were just starting seventh grade at Audubon Middle School.

Keshari was new to the neighborhood and Misha introduced her to all of her friends. Misha was the social butterfly of the two and Keshari quickly earned the reputation as "the brain." Misha was always something of a bossy know-it-all. Keshari was very strong-minded and obstinate when she'd made up her mind and wasn't having any of it. The two girls fought and sometimes wouldn't speak to each other for days, but they always made up. They were fiercely protective and supportive of one another as only sisters could be.

Keshari became a permanent fixture in Misha's household and, as she grew up, Misha's older brother, Ricky, began to take notice of his baby sister's friend. Some people have a certain aura about them, a charisma, something extremely special that even complete strangers seem to recognize and Keshari had that in a big way. Add her unexpected, green eyes in her flawless, brown skin and the fact that she seemed completely incognizant of what a stunningly beautiful, young woman she was growing into and Keshari was a force to be reckoned with even then.

Ricky was calculating and smooth in the way he went about inserting himself into her life. While he did not pursue her sexually, he did begin to take greater interest in Keshari's interests and introduce her to new things. He brought her books and suggested jazz and conscious hip-hop that he thought she would like. Misha was smart enough to see what was transpiring and she hated Ricky for what he was doing. Misha's brother was nearly ten years older than Keshari and he was a womanizer. He didn't care about anybody except himself and he was just biding his time until Keshari turned eighteen so that he could fuck her up in more ways than one. He'd been the black sheep in the family almost from the day he was born and Misha didn't want to see her best friend get hurt.

Misha implemented every weapon of distraction that she could to keep Keshari and Ricky's peculiar relationship at bay, but, with teenage hormones raging, combined with the thrill of having an older man like Ricky interested in her, Keshari was drawn to Misha's brother like a moth to a flame.

Misha was well aware of the fact that her best friend had eventually gotten caught up in her brother's illegal business dealings. When Keshari's mom passed away, Keshari seemed, for a period of time, to be hell-bent on trying to kill herself. Misha did everything that she could to sway Keshari away from "the game" and when she couldn't, Misha couldn't bring herself to judge Keshari too harshly. Keshari had lost so much in her life at such a young age and she'd made some very self-destructive decisions because of it and because of Misha's brother.

Misha Tierney's love for Keshari was unconditional. If there was any person in the world who Keshari knew would ride or die for her, she knew unequivocally that Misha Tierney was that one.

♪ 🎧 ♪

"What's up, girl?" Misha asked when Keshari joined her in the master suite's bath.

"There's not enough hours left in this day to cover all the shit that's going on in my life right now."

She sat down on the edge of the sunken whirlpool tub and proceeded to run herself a bath. She glanced over at Misha as she shook tea salts into the water and shook her head. Misha had stripped down to her bra and panties. She had Thaa Dogg Pound on the CD changer in the bedroom and the music was blasting. She'd pinned her wrapped-straight, gold-highlighted, brown hair on top of her head and stood in front of the mirror over one of the dressing room sinks, applying an avocado mask to her face while shimmying her perfect size 6 ass to the music.

"I am exhausted," Keshari said. "Feels like I haven't slept in a week. Add the fact that I think I'm about to give the green light to proceed on the biggest, single project that Larger Than Lyfe has ever done, and a meltdown has got to be just around the corner."

"Girl, please. You wouldn't know what to do with yourself if you weren't working your tail off for that record label," Misha said. "Exhaustion ceased to exist in your vocabulary probably your second year into this gig. You'll be okay. What's the project?"

"We're about to do a televised, nationwide talent search. I meet with Andre again about it this weekend and we're sure to go to press release in the next few days."

"Damn! That is major."

"Yeah...twenty million dollars major, and we're pitching the project to Cassandra Harrington and VIBE Network to pick it up. Let's just hope it's not the one project that I live to regret. I want you in on this, so clear a portion of your schedule for me."

"Cool," Misha said. "Once again, my girl's going to give the other record labels a serious run for their money. I can already see Puffy doing a remixed version of what you're about to do for his own label. You know the number. Just give my office a call when you're ready for my people to get to work for you."

Misha was a well-known, Los Angeles events coordinator. From the Soul Train Music Awards and Grammy Awards after-parties to birthday bashes for NBA players to upscale soirées at powerful, Black politicians' and businessmen's homes, Misha knew a thing or two about putting together big events with big price tags that everybody who was anybody wanted to be a part of.

"I went to see Rick today," Keshari said matter-of-factly, changing the subject.

"And?" Misha responded dismissively.

"He goes to trial in three weeks. He's still adamant that he's been set up."

"Like I give a damn," Misha answered, rolling her eyes. "Ricky's business is not my business and I make it a rule of thumb to keep his very existence as far away from my personal sphere as possible. Shit, I changed my last name to make it very clear that I want no connection whatsoever to that scum of the fucking earth. I will be so glad when you have the sense enough to do the same."

"If only it were that simple," Keshari said, slipping into the warm suds of her bath.

She put her head back and closed her eyes. She'd strongly considered telling Misha about the rest of her visit to see Ricky that day and what had transpired, but she quickly reconsidered. The timing didn't seem right. If she told Misha about Ricky threatening her life, Misha would have gone ballistic and her attitude would have become entirely too funky for the two of them to go anywhere together that night. Keshari rarely discussed that side of her life with Misha anyway and she did not want Misha to worry about her unnecessarily.

Misha went into the bedroom to change the CD that was playing, then filled a glass at the wet bar with ice, Coke, and a lot of Bacardi rum. She wanted to be in just the right mode to get her "swerve" on once she arrived at Rasheed the Refugee's party that night. Rasheed the Refugee's "Land of the Lost" filled the room with Rasheed's deep, laid-back, apocalyptic lyrical flow and bass-laced, "sumthin' you can ride to" rhythms.

"Well, Miss Thing," Misha said as she stood in the mirror patting her face dry after rinsing off her mask, "I think this party will be exactly the distraction you need to take your mind off business for at least a little while. It's going to be wall-to-wall brothas."

"That's the least of my priorities," Keshari said without opening her eyes. "With Rick's upcoming trial and this talent search project about to get underway, I'll soon be playing both ends against the middle. I don't have time for any romantic entanglements. Besides, I think you've got that little 'hoochie mama' routine hemmed up all by yourself. I'll leave the brothas to you tonight. What would I look like trolling around through record label executives and would-be rappers for a date?"

"Like a normal, young, red-blooded, extremely successful, damned woman," Misha said, glaring at her sarcastic friend's reflection in repose in the tub. "Furthermore, perhaps you should reassess your 'priorities' from time to time and make more of an effort to get yourself laid. That might take some of the pressure off. Deal with the talent search project tomorrow and let that fucked-up bastard ROT in jail for all I care. I haven't seen you in anything remotely resembling a healthy, romantic relationship since you made the mistake of getting yourself involved with him. What? Have you decided to stand by your man and serve him up with conjugal visits while he spends the rest of his sick-assed life behind bars?!"

"Shit, Misha! Don't start. I am SO not in the mood."

"You stubborn bitch!" Misha replied. "Tonight is the perfect opportunity for you to meet somebody...somebody fun...somebody who could very well prove worthy of you."

Keshari didn't even bother to respond. She wanted to sink into her bathwater until it covered her head. Sometimes Misha either intentionally dismissed or momentarily forgot who Keshari was.

♪ 🎧 ♪

At 10 p.m., Keshari's black Bentley convertible pulled into one of the congested valet lanes at the Mondrian Hotel in West Hollywood. She had two Suburbans with professional bodyguards escorting her. She also had a team of undercover security agents working the crowd.

Keshari had rarely traveled with the kind of security that many wealthy, prominent figures in the entertainment industry kept regularly in their employ. She had always been under protection of The Consortium's security and they were as professional and as adept at detecting and defending against danger as any of Los Angeles' most reputable security firms. The Consortium's security also had an advantage. Because they were a part of L.A.'s criminal underground, they virtually always knew, preemptively, who to watch, when to watch, and what was being planned. However, after Keshari's visit with Ricky that day, along with her desire to ultimately extricate herself completely and permanently from the affairs of The Consortium, she knew that she would have to begin implementing different measures regarding her security immediately. When Misha looked at her quizzically as they rolled out of the gates of Keshari's home, heavily secured as if Keshari was the new Suge Knight, Keshari quickly brushed it off with an offhand excuse about the label advising it for the party.

The two women stepped from Keshari's car simulta-neously and stopped the hotel's parking attendants in their tracks as they walked past. Clad in a form-fitting, backless, chocolate-beaded, Valentino jumpsuit with matching, chocolate satin, Jimmy Choo heels that wrapped and tied around her ankles, Keshari was positively stun-ning. Misha, hair pulled back in a sleek ponytail, wore a black, strapless, Calvin Klein column dress with spike-heeled Manolo Blahnik sandals. As always, she produced a diva's attitude to match her drop-dead gorgeous look and worked a calculated, feline, almost sexual strut like nobody's business.

An assortment of exotic sports cars, Range Rovers, and limousines crowded the valet lanes. Jermaine Dupri, Damon Dash of Roc-A-Fella Entertainment, Nas and Kelis, Xhibit, Lisa Raye, Alicia Keys, virtually all of the artists on the LTL label, Jamie Foxx, Jay-Z, Snoop Dogg and his sizeable entourage, Will Smith and Jada Pinkett-Smith, Queen Latifah, LL Cool J, Fat Joe and members of Terror Squad, and a host of Los Angeles Lakers and Clippers were spotted in the incoming crowd. Keshari paused and smiled for the cameras, causing the cluster of photographers who'd received access passes to shoot the event to flash shot after shot in a frenzy, knowing that it was a rare opportunity to get her to pose for pictures.

The media, as well as the public, were completely mesmerized by Keshari Mitchell's mystique. She remained something of an enigma in the industry. In a business where entertainers and record executives thrived on feeding their huge egos by being seen, Keshari seemed most content steering clear of a lot of personal media attention. She promoted her artists and her record label through an extremely competent executive team, she allowed a magazine or television exclusive from time to time that depicted her meteoric rise to professional success, her attorneys sending a very specific list of topics and questions to the interviewer's network or magazine in advance that Keshari absolutely would not discuss, and she worked to keep the rest of her life entirely private, which only made the media and the public hungrier to find out more about who she was.

In the beginning, as Keshari and her newcomer record label began to rapidly achieve success, a few rumors circulated that the beautiful, Wharton-educated record mogul might have an organized crime affiliation. Keshari's attorneys and public relations team threatened multi-million-dollar libel suits against virtually every form of entertainment media on the market before a story could ever be fully researched and drafted to reach the public and, thus far, no other renegade journalist had ever ventured into that territory again. Keshari was bound and determined that Larger Than Lyfe Entertainment would only be seen as the completely legitimate business enterprise that it was and anything else about her life that was not associated with her record label would never get the opportunity to be served up for public consumption.

A handful of rappers in the industry did know that Keshari was connected...very connected...and it was a subject that none of them dared to touch. One of the biggest codes of the streets was SILENCE and they knew that talking too much could very easily jeopardize their lives. It wasn't just about exposing Keshari Mitchell. Exposing her also, ultimately, exposed her very dangerous business allies.

An elevator arrived at lobby level and whisked Keshari, Misha and Keshari's bodyguards to the rooftop's ultra-chic Skybar. The record label had booked Skybar, the outdoor living room and the pool area for their party that night and a remixed track by Rasheed the Refugee had the heads of the men bobbing back and forth and the women swiveling their hips to the beat as bottles of Cristal and Courvoisier circulated. Waiters passed through the crowd with appetizers and decadent, miniature desserts. Gift bags containing shiny, platinum-colored iPod minis, programmed with tracks from Rasheed the Refugee's debut and sophomore albums, along with tracks from his now certified platinum third CD, were passed out to the VIP guests as they arrived at the party.

"Girl-l-l," Misha grinned, "you do know how to represent your label's name. Who put this together?"

"Andre's team worked directly with the hotel's event planners," Keshari said, looking around, appreciating Andre's usual attention to detail.

She lifted a glass of the bubbly Cristal from the tray of one of the passing waiters and took a sip. Misha enjoyed a couple of the tiny canapés, then gulped a glass of the expensive, chilled champagne as she simultaneously began giving the eye to a tall, dark and handsome player for the Sacramento Kings.

Definitely not a woman to waste any time, Keshari thought as she watched the familiar "mating ritual" go into effect. Misha's latest conquest strolled over and exchanged words with her. He greeted Keshari warmly. Then he and Misha slid off toward the dance floor.

Keshari laughed to herself as Misha shimmied to the music, teasing her rhythmless giant of a partner as she strategically rubbed parts of herself against him and then danced away again.

Keshari spotted Rasheed the Refugee in a corner outside near the pool, giving an interview to a writer for *VIBE* magazine while members of his entourage sat at tables all around him. LTL's PR department had advised Rasheed's managers to have Rasheed do the interview that night at the platinum party for his hugely acclaimed third album, *Ghetto Proverbs*, where he could be seen basking in the overwhelming success of his creative work. Rasheed, dressed in oversized, navy military fatigues and expensive combat boots, possessed the calm, collected, and regal demeanor of African royalty. He was warm and engaging, a natural conversationalist. He wasn't the bling-bling persona that seemed to prevail in current hip-hop. He was the West Coast's version of the East Coast's "Nas." His music was all about Black consciousness. He gave a strong, unapologetic, political voice to the art form of hip-hop and he compelled mainstream America to think seriously, at least for a moment, about the state of things in the U.S. and beyond. He was one of the smartest brothas Keshari had ever met. He could speak with depth on everything from American politics and economics to Nostradamus and Illuminati.

Rasheed had been a force in Los Angeles' hip-hop underground for several years and had built a strong following before signing with Larger Than Lyfe Entertainment. His controversial debut album turned him into an overnight, nationwide sensation. He sold a record-making 1.5 million units in the first two weeks of the release of *Land of the Lost*. His second album made him a superstar. To date, he'd sold 1.6 million units of his third album, *Ghetto Proverbs*, and SoundScan was still counting. He was asked to make appearances on everything from *The TODAY Show* to *Larry King Live* to discuss his scathing indictments of George W. Bush and his entire family, racial profiling, affirmative action, reparations, and the September 11th tragedy.

He stood poised as if he was prepared to do battle, a serious, contemplative expression on his face, the night lights of West Hollywood serving as the backdrop, while the *VIBE* photographer captured shots of him. Keshari couldn't be any prouder of him. His success was her label's success and they'd accomplished that success by dropping pearls of wisdom into consumers' ears at the same time that they entertained them with lyrical genius and hit-making tracks from some of the hottest producers in the industry. Of all the artists on the LTL roster, Rasheed the Refugee was, hands down, her favorite.

The party was the typical L.A. affair—too much money and ego concentrated in one place, executives networking, industry gossip everywhere, rap stars holding court with their entourages, nursing snifters of cognac while typing on iPhones, Sidekicks and BlackBerrys or arranging booty calls on their cell phones, and music video models sprin-kled throughout, working the scene like professionals, hoping to leave that night with somebody with clout.

Keshari began making her way through the crowd, stopping here and there to exchange pleasantries with music executives from other record labels.

"Keshari Mitchell," Sean "Diddy" Combs said, hug-ging her. "How are you?"

"I'm good...I'm good." Keshari smiled. "I'm so glad that you could make it to L.A. for Rasheed's party."

"I had a couple of business meetings and I'm shopping for some property, so I'm kinda killing two birds with one stone. Ra's party is the perfect place to blow off some steam. Congratulations, by the way, on your success."

"Thank you," Keshari answered. "I'm preparing for the same success with my new girl group, so expect an invitation for their album launch party."

"I hear that you've been getting your feet wet for your own fashion line. One of my designers saw you at a show in Milan. I might be able to give you some pointers."

"Actually, the fashion line's a ways out, but I'd appre-ciate your insight. I'm sure that it'll prove invaluable. We'll definitely have to get together about it. I've got another major project underway that's going to consume the bulk of my time for the next several months. I'm doing a press release about it in the next few days."

"What's the project?" Sean asked, his interest piqued.

"Keep your eyes on the news." Keshari smiled, not divulging anything. "Listen, I know that a table has been reserved for you and your people, but why don't you join me at my table? I'd love to have you. Executives from RIAA (Recording Industry Association of America), if they're not here already, should be arriving shortly."

"I'll do that," Sean said and shook his head as he watched the switch of her perfect ass walking away.

Keshari spotted Misha still shimmying her hips to the music with her Sacramento Kings players on the transparent dance floor that covered the pool. Misha was wearing the hell out of her dress. She saw Keshari and waved to her. Keshari could tell that her friend was building up a nice, little buzz from multiple glasses of champagne.

Dante Peterson, a writer for *The SOURCE* magazine, tapped Keshari lightly on the shoulder.

"Ms. Mitchell, would you spare me a couple minutes of your time? I've been attempting to get in touch with you. I'd like to arrange an interview. I'm putting together a story on 'power women' in the music industry and the story certainly wouldn't be complete without including you."

"Dante, you know the protocol for securing an interview. Contact my publicist. This is a party," Keshari said, barely pausing long enough to fully acknowledge the writer's presence.

Shaquille O'Neal rushed up and picked Keshari up from the floor, grinning his 2,000-watt, trademark "Superman" smile. Keshari and Shaquille had been friends since Misha had introduced the two of them at a nightclub party that she'd promoted a couple of years before.

"What's up, girl? How you been?"

He set her down and kissed her on the forehead.

"I'm cool. Busy as hell."

"You look good. Damned good. Almost as good as me."

"You're so silly," she said, smacking him. "How're Shaunie and the kids?"

"Everybody's good...can't complain. They all just got back from Miami. I'm taking you to dinner next week. Where do you want to go?"

Keshari laughed and shook her head. "NO" was definitely not a part of Shaq's vocabulary.

"Italian food...your house. 'Street Ball' on the Play-Station and make sure to order tiramisu. But let me call you. I'm gonna be in and out of town for the next few weeks. I'll hit you the moment I wrap things up."

Shaq beamed. The giant, dark brown brotha had a smile that could light up a room.

"Alright, girl," he said, "but don't keep me waiting."

He kissed Keshari again before moving off through the outdoor living room with his friends.

Coming through Skybar toward the patio, a very familiar face smiled and headed in Keshari's direction. A wave of uneasiness came over Keshari. It was Marcus Means. Ricky had to have sent him. Marcus Means, nor anyone else affiliated with The Con-sortium, had ever set foot inside Larger Than Lyfe's offices nor any Larger Than Lyfe function since the record label's doors opened.

Keshari smiled back at him and waved him over.

"Hey, girl," Marcus said amiably.

Keshari played it cool.

"What's up, Mark? Since when did hip-hop become a part of your repertoire?"

"Maybe I'm expanding my repertoire." He smiled.

The two of them strolled over to one of the more secluded areas of the dimly lit outdoor living room and sat down.

"So, what's up? Are you alone? What brings you here?" Keshari asked.

"Yeah, I came alone," Marcus answered.

They were both silent. Marcus took in the flashily dressed partygoers across the patio and their narcissistic party ritual. He appeared to be somewhere between feeling mildly repulsed and amused as he watched them.

"I saw Rick today," Keshari said. "Trial commences in three weeks. His attorneys are beginning to suggest that they, at least, consider a plea bargain with the D.A. Rick is livid and totally against it."

"I know," Marcus responded. "A plea bargain wouldn't happen anyway. This is a high-profile, first-degree murder case. The victim is a prominent, White attorney and the accused is a high-profile, Black, alleged gangster who's managed to escape indictment for YEARS. The D.A. wouldn't even consider plea bargaining with Rick unless he turned informant on every connection he's ever had."

"When's the last time you talked to Rick?" Keshari asked.

"I saw him today."

Keshari knew that Ricky had to have told him about their discussion, about her wanting out of The Consortium. Marcus stared at her long and hard before he finally commented.

"Be careful, girl," he said. "You're skating on thin ice. I'm very serious when I tell you this. Rick loves you. We all know this...but this is business and you know the business."

Keshari stared back at him, but didn't respond. Marcus knew that she understood him and he made no move to further elaborate. A moment later, he was gone. Although Keshari was sitting directly under one of the heating lamps lining the chic terrace, goose bumps stood out on her arms. She could do one of two things. She could get through the rest of the evening and be confident that she could come to some acceptable compromise with Rick, or she could become so paranoid and stressed about her situation that she began making the kind of serious mistakes that could get her killed.

"What in the hell are you doing over here alone?" Terrence, Keshari's assistant, said. "You look like one of these fish tales just stole your man. This party's fierce! You run this! Why don't you get yourself in the mix and enjoy yourself?"

"I just needed a minute to myself to clear my head," Keshari said, smiling at Terrence reassuringly.

He sat down next to her and wrapped his arms around her. She put her head on his shoulder.

"It's been a long and fucked-up day," she told him, "and I don't even want to begin to try to tell you about it."

Terrence looked down at her with concern.

"Are you sure you're okay?" he asked. "You're shaking."

"YES," Keshari said emphatically. "I'm fine...I'm fine. I just need a good night's sleep. I'll be prepared to suit up and conquer the world again tomorrow."

Terrence wasn't sure that he was convinced, but he let it go.

"You're on in about fifteen minutes," he said gently. "Michael Webb and Christina Perlmann from RIAA just arrived."

Keshari, along with representatives from the Recording Industry Association of America, would be presenting Rasheed the Refugee with a platinum plaque for his third album, *Ghetto Proverbs*.

"I'm ready," Keshari answered.

"Anytime you need to talk, I'm here," Terrence said, reaching over and brushing back the curls that had blown into Keshari's face.

"I'm cool," Keshari said. "Stop being a mama bird." She reached over and squeezed his hand. "Thanks for the concern, though."

"Hey, babygirl, that's what I'm here for."

A sexy, dancehall track from Rasheed's album featuring Wyclef Jean called "Respect Her" was playing. Terrence went to check on his date and Keshari started toward the cluster of VIP tables that had been reserved for her. Her BlackBerry had been ringing nonstop and she thought that she'd quickly check her messages and chat for a bit with the RIAA execs and Sean Combs before presenting Rasheed with his platinum plaque. Not quite paying attention to where she was going and still more than a bit preoccupied with Marcus's unexpected appearance and the veiled threat that he'd delivered, she collided with a tall, broad-shouldered Boris Kodjoe lookalike and his full glass of champagne.

"Oh, damn! I'm sorry," he said. "Are you okay?"

"Fuck!" Keshari snapped under her breath.

One of Keshari's bodyguards appeared out of nowhere, his hand on his jacket as if he were prepared to shoot the man for his mistake.

Keshari sighed with exasperation as she felt Mr. Apologetic's champagne trickling between her breasts and down the front of the lace, La Perla bikini she wore.

"Ms. Mitchell, is everything okay here?"

"I'm fine. It was just an accident," she snapped irritably at the bodyguard, waving him off.

Mr. Apologetic seemed absolutely determined to set the situation right. He grabbed a handful of cocktail napkins from a passing waiter and handed them to Keshari.

"Thank you," she said quickly, dabbing agitatedly at her damp chest and down the front of her intricately beaded jumpsuit.

"Are you sure you're okay?"

"Yes," she said. "I told you, I'm fine."

He reached into the inner jacket pocket of his nicely cut, Armani suit and removed one of his business cards.

"Please forward me the bill for your dry cleaning and I'll reimburse you. Better yet, here. Take this. It should cover the cost of cleaning your outfit. I am truly sorry."

He held out two, crisp, new hundred-dollar bills to her. Keshari waved his business card and the money away with growing frustration. If this man apologized one more time, she was going to scream and start scratching at his eyes.

He stood watching her with genuine concern as she continued to dab at the damp but nearly invisible spot down the front of her outfit. Then, out of nowhere, it finally dawned on him who she was.

He smiled a sexy, disarming smile. "Keshari Mitchell."

"The only one I know," she replied.

"Of Larger Than Lyfe Entertainment?"

"YES," she said, looking off distractedly through the crowd of people for Terrence, ready to brush past Mr. Apologetic before he went into player mode or tried to persuade her to listen to some artist's CD.

"I'm Mars Buchanan," he said. "I'm the new general counsel for the Western Division at ASCAP."

Keshari let her guard down a bit, smiled and shook his hand.

"It's a pleasure meeting you," she said, looking down to inspect the virtually invisible champagne damage to her outfit.

Mars Buchanan went to apologize again and Keshari quickly cut him off.

"Look, this was as much my fault as it was yours. My mind was someplace else and I wasn't looking where I was going. Let's just forget about it. Okay?"

"Not a problem," he said with a bit of reluctance. "You know, I've read coverage of you in the trade papers and in several of the music magazines. I've also met your attorney and several A & R execs from your label at various industry functions, but this is the very first time that I've encountered you in person and let's just say that entertainment magazine photos don't even begin to have the same...striking...effect as seeing you up close and personal."

He was clearly flirting with her. A faint smile seemed to play at the corners of Keshari's lips. *This is definitely not the time*, she thought.

"It was very nice meeting you, Mr. Buchanan," she said, "but if you will excuse me, I'm expected up front."

"The pleasure was meeting you," Mars replied graciously, "despite the unfortunate way that we did meet."

Moments later, Mars heard Keshari's sultry voice.

"Ladies and gentlemen, I hope that you're enjoying yourselves this evening.

"We are here to give honor and recognition to one of the music industry's premier artists, one of the most prolific voices in today's hip-hop.

"This young brotha, with his extraordinary talent for flipping a metaphor, brings back the days when hip-hop involved knowledge-dropping and was used as a political tool for consciousness and empowerment...the days of

Chuck D. and Public Enemy, X-Clan, Poor Righteous Teachers, KRS-One and Boogie Down Productions..."

Loud applause. Excitement was building.

"*TIME* magazine asks if this brotha is a 'prolific phenom or a threat?' *Rolling Stone* calls this brotha 'Hip-Hop's Messiah.' *The SOURCE* gave him an unbelievable five mics on all three of his albums. And, in my opinion, he's got to be one of the most AMAZING brothas I've ever met in my entire life. Without further ado, let's give the man of the hour his props. RASHEED THE REFUGEE!!!"

The crowd went wild. The men "let loose their dogs," whooping it up throughout the packed outdoor living room, and the females screamed in sheer delight as Rasheed the Refugee took the stage.

Mars Buchanan secured a fresh glass of champagne, then maneuvered his way toward the front of the crowd. He stood amongst the partygoers, his eyes riveted to the stage, not at Rasheed the Refugee receiving his platinum plaque, but at the president & CEO of Larger Than Lyfe Entertainment.

He smiled a very satisfied smile to himself and sipped his drink.

-7-

"Looks like Miss Thing's got a secret," Keshari's assistant said when she arrived at the office the next morning.

"What are you talking about, T? I am really not in the mood."

"Check your desk," Terrence answered coyly as Keshari passed his workspace and went into her office.

On the corner of her desk was an exquisite, Baccarat vase filled with three dozen, long-stemmed, hot pink tulips. She pulled the card from the tiny pitchfork sticking from the arrangement. She already knew that her busybody assistant had sneaked and read it.

"Here's to the two of us meeting again under much less awkward circumstances. Mars Buchanan."

Keshari smiled to herself and rolled her eyes as she thought of the gorgeous, apologetic general counsel from ASCAP (American Society of Composers, Authors and Publishers) who'd spilled champagne all over her $5,500 outfit the night before. She dropped the card into the trash.

There was a small stack of CDs on her desk in an interoffice envelope from the A & R department. A & R received literally hundreds of demo CDs every single month from aspiring artists, hoping to sign recording contracts with Larger Than Lyfe Entertainment. A & R forwarded the most promising CDs to Keshari. When Keshari liked what she heard, A & R would often contact the artist to arrange to hear more of their music. Sometimes the record label requested that an artist go into the studio to lay down another track...a "no strings attached" arrangement to see how the artist worked and if the artist showed consistency in their likability and talent. Ultimately, Keshari decided whether or not LTL would extend the artist a recording or production contract.

She popped the first CD on the stack into her stereo system. It was a female artist...Tanjika Miles...and she couldn't sing worth a damn. Keshari already knew what she looked like, the exotically pretty, hot, and tempting video model type whose demo CD had made its way to Keshari's desk because the girl had been so hungry to get her music heard by the right connection that she'd performed a whole host of sexual favors for the male A & R exec who'd promised her the world. The industry was filled with these young, beautiful, talentless creatures. They fit the sex-driven visual image that record labels generally marketed to the public and their voices were made to sound sellable in the studios via implementation of state-of-the-art recording equipment and techniques. Keshari removed the CD from the system, attached a note requesting that A & R try and find out the particulars of the producer, and then tossed the CD aside. She had no interest whatsoever in the singer. The music industry had overlooked enough true creativity and artistry in music already for these types and Keshari was bound and determined that Larger Than Lyfe Entertainment would never lower its standards to swim around in the cesspool with some of the other record labels, signing talentless creatures who only looked like stars.

She inserted the next CD. It was a male rapper, "Mack-A-Do-Shuz." Mack-A-Do-Shuz wove intricate, philosophical, lyrical storylines of an urban gangster and his oftentimes dangerous life in the streets. The total package was impeccable, impressive creativity in the lyrical stylings and an innovative producer who worked in perfect synchrony with the artist.

Keshari called Sharonda Richards in A & R.

"Sharonda, who is this Mack-A-Do-Shuz? I'm listening to his demo right now."

"Chuckie Townsend has run into him a few times at The Gate and at Savannah West and he's been begging Chuckie to listen to his demo. I take it you liked him."

"Definitely. Get him into our studios with the same producer who did his demo to drop a couple more tracks. No promises. If we like what we hear, we'll negotiate a contract. We'll even work out a production deal for the producer. Touch bases with me in two weeks."

"Key, here's something you'll really like. Mack-A-Do-

Shuz completely produced the entire demo. He's both rapper...he writes all of his own material...AND producer."

"Whoa," Keshari said. "Get him in here right away. It's a wonder that no one has snapped him up and signed him already."

She hung up and began going through the stack of documents that had also been delivered to her that morning. Some of them were very time-sensitive. She had checks to sign and return to accounting, a couple of artist management contracts to review and sign and return to the legal department, several video budgets that required her review and approval, and finalized invoicing from The Mondrian Hotel for the platinum party had been faxed over to Andre's attention just that morning. Andre forwarded copies to her for her review and signatures before he submitted the invoices to accounting for payment.

Every penny that was spent at Larger Than Lyfe Entertainment had documentation to come across Keshari's desk. Projects with large budgets always required Keshari's signed approval before they commenced; and she and her accounting department always kept a watchful eye on everything so that projects did not wind up going over budget. She ran a very tight ship.

As she sat there at her desk signing documents, taking phone calls, and considering taking a ride up to the Malibu mansion where a music video was being shot for

LTL's girl group, Cashmere, she glimpsed the heavy, cream-colored, parchment card that had been attached to Mars Buchanan's flowers to her. She lifted the card from the wastebasket and smiled to herself at its message. Then she dropped the card back into the trash.

Moments passed and, as she was checking her voice-mail and e-mail messages, something compelled her to pluck the card out of the trash again. She gazed at it for several moments, then rang her assistant.

"Terrence, get me Mars Buchanan at ASCAP on the line. He's in Legal Services."

"No problem," Terrence replied.

A couple of minutes later, Terrence buzzed Keshari back.

"Keshari, I've got Mars Buchanan on the line."

"Thanks, T. Put him through."

"Well, hello, Keshari Mitchell. What can I do for you?"

"Good morning, Mr. Buchanan. I received your flowers. They're beautiful. Thank you. But you really didn't have to do that."

"It was the least that I could do to compensate for our initial meeting...and since you liked the flowers enough to call and thank me for them yourself, perhaps I can persuade you to have dinner with me...tonight."

Keshari was already backpedaling away fast from her impulsive notion to call him.

"I don't think that that would be a good idea," she said.

"I strongly disagree...unless you're married or otherwise involved. Are you married or otherwise involved?"

"I don't think that my personal life is any of your concern, Mr. Buchanan."

"Please...call me 'Mars.' 'Mr. Buchanan' is my father. Is seven o'clock a good time to pick you up? And would you prefer if I pick you up at your home or at your office?"

Keshari laughed. "Mr. Buchanan...Mars...random drug testing of the legal counsel over at ASCAP might not be a bad idea. But, on a serious note, I really don't think that it would be a good idea for the two of us to go out. I only called to thank you for the beautiful flowers that were delivered this morning."

"Why don't you think that it would be a good idea for me to take you out?" Mars asked. "I'm a good guy."

"I'm sure you are." Keshari smiled. "I just have a lot on my plate, that's all, and I hardly have the time for any...entanglements."

"I expected that you would have a full plate, Keshari, but even the most powerful people have to set aside little blocks of personal time to eat. Look, I met...by accident...an extraordinarily beautiful woman last night and I want to get to know her better and, just for a split second, I saw a little glint of something in your eyes, felt a tiny bit of chemistry, giving me the impression that you might like to get to know me, too. You and I both know that you didn't call my office just so you could thank me personally for the flowers I sent to you. Your assistant could have left that 'thank you' with my secretary or mailed me one of those generic 'thank you' cards and we both could have gone on with our respective days without a moment's direct contact. So, stop fronting. You like me. Admit it."

Keshari smiled to herself. She had to admit that she was both intrigued and amused by the relentless and extremely attractive attorney.

"You really don't give up, do you?"

"Not when it counts," Mars answered. "Come on. Have dinner with me tonight. If we don't click...which, in my belief, is highly improbable...you will never have to be bothered with my presence again. My word is bond."

Keshari didn't say anything.

"HEL-LO?!" Mars said, loud enough to cause Keshari to hold the telephone receiver away from her ear. "Give me an answer. I feel pretty damned certain that you've closed major business deals in less time than this."

Keshari laughed. It felt good to laugh like that.

"Yes," she said. "Yes, I'll have dinner with you tonight."

She could feel Mars smiling triumphantly through the telephone.

"So, how are we gonna do this?" she asked. "I'm really not in the mood to do the...you know...the 'public' thing. I've had a tremendously busy week...plus the party last night...and I'd just like to kick back and relax. Why don't you drive up to my house and I'll have my cook put something together for us?"

"Nah, tell you what," Mars said. "If you don't want me to take you out for dinner, why don't you come to my apartment and I'll cook for the two of us?"

"Oh, you cook, do you?" Keshari asked, impressed.

"I dabble a bit," Mars answered.

"That settles that, then. We'll have dinner at your place. I have only one, small request. No pork or red meat."

"Not a problem there, my queen. I don't consume the stuff either. Seven o'clock?" Mars asked.

"Seven o'clock's fine," Keshari replied.

"Would you like me to pick you up?"

"I'll drive," Keshari responded.

Mars gave her directions to his condominium and they hung up. Keshari buzzed her assistant again.

"Terrence, run a full background check on Mars Buchanan."

"Hmmmmm," Terrence said coyly, "bouquet of flowers...background checks. New love interest on the horizon? It's about time."

"Don't be silly, T. Get back to me with the findings of that background check in a couple of hours."

"No problem," Terrence said, chuckling and clicking off his extension.

Terrence got back to Keshari in just over an hour with the background information that she was seeking. Keshari regularly used a Los Angeles intelligence agency that was able to provide fast, accurate and extensive details, from medical histories to criminal backgrounds and credit profiles, on anyone. She read the findings of the background check that Terrence had printed from his e-mail and smiled to herself. Mars Buchanan's background couldn't have been any more spotless.

Keshari wasn't naively deluding herself into believing that nothing could or would happen to her in regard to her current predicament with The Consortium, particularly after Marcus Means's entirely unexpected visit at the party the night before, but she certainly wasn't going to be fearfully crawling under any rocks either. It was time that she started living her life COMPLETELY on her own terms, from running her record label to getting up in the morning fully able to face herself in the mirror without having a constant, moral tug-of-war taking place in her head and maybe...just maybe meeting someone fun and smart and sexy and worthy of her and, as her best friend constantly admonished her, getting herself laid.

For the time being, at least until Ricky's trial wrapped, she would not deviate from the regular program of her obligations, including her obligations to The Consortium. But her mind would not be swayed in terms of her ultimate intentions.

She had a date that night...a real date...for the first time in she didn't know how long.

Keshari had no idea why her heart was racing a mile a minute as she rang the doorbell outside Mars's condominium in the posh, Los Angeles suburb city of Marina Del Rey.

"I bet you could make wearing a Hefty trash bag look like a fashion statement." Mars smiled when he opened the door.

"That's cute." Keshari smiled back. "That's really cute."

Keshari was very casually chic in skintight, cuffed Roberto Cavalli jeans and fire engine-red Jimmy Choo sandals. She walked into Mars's huge apartment and looked around, thoroughly impressed. Mars had a table set on his terrace complete with linen tablecloth, matching napkins, and floating candles. There was a gazeboed Jacuzzi at the far end of the terrace just begging for a middle-of-the-night rendezvous with chilled champagne and strawberries. Ceiling-to-floor windows gave a spectacular, 180-degree view of the marina from the huge, sunken living room.

"Who did your decorating?" Keshari asked. "Your apartment is beautiful."

"A friend of mine is an interior decorator. She owns the PFI Firm in Beverly Hills. She did it."

"She did a great job. The soft grays and black leather are very tastefully masculine and you have a very substantial African art collection. That large, Yoruba fertility statue is one of my favorites."

"I'm glad you like it. Actually, I purchased two of the condos, had an architect and contractors knock out a few walls, make the floor plan flow, and make it my own. I'll show you the rest of it later. Let's go outside, kick back, and get better acquainted."

Mars poured Keshari a glass of chardonnay, then went to attend to their meal. He brought back salads, handmade chicken ravioli with a spinach and cream sauce, and fresh Italian bread with extra virgin olive oil.

"You said that you dabble a bit in the kitchen. You didn't tell me that you'd been to culinary school. Did you really make all of this yourself? And how did you prepare it so fast? What? Did you leave your office to start cooking as soon as we finished talking on the phone earlier today?"

Mars laughed. "Cute," he said. "Very cute. I made the ravioli a couple of weeks ago. I vacuum seal it and freeze it. The cream sauce only takes a few minutes to make. My housekeeper picked up the bread for me. And, no, I haven't been to culinary school. I took a few cooking classes at Williams-Sonoma. You know, a little sumthin' sumthin' to add to the ol' repertoire.'"

"A New Millennium Black renaissance man," Keshari said as she tasted the food. "Ummmmm…, this is really good."

The sun had almost completely set and the burning candles on the table illuminated Keshari's face with a warm glow. Mars stared across the table at her and took in everything that he possibly could about her, from the mystery in her almond-shaped, green eyes to the curve of her beautiful, full lips when she smiled and savored her food. Everything about her attracted him to her. He sipped his wine and began to talk animatedly about growing up in Brooklyn, New York.

He was the younger of two children. He had an older sister, a professor of African-American Studies at Columbia University. His mother and father, who still lived in Brooklyn, were happily married after more than forty years together. His mother was a retired schoolteacher and his father was a recently retired attorney.

Mars had lived in Los Angeles ever since graduating from Stanford Law School. He'd never been married, had no children, but was certainly not averse to commitment. One day, he said, he hoped to have a wife and family.

"So Keshari Mitchell, tell me all about you."

"Well," Keshari said, gazing out at the man-made lake outlining Mars's terrace, "I graduated with honors from UCLA. I got my MBA from Wharton. I began setting the groundwork for my record label while still working on my master's degree. I've been in love with hip-hop since high school and am currently delving on a serious level into the genres of jazz and R & B at my record label..."

"Okay," Mars said. "Now, that's the professionally prepared bio from your PR department. Tell me more about Keshari Mitchell. We're off the record. You can tell me anything."

"Anything?" Keshari asked half-jokingly with an eyebrow raised. "We just met. I'll give you an abbreviated version and allow you to build up some trust points for more."

Mars chuckled. "Sounds cool. How did you get your start in the industry?"

"I think I've always been in love with music," Keshari said, "especially jazz. Miles, Mingus, Bird, Billie Holiday, Dinah Washington, Ella and Coltrane, some of the contemporary stuff, old school R & B. Before my mom passed, she listened to jazz almost all the time. I guess the fond memories of her cooking and playing cards with her girlfriends with good jazz in the background made me become especially attached to the music too.

"Then, along came hip-hop," Keshari continued. "MY music...OUR music...music that had its start in my generation, created by my very own peers. I couldn't get enough of it. Eric B & Rakim, A Tribe Called Quest, Brand Nubian, EPMD, Das EFX, X-Clan, Pete Rock & CL Smooth, LL, Big Daddy Kane, Nas... I could put my hip-hop collection up against any DJ's, East or West Coast, and win hands-down.

"I did internships at MCA and Sony during undergrad. My best friend started doing party promotion while we were at UCLA. She knows some of everybody and I made quite a few industry connections that way. When I started in the Masters program at Wharton, I knew what my ultimate goal was. I wanted to start my own record label and turn my passion for music into a lucrative business enterprise."

Mars smiled as she spoke candidly. He was too impressed with this woman for words.

"I did extensive research on every facet of the music industry and my internships provided some inside knowledge. I formulated a solid business plan and submitted a proposal package to several corporations who had programs that awarded business start-up grants to minority entrepreneurs. The corporate board of directors for TCG Management and The Enrichment Project, Inc. took a huge risk on me. I took a huge risk on a VERY talented artist..."

"And the rest is history. Well...history still in the making," Mars said. "You're thirty years old and the most powerful woman...the most powerful BLACK woman...in the music industry. Now, tell me a little bit about the phenomenon's personal side."

"The phenomenon?" Keshari mused, and then smiled at the compliment.

She sipped her wine, hesitating before she proceeded to tell him a bit about the side of herself that so few people knew.

"Well," she said, "I certainly don't have the whole Cosby-like familial background that you have. My mom died of cancer when I was a teenager. I never really knew my father. My grandmother took over trying to raise me when my mother passed away. She died a year ago. We were never really that close, even though I was her only child's child. Other than that, I don't really have any biological family to speak of. I've got no children... and I'm not sure if I'll ever meet the man I love enough to want any...and I'm definitely not sure when my life will slow down enough to even be a parent. I've got two purebred Rottweilers, Hannibal and Marcus Garvey. They're probably the closest I'll get to having children. Then, there's my best friend, Misha, who's always been like a sister to me."

"Damn," Mars said seriously, sipping his wine, "that's deep. It's amazing where you are now, considering your losses and all else that you've been through so early on in your life."

"I have to admit that I never fathomed achieving the kind of success that I have. I often wonder if my life would have taken even remotely the same direction if my mother were still alive. I wonder if my life would be anything like it is now if I'd made a few different choices along the way."

Mars made eye contact with Keshari across the table and held her gaze for a lingering moment. He seemed to look through her, into her, and take an unobstructed view all the way to the heart of her, and his eyes said,

I'm here for you. I've got you if you need me. For some-one who literally rubbed elbows with some of America's most dangerous on a regular basis, Mars Buchanan put her completely off balance. She gulped a huge swallow of her wine and got up from the table. She strolled down the dimly lit terrace toward the gazebo where the Jacuzzi was situated. Mars watched her intently and wondered what she was thinking.

"Tell me," Mars said, coming up behind Keshari and playing with a lock of her hair, "just how is it that a breathtakingly beautiful, single, extremely successful sista like you has managed to escape getting married? Or being hemmed up in an exclusive relationship with some understandably overprotective boyfriend?"

Keshari spun around, surprised at Mars's closeness to her. Her heart was racing again like it had been when she arrived at his apartment.

"Do you really have to ask that question?" She laughed. "It's like I told you. I'm married to my career. There has not been time...in years...for me to get seriously involved with anyone."

Her and Mars's eyes met again. He was close enough to her now to practically feel her heart racing. His closeness made her feel as if all of her vulnerability was exposed like physical nakedness. It made her awkward and anxious and wanting to put some space between her and this man.

"Am I making you uncomfortable?" Mars asked as if he was reading her thoughts.

"What makes you say that?" Keshari said.

"Your body language. You look like a deer in head-lights."

"No, you're not making me uncomfortable," Keshari responded.

In actuality, the whole situation was taking her way out of her comfort zone. There was a serious amount of attraction building quickly between the two of them, far more quickly than Keshari would ever have anticipated.

She moved away from Mars back toward the dinner table and he quickly followed. He caught her by the wrist and brought her around to face him again.

"Keshari, I'm only trying to get to know you. So, why don't you relax, stop over-analyzing the possibility of what will happen between the two of us before anything even has the chance to happen, and just play things by ear. For now, we're having dinner...no pressure. If I'm delving into territory that you really don't want to talk about, tell me that it's none of my business and I'll back off. I'm not trying to make you uncomfortable."

Keshari smiled and relaxed a bit. It was just dinner, she thought, and she had no idea why she felt so out of control of herself. It was probably because she was having dinner with this gorgeous, successful, funny, cool, con-siderate, intelligent brotha producing vibes from the very start that she'd never, ever felt before...not even with Rick.

Boney James's *Sweet Thing* filtered out onto the terrace from Mars's Bose sound system. The breeze that whisked across the terrace blew Keshari's tousled curls into her face. Mars reached out and gently stroked them away and she was wide open all over again like a deer in headlights.

"Damn," he said, "you really don't seem to have any idea how beautiful you are, do you?"

He took a huge gamble and kissed Keshari. The moment just seemed right, and during that moment when his lips, all warm and soft and perfect, touched hers, a fiery charge rocketed through Keshari's entire body... CHEMISTRY.

It had been a bad idea to accept his dinner invitation. The timing...she had some very significant issues to resolve before she could start living her life like this, with her guard down.

"I'm sorry. I have to go," she said quickly, pulling away from him. "I really have to go."

"What's the matter?" Mars questioned. "Did I do something wrong?"

"Of course not," Keshari said. "I just...I can't do this. My life is complicated enough as it is. I don't need a romantic entanglement in my life to further complicate things."

She grabbed up her purse and was out of Mars's apartment in a flash. Mars was left standing in complete bewilderment, wondering WHAT had just gone down.

When Keshari arrived at her Range Rover parked in the subterranean garage outside Mars's condo, all four of her tires were slashed and the body of the truck had been viciously keyed all the way around.

=9=

Mars was grinning as sweat poured down his face and chest. He dribbled the ball. He was an agile, left-handed player. He did a couple of crossovers, some fancy footwork, and then plowed straight up the court.

Swoosh! Another basket. Twenty-one. Mars's game.

"Man, you must be gettin' old," Mars gibed at his best friend, Jason Payne. "Either that or married life has fucked up your game. It's been a LONG time since I kicked your ass on the court two weeks in a row."

Every week, the two men, who'd attended Stanford Law School together, got together to play some one-on-one or get in on a pickup game with some of their boys at The Spectrum Club in Culver City or at the exclusive Los Angeles Sporting Club.

"Man, fuck you," Jason snapped with a toothy grin. "Married life is just fine...and so is my game. Don't knock what you don't even have the guts to try."

Jason popped Mars in the back with his sweaty towel. They headed for the locker room showers and the next group who'd reserved the basketball court took the floor.

"Guts," Mars said, "has nothing to do with the reason that I'm not married. You know that I'm not knockin' marriage. I have yet to meet the woman qualified to become Mrs. Buchanan."

He stepped out of his workout clothes and under the steamy jets of shower water. Jason laughed, and then turned around to rinse off.

"The woman 'qualified,' as you put it, to become 'Mrs. Buchanan' doesn't seem to exist. You keep raising the bar or changing the rules."

The two men stepped out of the showers simultaneously and cinched towels at their athletically chiseled waists.

"Whatever happened to the sista who decorated your condo?" Jason asked. "What's her name? Portia something. She was a runway model or something before starting her own design firm. Now, there's a beautiful sista."

"Portia and I still see each other off and on," Mars answered. "She wants a lot more than I'm capable of giving her. She wants commitment and I'm just not feeling that with her."

They stood at their adjacent lockers and began to dress. Mars slipped into a cream-colored, velour Sean John sweatsuit and zipped the jacket over his bare chest. Jason slid on black Armani trousers and a black silk knit tee.

"I met somebody," Mars said suddenly.

"And?" Jason said disinterestedly. "You meet women all the time."

"Jay, man, you're not listening. This is different. I think this one could be 'Mrs. Buchanan.'"

Jason spun around to look at his friend. He saw the look in Mars's eyes and knew that he was serious.

"Ahhhhhhhh shit," Jason said. "My brother looks like he's already on the verge of buying the five-carat rock. Who is she?"

"Keshari Mitchell," Mars said.

"Why does that name sound so familiar?" Jason said. Then his eyes bugged out. "You mean, the head of Larger Than Lyfe Entertainment?"

"The one and only," Mars said proudly.

"DAMN-N-N-N," Jason said.

"I've never met anyone like her," Mars went on. "I mean, she's the most powerful woman in the music industry, but when we were alone...she was SHY, vulnerable, innocent even, and so-o-o-o-o damned sexy at the same time."

"Yeah, I've seen her in a few photos and I sat behind her at last year's Grammy Awards. Many have said that ol' girl makes Halle Berry look like your average, around-the-way girl. I'm jealous."

"She is the most beautiful woman I've ever seen in my life," Mars said.

"You're GONE!" Jason laughed. "So, when's the wedding?"

Mars laughed. "It's not that deep yet."

"You know, I don't want to piss all over your good vibes. I'm always happy to see my bro find happiness. But there are a few rumors in the industry about your new paramour."

"I cannot believe that you're about to try and feed me some industry gossip," Mars said.

"Nah, man, on the real, there's been talk that Keshari Mitchell's record label is a front for drug money, that she's involved in organized crime on a MAJOR level."

"That's ridiculous," Mars said. "I don't believe that shit for a minute and you know as well as I do that anytime a brother or sister achieves the massive level of success that Keshari Mitchell has in an arena that has typically been dominated by White folks...especially when this brother or sista didn't resort to selling himself or herself out in the process of achieving success... the rumor mill becomes inundated with lies to try to character assassinate them. You KNOW this and I would think that you would be a whole lot more supportive of a sista making major strides in the industry, rather than becoming party to malicious gossip meant to tear her down."

"Yeah, you're right, black," Jason said, grabbing his duffle bag and keys. "Hey, I'm sorry. Just...be careful. Keep that third eye open."

"Always," Mars said, giving his best friend a brotherly "pound" in that cool way that Black men do.

They said their goodbyes in the parking lot and went their separate ways. Mars had no plans for the day and was headed back to his condo. Jason was headed to a lunch date with his beautiful, pregnant wife.

Mars slid behind the wheel of his Mercedes and picked up the phone to check his voicemail messages at home. There were several, business-related calls, a message from the housekeeper about his dry cleaning, and a final message from Portia Foster.

"Hi, sweetheart. I'm back in town. I've got a bottle of Perrier Jouët, some food from our favorite, little spot, a purse full of condoms, and I'm coming your way. I hope eight o'clock is okay. Bye."

Mars shook his head as he hung up and pulled out of the parking lot into the busy, Saturday afternoon traffic. He was growing increasingly annoyed by the presumptuous way that Portia conducted herself with him. She acted as if the two of them were involved in an exclusive relationship. It was high time that he removed any possibility of confusion about what the two of them really were to each other. He needed to establish some easy-to-comprehend parameters in regard to their dealings immediately.

♪ 🎧 ♫

At 8:15 that evening, Mars's doorbell rang. Portia Foster had arrived.

"Hi, sweetie," she said, planting a kiss on Mars's lips and breezing into his apartment on a cloud of Christian LaCroix perfume.

Portia Foster had a very strong resemblance to the model and actress, Kenya Moore. She was thirty-two years old with deep, flawless, mahogany skin, smoky, bedroom eyes, beautiful, jet black hair that usually cascaded down her back in huge curls and she currently wore in a short, funky, pixie-type cut, and legs that went on for days and days.

She was six feet tall, yet possessed an affinity for four-inch heels. She'd been a runway model for Yves Saint Laurent and Emanuel Ungaro in Paris and Milan prior to establishing a successful interior design firm in Beverly Hills. Mars and Portia had been seeing each other off and on for nearly two years since meeting at a book signing for Tavis Smiley at the Beverly Center.

"So, where've you been for the past couple weeks?" Mars asked.

"I went to Ghana to pick up and purchase some art work from my contacts there." Portia grinned. "It was beautiful. The people are beautiful. We have to go there together. What? Did you miss me?"

"Yeah... somethin' like that," Mars said, smacking her on the butt.

She set the food on the living room's huge, abstract-shaped, cracked-glass table and went out to the kitchen to get plates and silverware and flutes for the champagne she'd brought. Mars turned on *SportsCenter* and steeled himself for the evening ahead.

Portia returned to the living room, kicked off her Gucci heels, went over to the stereo, perused Mars's carefully organized CD collection, and put on Miles Davis's *Bitches Brew*. Mars looked at her back as if she was losing her mind.

"Portia," he said, "I'm watching the highlights of the game."

"Yeah, yeah, sweetie," Portia said quickly, turning down the volume on the television set, "and those highlights will be on at least three more times before the weekend is over. How can you possibly say no to Miles?"

She turned up the stereo volume, lit some freesia incense, and poured Mars a glass of champagne. Then she hiked up her skirt, sat down Indian-style on the floor at the cocktail table, and commenced to roll a joint from the ounce of premium, Indonesian marijuana she pulled from her purse.

"I brought you something back from my trip," Portia said.

"Oh, yeah? Where is it?" Mars asked, his attention never leaving the basketball highlights.

"It's a piece for your bedroom. You can pick it up from the gallery sometime next week or have the housekeeper or your secretary arrange to pick it up."

"Thanks," Mars said absently.

He gulped down his champagne, and then poured himself another. Portia took a deep drag on her joint, and then passed it up to Mars. He hit it and passed it back to her. He served himself a dish of the steamed broccoli and pan-fried dumplings she'd brought and dipped one of the dumplings into the spicy, Szechuan sauce. Portia put her head back on Mars's knee and vibed to Miles Davis's horn and the intricate rhythms of *Bitches Brew*. Mars popped a bit of dumpling into her mouth and she smiled at him as she started to get herself completely faded on the thick, pungent smoke of her joint and the expensive champagne.

"How's work?" she asked.

"Fine," Mars responded.

"You really should go ahead, take that leap of faith, and start your own firm," Portia said. "You've talked about entertainment management and legal representation for too long. It's time to put your plans into action."

"Not yet," Mars said. "I'm still doing some fine-tuning."

Mars finished eating and poured himself a third glass of champagne. He had no idea why he was downing so much of the bubbly liquid so fast. Perhaps, subconsciously, his drinking was an escape tactic. He couldn't be held totally accountable for whatever happened that night if he was drunk.

He knew that he should initiate dialogue with Portia as soon as possible that established some parameters between them. He had serious intentions of pursuing a relationship with Keshari Mitchell, despite the way that she had run out of his apartment, and he did not need Portia to be functioning on any mixed messages nor continuing to show up at his home uninvited. But, knowing Portia's typical mode of operation on her surprise visits on nights like this one, the totally male part of him, his little head doing all of the thinking while his big head took a lunch, would not allow the logical, rational side of him to speak, to clear the air once and for all.

The next thing Mars knew, Portia was tugging down his Sean John sweats and Calvin Klein underwear. She took his manhood into her mouth before he could utter a single word. The only sound that he could muster was a deep groan. She caressed and teased his male part with her tongue until he was as hard as solid rock. He reached for her and she stood up, shedding expensive, designer garments like leaves from a tree in fall.

Her body was the perfection of an African goddess and she was not very big on foreplay. She straddled Mars as he sat there with his sweatpants around his ankles. She took him inside her in one, smooth glide and began to rock slowly back and forth, up and down with the expert precision of a woman who knew exactly which buttons of his to push.

Mars worked his hips to thrust himself deeper into her. He squeezed her perfect, round ass and guided her up and down on his male part aggressively. She pulled Mars's face into her ample breasts and he took an erect nipple hungrily into his mouth.

"Fuck me like you mean it, sweetie," Portia moaned.

Mars was more than happy to oblige. He maneuvered the two of them onto the floor and, with Portia on her knees, took her from behind doggystyle in deep, shuddering thrusts that she loved.

The intensity of their lovemaking quickly built to a crescendo. Portia dug her manicured nails into the plush, gray carpet as she screamed out in ecstasy and Mars gave her what she'd come for faster and faster. He shuddered deeply as he climaxed and collapsed onto Portia's back. Portia smiled at him as she got up and went to the bathroom.

The unbelievable sex was the one thing that kept Portia Foster in Mars's life. Sexually, the girl had mad skills. She was as uninhibited as they come and she turned him out every time that they connected.

He went into his bathroom and watched her as she soaped herself with his loofah from her breasts to her ankles in his shower. Watching her bathe was a sensual event in and of itself. He stepped into the large, glass compartment with her and took her again, her back pinned against the black-tiled shower wall, her legs in a vise-like grip around his waist.

When they made love a final time in the wee hours of the morning in Mars's huge bed, the face that Mars saw in place of Portia's was Keshari's. As he fell asleep with Portia lying contentedly asleep beside him, vivid dreams of Keshari drifted about in his mind.

W hat the FUCK is the matter with you?!" Keshari yelled. "What the fuck would make you do something like that?!"

"Ma'am, I am going to have to ask you to quiet down or I'll have to ask you to leave," the sheriff's officer standing guard across the room advised Keshari.

She nodded in acknowledgment without looking back at him and lowered her voice to an embittered whisper. She was positively livid and couldn't even contain her fury when she arrived at Men's Central Jail to see Ricky that morning.

"You know, that was some hot-headed, immature, patently dumb shit that the junior gangsters on the street corners do. I would think that, after all these years, you would be a lot more evolved than this brand of shit. That IS what you've always upheld, that The Consortium is composed of the 'thinking man's' gangster."

All four of Keshari's tires had been slashed and the body of the Range Rover from the hood to side panels to the rear had been very badly damaged with something that had to have been like a power drill. The gas tank had been filled to overflowing with some sort of a sugary substance. Keshari had had to call a tow truck and a car. She sat, fuming, inside the vandalized Range Rover and waited nearly an hour for it to be picked up before her chauffeured car dropped her at home. She wasn't about to go back up to Mars's apartment and have to reveal to him what had happened.

Despite the many heinous acts of extortion, revenge and intimidation that Keshari had seen in action over the years, it never ceased to dumbfound her the kinds of things that Ricky and those he employed could pull off and get away with. The maneuver implemented was one that The Consortium had used many times. The vandal had been a police officer from the local precinct who'd "come to respond to a resident's call" for which the security office, who typically handled calls pertaining to residential problems prior to involving the police, would have no record. The officer was, undoubtedly, on The Consortium's payroll, had received instructions, some promise of monetary compensation, and had done the damage himself. He'd left the premises after carrying out his mission without a moment's suspicion because he was operating under the color of law.

"To protect and serve" was nothing more than a farce. Police officers, in growing numbers, were mainly in the service of usurping their authority and corruptly lining their own pockets. The Consortium had so many police officers regularly in its employ that it would make the Los Angeles Rampart scandal look like a typical day of the secretary making off from work with a purse full of the business's office supplies.

The security guards at the gated entrance of the condo community didn't question a thing when Keshari told them that she was having car trouble. They provided courteous access to her tow truck and her chauffeured car, notated in their logs the resident that Keshari had been visiting, and then bid her a good evening.

All night long, Keshari tossed and turned in anger until she finally gave up on sleep and sat in the solarium on a slow fume with her two Rottweilers at her side, barely able to wait until visitation hours commenced at the jail so that she could confront the sadistic asshole who'd orchestrated what had happened. She asked herself over and over again how she had ever been in love with him. She'd now received two warnings. Most people in her line of work were never as lucky. She knew that there would not be a third.

"So, what's next, Ricky?" Keshari snapped venomously. "You gonna order a hit on me?"

Thus far, Ricky had not responded. He'd sat quietly and allowed her to vent.

"That's a funny question," he responded. "What do you think?"

"It was a rhetorical question," Keshari said.

"Of course, it was. You really, really, really have allowed

the history of our personal relationship make you forget what the hell you're fucking with, what the fuck you're involved in. This is not just about me. And now you've gone and gotten some square-assed, pretty boy caught up in your shit. Are you losing your mind?!"

"Is that what this is about?! You had my car vandalized because of him? I'm NOT involved with him, Rick. We JUST had dinner!"

"Yeah, you're involved. You just don't know it yet. It's written all over your face. But don't be stupid. What happened to your car had absolutely nothing to do with him. For the very last time, you'd better wake up and snap yourself back into the nature of this business. You keep trying to play Little Miss Roberta Regular Life and it's going to get you and other completely unassuming people in a very bad way."

"Rick, I want out of this," Keshari reiterated in exhausted exasperation. "Right now, there is NOTHING that I want more in my life."

Ricky gave her a look so scathing that it was clear that he would have hit her had the venue been different.

"Do you really think that you would be having this conversation a second time if it were anybody other than me?" Ricky asked. "What I strongly advise is that you set aside whatever it is that has been troubling you ONCE AND FOR ALL, contact your insurance company and take care of the damages to your Range Rover, or take yourself over to the dealership along with your checkbook and purchase yourself a new one. Then put your mind back on the fact that I'm in here preparing to go to trial on murder one charges and you need to be out there with your A game in place to handle my fuckin' business affairs. If I hear one more word about your desire to leave this organization, I'm gonna sink your beautiful ass in a hole in the ground. Do we have a full understanding?"

"Of course," Keshari replied succinctly. "I got a call from Javier," she said, changing the subject. "They want a meeting."

"When?" Ricky asked.

"Immediately... I told him tonight."

"I hope it has nothing to do with the upcoming shipment."

"Come on, Rick. It has everything to do with this trial. Javier already expressed that his bosses are extremely concerned."

"I want you to follow up with me as soon as that meeting wraps. Get a message to me through my attorney. Today is your last visit. The media scrutiny is steadily increasing and we need to take all safeguards now. I need to know, Keshari...particularly with what I'm currently facing and all that I stand to lose...are you with me?"

Keshari looked him directly in the eye and answered without hesitation, "I'm with you, Rick."

"Are you sure?" Ricky asked.

"Yes," Keshari responded. "I'm with you."

Just after Keshari walked out of Men's Central Jail and sped off up Vignes Street, a young man who didn't appear to be much older than twenty-five approached the sheriff's officer at the counter.

"Excuse me," he said. "Wasn't that Keshari Mitchell just leaving?"

"Who?" the sheriff's officer responded.

"Keshari Mitchell...the record mogul. What was the nature of her business here? Was she visiting Richard Tresvant?"

"Sir, that is not public information. Now, if you'll excuse me."

The sheriff's officer moved down the counter to assist the next person.

♪ 🎧 ♪

Javier had driven up to Keshari's home in Palos Verdes by himself to meet with her. He sipped his espresso thoughtfully after delivering his mind-blowing message—Machaca would not be transacting any more business with The Consortium until Ricky's trial had ended and he was no longer the focus of media attention.

"This decision will be absolutely detrimental to our business, Javier," Keshari said. "There must be some means of compromise. Perhaps, until the trial concludes, we can renegotiate our terms...say, a twenty percent increase on the product price in your favor."

Javier shook his head. "The bosses are firm. There will be no compromise."

"Javier, if Machaca cuts The Consortium off like this now, you must know that it shall adversely affect ALL of our future business together."

"Believe me, Keshari, the bosses have turned all of that around and around to review it from every angle and, just as you want us to understand your position, surely you must understand our position as well. The risk is too great for us to jeopardize our interests. If federal law enforcement launches an investigation, a lot of people will get hurt."

"The Consortium is connected at the federal level, Javier. I gave you my assurances before and I assure you now that we are covered."

"Machaca is connected federally, Keshari. Yet, we take nothing for granted. Nothing is a hundred percent. Ultimately, and I do extend my apologies, this is not a negotiation. I was advised by my superiors to deliver the news. We will complete the upcoming delivery and then our business relationship, for the time being, must be terminated."

"Do you know what you are starting here, Javier? This could result in a turf war."

Javier shrugged.

"That is not our concern, Keshari. Your turf wars would in no way involve our organization."

-11-

It had been a week since the night they'd had dinner. Mars hadn't called Keshari Mitchell and she had not called him. Mars cancelled all of his morning meetings and decided to stop by Keshari's office in Century City. He had no idea what had come over him. He had no idea what Keshari's schedule was like that morning, whether she was in meetings, whether she was even in town. He needed to see her and he had decided that he intended to remain at her office until he did.

Mars arrived at Keshari's office at 9:30 a.m., like he was going to work for Larger Than Lyfe Entertainment. Terrence, Keshari's assistant, seated him in the huge, ultra-modern reception area and had the label's in-house catering service bring him coffee and a scone. Ten o'clock came and went without Keshari's arrival.

"You know, I can take a message from you and relay it to Keshari once she arrives," Keshari's assistant told Mars. "I've tried reaching her a couple of times on her cell phone and she's not answering. I honestly don't know when she's coming."

"Nah." Mars smiled. "I'll wait."

"O-kayyyy," Terrence said, heading back to his workspace.

Ten thirty rolled around and Mars started to get a little antsy. It began to dawn on him how presumptuous it had been for him to show up at this very busy woman's office without an appointment, or an advance phone call or anything, and expect to see her without a problem. He checked his watch and considered leaving. He decided to wait a few more minutes.

At 11 o'clock, Keshari strode through the reception area. She was as beautiful as always in a single-breasted, black, Armani pantsuit, black flip-flops exposing a diamond toe ring, and dark, Cartier sunglasses. She had a Starbucks latte in one hand and she was pulling a large, rolling briefcase behind her. She stopped dead in her tracks when she saw Mars seated casually on one of the sofas thumbing through a *Billboard* magazine. He looked up and felt his mouth spread involuntarily into a huge smile.

"What are you doing here?" Keshari asked abruptly.

"I thought I'd stop by and check on you. I didn't like the way things ended the other night. I wanted to make sure that you were okay."

Keshari looked around her, self-consciously. Terrence poked his head around his computer monitor and grinned at her. She rolled her eyes. She refused to allow herself to become the hot topic of water cooler gossip. The receptionist at the front desk sat, ogling Mars from a distance. The brotha was FINE, she thought. He looked just like the attorney's sexy boyfriend on SHOWTIME's *Soul Food*.

"Come on into my office," Keshari said and closed the doors behind them.

Mars sat down on the office's leather and chrome sectional. Keshari set her briefcase down and glared at him with her hands on her hips.

"Why are you doing this?" she asked.

"Doing what?" Mars asked innocently.

"Pursuing me...relentlessly."

"If I was absolutely certain that I had no reason to be here, I wouldn't be here," Mars responded.

Keshari thought of what Ricky had told her when she had gone to confront him at the jail: "Yeah, you're involved. You just don't know it yet. It's written all over your face." She quickly dismissed the thought.

"I'm probably the last person in the world who needs to be getting romantically involved with anyone right now. I don't have time for this."

"You need to make the time," Mars said seriously.

"I wish it was that simple."

"It is," Mars said.

Keshari shook her head at the ridiculousness of the man's persistence. The entire situation that appeared to be transpiring between the two of them was ridiculous, especially considering the steadily mushrooming set of circumstances in her life that remained barely within the fringes of her control.

"There is no way that you can deny that there was a connection made between the two of us the other night," Mars said. "No...not just the other night, but from the moment we met. I can honestly tell you that I don't ever remember a time when I've felt such...compulsion...to get to know a woman, spend time with her, be a part of her world, and have her be a part of mine. I mean, let's be very clear here. I don't make a habit of showing up at powerful women's offices unannounced and throwing myself at them."

Keshari allowed herself to smile at Mars's last remark.

"Look," Mars said, getting up and going to Keshari, "just tell me that you don't want to see me again and I assure you that I will make myself cease to exist for you. Look me in the eye and tell me that I made a mistake coming here today, that you have absolutely no interest in me, and you will never be bothered by my presence again."

Keshari didn't say anything.

"Tell me," Mars insisted.

He got no response.

"Tell me," he said again, backing Keshari up against her office door.

Still, she said nothing.

"Yeah. Like I thought," Mars said.

He kissed Keshari as he had the night they'd had dinner, spontaneously, passionately, and Keshari found herself kissing him back. Ricky had been right. She couldn't explain it and it would be so corny and ridiculously cliché to call it "kismet," but there was a strong connection between the two of them that had started on the night that they'd met entirely by accident. She was so fucking attracted to him and she was so tired and frustrated with living a life that was so damned restrictive that she constantly had to shut off her emotions and the possibility of forming an emotional connection with someone else.

For a moment, she lost herself in the amazing feeling of him kissing her. Then, just as quickly, she pulled away, completely conflicted, her heart screaming one thing and her mind calmly and rationally telling her the safest, wisest thing to do.

"Okay, now what?" Mars asked in exasperation.

Thoughts flashed through Keshari's mind about what had happened to her Range Rover, what Ricky had said to her, and she didn't even have to think about what would happen if she continued to try him. Even though her entering into a relationship with Mars Buchanan would have nothing at all to do with the affairs of The Consortium, Ricky would make it an issue. It was all about control with him and what he called "loyalty."

"Serious romantic relationships cause crime bosses to slip," Ricky would say. Quite a contradiction since Keshari and Ricky had once been very seriously involved and had emotional ties that continued to exist from their relationship to that day.

"I can't do this," she said, as much as a huge part of

her wanted to. "I'm serious. You have no idea what you're getting yourself into, trying to get involved with me... and I'm at a place in my life right now where getting involved with you is simply not feasible."

"Tell you what," Mars said, equally seriously. "I'm not going to continue to engage in this very circular discussion with you. I have to fly to our New York offices for two weeks and I have a speaking engagement at Howard University in D.C. You've got fourteen whole days to get the most pressing matters on your schedule squared away. When I get back, I'll call you and we'll get together and do something...and I won't accept 'no' for an answer."

"You know, you make a lot of aggressive demands for a man whose position in my personal sphere is new, extremely precarious and very expendable," Keshari said semi-jokingly.

"Oh, it's like that?" Mars asked teasingly.

"It's like that," Keshari responded.

She was already relenting.

"Well, let's just say that I know what I want, I go after what I want, and I am abundantly aware that the really good things in life generally only come through hard work and much persistence."

"Your pursuit of the really good things in life is going to wind you up with a restraining order against you," Keshari quipped.

"Oh, you've got jokes." Mars smiled, completely undaunted by the remark.

He planted a kiss on Keshari's forehead.

"I've got to go. I cancelled my schedule to come here this morning. I'll call you as soon as I get back into town and you'd better be prepared to deal with me."

After he was gone, Keshari was still very conflicted.

"You know you should have ended it," she said to herself.

♫ 🎧 ♫

LTL's PR and legal departments had reviewed the information contained in the press release and Terrence was busy at the fax machine, prepared to launch the news to media. The nationwide talent search was a go. It would be the largest, most expensive single project that Larger Than Lyfe Entertainment had ever undertaken. The project would conduct auditions in ten U.S. cities and the auditions would kick off in one month in Los Angeles, at Universal Studios. The first billboards were going up that day on Sunset Boulevard in Hollywood and at Universal Studios. Then an enormous, digital billboard on top of the Sony building on the world famous Times Square in New York City had been leased to announce the event to the East Coast. Keshari had a meeting in LTL's main conference room that day with a senior staff writer for *Billboard* magazine to discuss the launch of the talent search project. A & R executives were visiting major, urban music radio stations across the country over the next four weeks to hype the launch of the talent search project to radio listeners.

♪ 🎧 ♪

Ricky received notification of Machaca's decision to terminate their business dealings with The Consortium via a letter from Keshari delivered by his attorney. The letter was written in a cryptic numerical code that many crime organizations developed to communicate, particularly when members were imprisoned. Ricky had learned the code, which changed constantly to keep law enforcement from learning to decode it, during his early gangbanging days and, in turn, he had taught the code to Keshari.

The news regarding The Consortium's exclusive supplier so infuriated Ricky that he hurled a chair against the window of the small room that he and his attorney used to confer about his case. He yelled obscenities in fury and was immediately restrained and escorted back to his cell. Ricky's attorney was instructed by the sheriff's officers to strongly advise his client to control himself and the attorney was told that he could return to meet with his client, provided that Ricky had his temper fully under control, the following day during visiting hours.

-12-

I t is an everyday occurrence for cocaine to be transported into the United States and circulated throughout the country. In the United States alone, on average, about 250 tons of cocaine are consumed by users annually. Benjamin Arellano Felix of the infamous, Mexican Arellano-Felix cartel once stated that "as long as there exists that kind of demand for cocaine, there will always be a supply of it" and virtually every conceivable group engaged in the business of organized crime participates.

The United States is one of the only nations in the world with an organized tactical force of law enforcement agents numbering in the thousands who are engaged in a continuous "war on drugs," yet, after more than twenty years of a changing political arena, stiffer laws and sentencing for drug-related offenses, along with millions and millions of dollars earmarked specifically for the fight, the so-called "war on drugs" is still no closer to being won than it was when the whole war started. A number of factors weigh into such a dismal outcome, one of them being the United States' covert and not-so-covert involvement in, and profit from, the international drug trade since the beginning.

♪ 🎧 ♪

A freight trailer backed up to the loading dock at FLOSS Auto Customizing in Inglewood. The driver hopped from the truck's cab and opened the trailer's rear doors. Three FLOSS employees came out to the loading dock to help the truck driver and his partner unload. Twenty-six pallets containing stacked cases of eighteen-, twenty- and twenty-two-inch designer auto rims, along with 300 well-concealed keys of 80 percent pure Colombian cocaine, worth nearly $15 million once it was completely distributed to The Consortium's client base, had made its way unscathed from Bogota to Mexico, from Machaca's warehouses right outside Mexicali, all the way to the first point of delivery in Los Angeles.

Keshari arrived at FLOSS with Marcus Means. Javier Sandovar, along with four of his men, arrived shortly thereafter. It was the first time that Keshari and Javier had come together since their two organizations had parted ways and the meeting was tense, but Javier needed to be present to confirm that each segment of the shipment arrived in full and intact. They talked briefly before they each went to their separate corners to conduct discussions on their cell phones and wait for the offload work to be completed. It would take two to three hours

for all of the auto rims to be unloaded, unpacked, disas-
sembled and all of the valuable product removed from
them by FLOSS employees. Once the delivery had been
counted, it would be loaded into the door wells, bum-
pers, wheel wells, and secret compartments of various
automobiles owned by Consortium members, including
the black Suburban that Keshari was driving. Then the
product would be transported and delivered to several
"processing houses" owned by Ricky and The Consortium all over Los Angeles, where the keys would be
broken down, most of them diluted, repackaged in accor-
dance to the orders of the client base, and then flown to
various areas of the country for delivery and collection
of payment.

It was 1 p.m. when Keshari and Javier confirmed the
count of the shipment. The two also confirmed their next
meeting in two days at AESTHETIC, Ricky's Baldwin
Hills art gallery. Javier and his men left. Keshari began
issuing instructions to the small group of men and a
woman who'd arrived to assist in driving the divided
product to the processing houses.

It was a very bold and dangerous mission, moving
that much cocaine across the city in a relatively small
time window on a single day, both from a law enforcement standpoint and from the standpoint of rival gangs
gaining access to information and attempting an ambush.
Everyone, including Keshari and Marcus, wore bullet-
proof vests. All of them carried scanners in order to hear

communication between police officers in the field and dispatchers at nearby precincts. The Consortium had acquired special coding that enabled them to switch from channel to channel to pick up the police communications at more than one precinct. All of them came heavily armed, prepared to do battle in the unlikely event of an ambush. They all worked with the full understanding that they were required to guard the product with their lives. If there was a loss of product and it was determined that the product was lost due to someone's own negligence, the repercussion would be a final one. The Consortium's loss ratio was a very small one.

"Okay, let's move," Keshari ordered. "I need an update from all of you in thirty minutes. I'll contact each of the processing houses in precisely two hours. Each of the segments must have been delivered, fully received and documented by then. No exceptions. You need to call me immediately if you think you even smell what might be a problem."

A little way up the alley from FLOSS, a telephone repairman sat, belted near the top of a utility pole directly outside his open repair van, with a high-powered camera, snapping shot after shot of the seemingly routine delivery at the auto customizer, from the moment that the freight trailer backed up to FLOSS's loading dock to the moment that the black Suburban that Keshari was driving pulled out of the garage, followed shortly thereafter by five other customized SUVs, a sports car and a sedan, headed for The Consortium's processing houses.

-13-

In a serious, navy Armani Collection suit, Richard Tresvant, surrounded by his personal "dream team" of attorneys and a team of professional bodyguards and sheriff's officers, made his way into the side entrance of Superior Court in Downtown Los Angeles. A throng of newspaper and television reporters, all of them posing questions at once, scurried quickly after the group.

"No comment," Larry Steinberg, Ricky's lead attorney, told the media, and then the group quickly hustled into the building, the reporters barred from entry by the sheriff's officers who maintained the busy courthouse's security.

It was day one of *People and the State of California v. Richard Lawrence Tresvant*. His charge was first-degree murder. The victim was prominent, Los Angeles corporate attorney Phinnaeus Bernard III of the prestigious Carlyle, Brown, Von Klaus & Pennington Law Firm. The Honorable Phelton Bartholomew was presiding.

"All rise," the bailiff said to the packed courtroom, and court was in session.

Ricky sat at the defense table, suavely poised as if a

camera was directed at him. He stared straight ahead, except when he leaned over from time to time to converse with one of his attorneys. His facial expression was grave, as it should have been in consideration of the gravity of his charges, but his reputation for arrogance and a hair-trigger temper when crossed had far preceded him to the first day of his murder trial. Spectators in the courtroom watched his every move, his every gesture, waiting for his facade to slip and expose the murderous gangster who'd managed over and over and over again to slip through the grasp of law enforcement for numerous, heinous crimes to which he was reputedly connected or for which he was directly responsible.

Members of Phinnaeus Bernard III's family sat right behind the prosecution table. Phinnaeus Bernard's wife was elegant and dignified, her suit and hair flawless. Phinnaeus Bernard's two children, were polished and well-educated and seemingly beyond immediate reproach, like a politician's family.

Partners at Carlyle Brown, Phinnaeus's law firm, had mutually come to the decision not to make themselves visible in support of the Bernard family over the course of the trial until completion of the firm's independent investigation into the scandal surrounding Phinnaeus's death, particularly since the scandal may have been linked to the business affairs of the firm. Carlyle Brown maintained a stellar reputation in the field of corporate law and they would not have that reputation tarnished by one attorney gone bad, even if he was a partner. Partners and associates at the firm sent their condolences and words of support to the Bernard family, but all were noticeably absent at the opening of the trial.

Richard Tresvant's support system was noticeably absent as well. With the exception of his very sizeable legal defense team, no family, friends, nor business associates were present, although several of his business associates were expected to testify on his behalf, including one business associate who would corroborate Ricky's alibi.

Although neither the prosecution nor the defense had any objections to live television coverage of the trial, Judge Phelton Bartholomew promptly banned live coverage in his courtroom and granted only a handful of press passes to media, without the presence of cameras, to cover the trial. Judge Bartholomew remembered the O.J. Simpson trial and was adamant that neither the judicial process nor his courtroom would be turned into a three-ring circus.

Los Angeles County District Attorney Steve Cooley stood and took the podium. His team of supporting attorneys stopped whispering among themselves and looked on. The opening statement was a crucial part of the trial. It was the one part of the trial, with the exception of the closing statement, in which both the prosecution and the defense had the most latitude to swing the jury in their favor without objection or rebuttal.

The prosecution knew that spectators, as well as members of the jury, were anxiously awaiting the defense's opening statement. Therefore, the prosecution's opening had to have maximum motivating impact on the jury. Richard Tresvant had a team of legal "all-stars" defending him, from Larry Steinberg, Richard's lead attorney, to Barry Scheck, on forensic evidence. These people were some of the greatest legal minds in the country and were guaranteed to bring as much drama to the trial as the highly sensational murder case itself.

"Organized crime is complex beast," Steve Cooley stated. "Organized crime is so complex, so insidious, that it is becoming more and more difficult to prove, and organized criminals are becoming more and more difficult to apprehend, indict, and convict. Millions of dollars are spent annually by local, state, and federal law enforcement to bring down organized crime. Millions of dollars more are spent by organized crime rings to continue building their empires of dirty, often blood-soaked, money without interference. It's a never-ending battle that is glamorized in books, movies and in current rap music.

"And what does any of this have to do with the execution-style murder of prominent, Los Angeles, corporate attorney Phinnaeus Bernard III? In the complex and vile machinations of criminal business enterprises and the laundering of criminals' dirty money, innocent people sometimes get caught most unfortunately in the under-tow. One of those people was Phinnaeus Bernard III.

"On March 11, 2005, at approximately 10 p.m., Phinnaeus Bernard III was murdered in the underground parking garage of his workplace at 300 South Grand, right here in downtown Los Angeles; two bullets to his chest and one bullet to his head."

Steve Cooley stepped over to a giant, life-sized photograph of the crime scene. Spectators in the courtroom gasped in horror. A close-up, blood-spattered view of Phinnaeus Bernard inside his Mercedes with its driver side door ajar glared like a spotlight at the courtroom. Phinnaeus Bernard's wife wept quietly while the family comforted her. Steve Cooley moved back to the podium and the crime scene photo was removed.

"Phinnaeus Bernard III had a thriving career as a corporate attorney. He was a partner at one of the most prestigious law firms in the country. Phinnaeus Bernard III had no criminal record, no criminal history. Nonetheless, he came to know Richard Lawrence Tresvant... and Mr. Tresvant possesses a lengthy history of run-ins with the law. He sits here now in his expensive suit, with his legal 'dream team' and he looks almost like he's a pillar of the community. But, I repeat, Richard Tresvant has had NUMEROUS run-ins with the law and there have been repeated allegations, complete with indictments, that have brought him to court on multiple prior occasions to fight charges related to major involvement in California's narcotics pipeline, as well as major affiliations to various other organized criminal enterprises. Each time, he comes to court with high-priced, well-known defense attorneys to fight his case and, every time, he manages to slither right under the radar of conviction. He'd like you to believe that he is a legitimate, affluent businessman with multiple, lucrative business enterprises, who is perpetually persecuted by Los Angeles law enforcement because he is Black..."

"Objection! Objection, Your Honor!" Larry Steinberg stood up and erupted angrily. "Mr. Cooley's statements are inflammatory and entirely conjectural!"

"This is an opening statement by the prosecution, Mr. Steinberg," Judge Bartholomew admonished, "and you are well aware of this. Please retain your rebuttals for the argument. Please continue, Mr. Steinberg."

"Cocaine and a substantial amount of money were found in Phinnaeus Bernard's car trunk," Steve Cooley said. "To most, it would appear to have been a drug deal gone bad. All evidence indicates that Phinnaeus Bernard III's murder was the result of a professional hit. The People and the State of California have every reason to believe that Richard Lawrence Tresvant personally orchestrated and committed the murder of Phinnaeus Bernard III. We have substantial evidence to support this, including Richard Tresvant's fingerprints all over the murder weapon. We ask that the jury bring forth a unanimous guilty verdict following the presentation of the evidence in this trial and convict Richard Tresvant for first-degree murder."

Spectators glanced over at Ricky at the defense table. He didn't so much as flinch at the prosecutor's words.

♫ 🎧 ♫

Spectators filed back into the courtroom after lunch and quickly claimed a seat. Live news coverage of the scene outside the cour-thouse and highlights of what was transpiring inside had been taking place all morning. Legal commentators had begun to discuss the murder case on CNN and truTV. Opening statements by the defense were set to begin immediately.

Larry Steinberg's courtroom theatrics were legendary. It was like getting front row tickets to the Rolling Stones' farewell concert to get to see Larry Steinberg in action that day. He launched into his opening statement of the case with his usual flair. It was not just what he said to the juries he faced, nor the way in which he presented his very provocative arguments. It was the amazing charisma that accompanied his obvious legal genius. It had been a very strategic move on Ricky's part to put Larry Steinberg on retainer to represent him.

"This is an open and shut case," Larry Steinberg stated calmly to the jurors. "As much press coverage as my client and this case are now receiving, as much as the prosecution will valiantly attempt to make you all believe that they have their man and that Richard Tresvant is this ruthless, ego-driven 'gangster'...some 'high-ranking drug trafficker' who gets away with committing 'numerous' heinous crimes, this is an open and shut case and I intend to prove to you, without a lot of smoke and mirrors and other skillfully crafted distraction techniques, that you have the wrong man in front of you. Richard Tresvant did NOT murder Phinnaeus Bernard III.

"There are three significant elements...prerequisites... that must be met in order to indict and convict in any criminal case. They are MOTIVE...TIMELINE and OPPORTUNITY...and EVIDENCE. Of all three of these prerequisites, I, and the other attorneys comprising Richard Tresvant's legal defense team, intend to show you that the prosecution failed to satisfactorily meet a single one of the prerequisites required to indict and convict. Number One...there exists no motive for Richard Tresvant to have murdered Phinnaeus Bernard III, other than a molehill made into mountain of circumstantial evidence and the flimsy concoction of the prosecution's mind.

"Number Two...Richard Tresvant has witnesses who shall come forth over the course of the trial...prominent, upstanding, law-abiding citizens...who will testify to Richard Tresvant's whereabouts on March 11, 2005, during the time window of the murder of Phinnaeus Bernard III, and Richard Tresvant was nowhere near the crime scene.

"Number Three...the defense has evidence, including two passed polygraph tests, one from a polygraphist hired by the defense and a second administered by a State-appointed polygraphist, as well as testimony from nationally renowned forensic and legal experts to prove Richard Tresvant's innocence, along with the very real possibility that this man has been very masterfully set up...framed...for the murder of Phinnaeus Bernard III.

"After full presentation of the facts and evidence of this case, I ask that you, the jury, bring back a unanimous verdict of 'not guilty' for my client."

-14-

"Have you been following the trial?" Marcus asked, joining Keshari in the solarium at her Palos Verdes home.

"Of course, I have," Keshari responded. "I cancelled my schedule and have been glued to this television all day. Ricky and his trial both are getting heavy coverage. truTV has been discussing him all day. None of this looks good."

"I agree," Marcus said. "The feds are on this now. Rick remains confident, though, that the matter is fully under control."

"Rick cannot buy all of federal law enforcement. Can you now understand why I am so adamant that it's time to get out of this?"

"We don't have time to keep going there, Keshari. We've got new people in our client base, which presents an increased demand for product, and we've severed ties with our exclusive supplier. We've got a business to run and, clearly, more pressing issues to deal with here than your personal desire to go straight."

"My intentions are serious, Marcus. I am separating myself from The Consortium. If, after all that I've done for this organization, the organization's decision is to place an order or a price on my head for that decision... I'm at a place in my life now where it's a risk that I am fully willing to take. I'm getting out of this business."

"You know why I'm here, Keshari," Marcus said. "We must locate a new supplier and, because of Rick's current situation with this trial, the matter is yours to handle. Where are you with that?"

"I've narrowed the list down to a few, very solid prospects. However, transport is a major and very expensive factor with all of them. That was the reason that we negotiated a deal with Machaca in the first place. You know that. Our best bet right now is with the Jamaicans, or the Colombians out of Miami. I have meetings scheduled with heads of both organizations prior to launch of auditions for my record label's nationwide talent search project in another week and a half."

"Good," Marcus said. "I'll let Rick know. Do you need me to accompany you?"

"I've already let Rick know," Keshari said, staring at Marcus pointedly, "and, no, I'll manage these meetings on my own."

For a moment, the two grew dangerously silent.

"Marcus, following completion of negotiations with our new supplier, I am stepping down from any role that I currently play with The Consortium. If, at that point, you want my position in this organization, you will certainly get no contention from me about it. Until then, I am second in command in this organization and you need to remember and respect that at all times. Do we have an understanding?"

Marcus didn't respond. He stared at Keshari ominously and Keshari glared right back at him, clearly challenging him to make another mistake of forgetting who she was and how she had come to be second in command in The Consortium in the first place.

"Are we clear here?" she repeated. "It's non-negotiable and non-debatable."

"Yeah," Marcus responded.

They were silent again, both of them seeming to contemplate the next steps in their increasingly uneasy alliance.

"Does Rick know of your plans to separate from the organization after securing the new supplier?" Marcus asked.

Keshari didn't answer.

"I didn't think so," Marcus said.

-15-

"On your most ideal second date, where would you go? What would you do?" Mars asked.

After two weeks of phone calls from New York and D.C. to Los Angeles, more bouquets of flowers delivered to Keshari's home and office, and numerous exchanges of e-mail and cute, little text messages, Mars arrived at Keshari's Century City offices, looking gorgeous in a crisp, white linen shirt and black linen trousers, fresh off a plane from New York.

"I don't know," Keshari said, thinking it over. "Maybe a drive up the coast with the top down and a good bottle of wine, some jazz on the CD changer, watch the sunset."

"That sounds really, really nice, but I've got something than that in mind."

"Oh, really?" Keshari asked, amused. "Like what?"

"You'll see."

Mars held her hand as the two of them rode the elevator down to ground level of the upscale office building on Century Park East. He held open the door of the chauffeured Lincoln for her and she slid inside.

"Straight to LAX," he told the driver.

Keshari looked over at Mars, confused.

"LAX? I can't think of a single good restaurant in the airport area. I've got a meeting in a couple of hours, so we'll have to wrap this up pretty quickly. I'll be able to give you my undivided time and attention on the weekend."

"Just chill," Mars reassured her. "I don't want you to spoil the surprise."

"I don't really like surprises, Mars."

"You'll like this one. I promise."

Mars looked over at her. Keshari was very quiet and the look on her face was very serious. She really didn't like surprises and the fact that she was suddenly riding off into the unknown without a clue was taking no time at all to render her fit to be tied.

For a moment, he was hesitant about telling her what he had planned.

"Negril," he said, kissing her hand. "We're going to Negril."

He had such a mischievous twinkle in his eyes after divulging that tidbit of information that Keshari couldn't be sure if he was making a joke or not.

"'Negril' better be the name of some new and trendy, Caribbean restaurant," she said. "I know very well that you better not have composed the very foolish notion in your head that you are gonna kidnap me away to Jamaica."

Mars smiled and said nothing. Keshari knew then that "Negril" was not the name of a Caribbean restaurant.

"Are you out of your mind?! Mars Buchanan, you take me back to my office right now!"

"Uh-uh. No can do. I told you that we were going to do something completely spontaneous when I got back into town and to clear your schedule in preparation for it. I also told you that I did not want any argument from you about it."

"Mars Buchanan, I have a twenty million-dollar nation-wide talent search in the works as we speak. The Los Angeles auditions launch in exactly one week! We are crunched for time as it is and there are still venues that need to be finalized, expenses that still require my review and approval. I have a four o'clock meeting with my attorney to complete a funds transfer that only my signature and voice authentication can authorize. God-dammit, I have a company to run!"

Mars smiled.

"Your assistant sent your laptop. NetMeeting is an excellent tool. We've got a state-of-the-art webcam, fax machine, laser printer, copier, phones, supplies, every-thing you need. You can issue orders as if you are right there at your record label. Any contracts or other docu-ments that you need can be faxed or overnighted to you at our hotel. You have complete control over this entire situation and you don't have to be in your office all day and half the night to exercise that control."

Keshari put her head back and closed her eyes. For many months, she'd been coveting what she liked to call a "normal" life. Was this "normal"? she asked herself.

"This is so ridiculous. I don't have any clothes with me... nothing. I don't even have my passport." She sighed. "I cannot believe that you would arrange for me to fly off with you to the Caribbean like I'm some rap star groupie without consulting me first! This is our second date! Why couldn't you just take me to lunch?!"

"First off," Mars said calmly, "of course, I'm not treating you like a rap star groupie...because I am not a rap star. Second, I asked Terrence if it would be too much of a problem to secretly put together the things that you would need for this trip. He told me that it would be no problem at all. He was actually excited about getting involved in the surprise. He coordinated with your house-keeper to get you packed. He cancelled your schedule. He also took care of providing me with your passport. He and my assistant were absolutely instrumental in putting all of this together."

"Terrence is going to find himself in search of new employment if he continues to show such readiness to appease the requests of someone who does not pay his salary," Keshari glowered.

Mars chuckled and squeezed her hand.

"You'll thank Terrence when you get back."

♪ 🎧 ♪

The two had first-class accommodations all the way. An attendant met them at curbside as soon as their chauffeured car pulled up to check their baggage and secured their boarding passes for them while the two of them sat and had lattes and sandwiches in one of the VIP lounges. Then the attendant escorted the two of them through security checkpoints and to their gate to board their plane.

Just before the flight lifted off, Keshari took out her cell phone and called her best friend, Misha Tierney.

"Where the hell are you?" Keshari asked.

"I'm at Manolo Blahnik in Manhattan, trying on shoes."

"What are you doing in New York?"

"Networking...shopping...taking care of me. Chris is meeting with a new sports management company. He asked me to come out and kick it with him for a couple of days."

Keshari laughed. "Girl, you are becoming a little NBA whore."

"Excuse you. I date a couple of NBA players and now I get classified as a groupie. Forget you! What's up with you, anyway?"

"I just thought that I'd call to tell you that I'm taking a couple of days off work to relax and get my bearings in preparation for the launch of this talent search. My flight is about to take off for Negril right now."

"Negril? You haven't taken a vacation since...well, shit, since...NEVER. What brought this on?"

Keshari lowered her voice to a whisper. "Well, you know how you've been so strongly demanding that I go and get myself laid? Maybe I'll just do that."

Mars overheard what Keshari said and chuckled. A woman across the aisle from them heard what Keshari said and chuckled, too.

"OH...MY...GOD!" Misha squealed. "Somebody's been keeping secrets. Who is he? Who is he? I'm sure that he's in the industry...because all you ever do is work. I want to know all the details...blow by blow."

"After I get back," Keshari promised. "Tell that brotha with the NBA's most gorgeous smile that I said hi."

-16-

Mars's secretary had taken care of all of the arrangements per Mars's very detailed instructions and had booked Keshari and Mars into an enormous River Suite right on the water at Sandals Negril. The hotel was amazing with a staff at the ready to fill their every need and a personal butler assigned to their suite to provide them with around-the-clock, personalized service.

When they arrived at their plush and tropical hotel suite, vases of pink, red and purple tulips, Keshari's favorite flowers, were all over the living room as well as in Keshari's bedroom. There was a bottle of Cristal on ice. There were also bottles of Keshari's favorite pinot grigio and white zinfandel stocked at the bar as well as in the suite's refrigerator. There were fresh strawberries and decadent, European chocolates on the cocktail table. Mars had even managed to acquire a box of Keshari's favorite Cuban cigars after finding out that she indulged in them from time to time. A corner of the expansive living room had been converted into a fully equipped office for Mars's and especially Keshari's use. A rented Jeep was at hand for them to drive and explore every corner of the beautiful island during their stay. Mars had thought of everything and he had clearly spared no expense where their elaborate "second date" was concerned.

Even though, technically, this was her second date with Mars Buchanan, this was the first time that Keshari could remember having taken anything resembling a real vacation in her life. She'd traveled with Ricky on many, many occasions to exotic cities on practically every corner of the globe, but the trips had always been connected in some way or another to the business affairs of The Consortium, and, since Larger Than Lyfe Entertainment's inception, Keshari had thrown herself completely into her work, building the success of her record label, without ever even considering taking a break. She'd been to exotic locales for artists' video shoots and had enjoyed Presidential Suites at luxury hotels, VIP treatment, and nights out with rap stars and their entourages and video crews at the hottest nightclubs in the area while entertainment media swooped in out of nowhere and lapped it all up with their cameras, depicting to the public the beautiful record label mogul living and loving the "glamorous life," but Keshari hadn't been so far as San Francisco simply to get away from it all and have some much-needed time to herself. This excursion was specifically intended for her enjoyment and she had no idea where to begin, particularly since it wasn't something that she had orchestrated herself.

"Why don't you go and get settled, maybe take a relaxing bath?" Mars suggested. "The masseuse will be here in a little while."

"I need to make some calls," Keshari said, heading over to the converted office space and picking up the phone. "I've definitely got to call Terrence and give him an earful. I still cannot believe that he knew all about this elaborate second date, helped to plan it and did not say a thing…as much as he runs his mouth. I also have to touch bases with a few of my people regarding my talent search project. We were actually working on some time-sensitive issues when I was kidnapped today."

She looked back at Mars and smiled coyly. She was still on the phone, issuing orders and jotting notes on a steno pad when the masseuse and the masseuse's assistant arrived.

Mars walked over, took the phone away from Keshari, and hung it up without even allowing her the opportunity to end the call.

"Enough work," he said. "It's time to start our date."

The two of them got full body, Swedish massages.

"I'm going to make a point of setting aside time for a massage at least once a month from now on," Keshari said, as she lay on the massage table across from Mars. "This is mind-altering."

Without even having dinner, Keshari fell asleep on the living room sofa after the masseuse and her assistant were gone. Mars picked her up and carried her into the bedroom, tucking her gently under the covers. He sat on the floor beside the bed, stroking Keshari's hair and watching her sleep until he lost track of time. She looked so peaceful and she slept soundly, as if she hadn't a truly good night's sleep in a very long time. Mars finally pulled himself away from watching her and took his laptop into the living room to check e-mail, make contact with his secretary and to make some needed phone calls of his own.

♪ 🎧 ♪

The next morning, Keshari was up before Mars, doing what she did best, running her company from their hotel suite in the Caribbean. She had faxes spread across the desk and living room cocktail table. She had the phone on speaker and her attorney was telling her which pages needed to be signed and faxed back to him right away.

Mars came into the room in black pajama pants and a black wifebeater, sleep still hovering around his eyes. He sat on the corner of the desk where Keshari was working and smiled down at her.

"You know, my intention for bringing you here was to take you AWAY from business..."

"David," Keshari said quickly, "I've got to go. Keep me posted. Keep the fax and e-mail pipelines open and we'll speak again in the morning."

Breakfast arrived and was set up on their private porch.

Keshari sipped her Blue Mountain coffee and savored the fresh, tropical fruit and Jamaican turnovers filled with chicken and spices while Mars laid out all of the colorful brochures that the hotel had provided and talked about some of the places that the hotel had recommended and that his secretary's research had turned up and were noteworthy of the two of them checking out.

Dressed casually in shorts, tennis shoes and designer sunglasses, Keshari and Mars headed out to explore the island. The day was sunny and warm. The landscape was lush and tropical, outlined by white sand and azure blue waters lapping at the shores. The entire setting was idyllic and it was understandable why couples flew to the islands year after year to ignite or reignite a love connection.

Keshari and Mars went shopping in the open-air marketplace and bought a host of intricately hand-crafted items and Caribbean artwork, souvenir T-shirts for friends, reggae and dancehall music CDs, incense, and scented candles. They went to one of the upscale, duty-free jewelers in the area and Keshari purchased a Ceylon sapphire-and-diamond bracelet and a Cartier watch, a shopping spree that quickly totaled $100,000. She even convinced Mars to accept the gift of a Piaget tank watch with a beautiful crocodile wristband that she pointed out to him and he fell in love with. He put up quite a struggle before finally and reluctantly conceding to accept the very expensive gift.

"You have excellent taste, but I can't accept this. This is too much. This is way-y-y too much."

Keshari waved off his protests and had the jeweler run the charge.

"So is what you went and planned for our SECOND date," Keshari promptly reminded him, "but I've gone along with it all without too much argument, so I don't expect to hear any argument from you where my gift is concerned."

They had dinner that evening at 3 Dives Restaurant and Cliff Bar on Negril's renowned and spectacular cliffside. They dined on lobster tails and callaloo and sampled several of the Caribbean-style alcoholic beverages. They animatedly discussed a couple of the publishing rights cases that Mars was managing at ASCAP and they talked about the current state of the music industry, especially hip-hop. They both agreed that music was an art form and that they both were strong proponents of free expression and strong opponents to censorship.

"But a level of responsibility must be assumed in the creation of any art form," Keshari expressed. "The greatest, noblest mission of the art form, of creative expression, is to ENLIGHTEN, to EDUCATE. It is not merely an artist's emotional release onto some medium. All of the greatest artists have the desire to change the world in some way with their art...and hip-hop has lost its way in that regard."

The two vibed on a level that was simply phenomenal. They talked more about themselves, their "likes" and "dislikes," and relationships. Mars was so humorous and he made Keshari laugh. Keshari was so tremendously intelligent and it rendered Mars absolutely in awe of her. They continued to build on the amazing rapport that had been established while they communicated long distance over the two weeks that Mars had been on the East Coast on business and they both worked valiantly to keep the intensifying sexual attraction between the two of them at bay...at least for the time being.

♫ 🎧 ♫

Later that night, both of them dressed in all black, Keshari sporting a tiny, sexy creation designed especially for her by Donatella Versace herself, a stretch limousine delivered them to the hottest nightclub on the island, The Jungle, where none other than dancehall reggae superstar Beenie Man was the DJ. Mars was absolutely intoxicated by the way that Keshari moved on the dance floor. He had no idea that she was such a good dancer. Keshari smiled and teased him relentlessly as she moved and he tried to keep up with her. She had hundreds of male eyes riveted to her amazing body as she danced. They bogled and butterflied to pumping dancehall rhythms until the wee hours of the morning.

They got back to their hotel suite and it was clear that Keshari was functioning on a contact high she'd acquired from the pungent cloud of ganja smoke that had circulated throughout the club that night. The rum-laced drinks they'd had were probably not helping matters much either. Her guard was way down; she'd done away with her typical, no-nonsense persona and began working what appeared to Mars to be a slow seduction.

Keshari opened the French doors that led out onto their private porch. The porch stepped directly down to the man-made river that outlined all of the hotel's River Suites. The warm, salty, night breeze filtered into the room. The moonlight was the dark room's only illumination. Keshari lit Blue Nile-scented candles along the window ledge, on the bedside tables, and in the doorway leading out onto the private porch. The candles sent a warm, golden glow around the room and over the walls and filled the air with their hypnotic fragrance.

"I'm gonna let you get some sleep," Mars said, kissing her on the forehead. "I had fun tonight."

"No," Keshari said, taking his hand, "don't go. Come on. Dance with me some more."

Bob Marley's "Is This Love" played on the bedroom's stereo system. The entire vibe in the room was surreal and Mars felt sure that he would soon be shaken awake from the obvious dream that he was having just as it was getting to the good part. Keshari kicked off her four-inch Versace heels as Mars pulled her in close and they "slow wined," their bodies in perfect groove with one another.

"I want you to know that, in my entire life, no one has

ever done anything for me as special as all this...this trip...our second date," Keshari said softly. "This means a lot to me. I needed it... more than you know."

"You deserve it," Mars said, "and I promise you that there's more to come."

"My business can't stomach you kidnapping me again. As much as I'm loving every moment of this trip, no more surprises like this. Okay?"

"Okay," Mars responded. "I'll make every effort to give you more notice the next time I want to take you away and have you all to myself."

Keshari laid her head against Mars's chest comfortably and they continued to slow dance by candlelight. Mars savored the feel of Keshari's skin against his fingertips. The scent of her Bvlgari perfume was now engraved in his memory. Then their lips met.

Keshari's body melted into Mars's as her fingers found their way underneath his silk T-shirt, gently caressing the bare skin of his back. Mars felt tense and almost frustrated with yearning for her as his manhood threatened to break the zipper of his expensive, Italian trousers.

"Are you sure you're ready for what you're starting?"

"I think I can handle it," Keshari whispered, kissing his neck.

That was all the invitation that Mars required. He slowly unzipped her strapless dress and let it fall to the floor and Keshari undressed him. Mars savored every single centimeter of Keshari's body with his kisses and caresses...her neck, the small of her back, her beautiful, voluptuous breasts, her navel, her luscious, brown thighs. Every place that Keshari's soft fingertips touched on Mars's body sent an electrical charge through him. She squeezed his perfect apple of an ass and almost brought him to climax.

Keshari arched her back and called out Mars's name when he let his tongue explore downtown. They made love on the huge bed with the moonlight and candle-light softly illuminating their naked bodies. Mars was a skillful and attentive lover. He entered Keshari with slow, deep thrusts as she wrapped her legs hungrily around him, craving the very essence of him.

"You're gonna make me fall in love with you," Mars whispered in her ear as he came.

He held her tight and kissed her face and wouldn't let go. It was so intense, probably the most satisfying erotic experience that Keshari had ever had. Mars's sole objective seemed to be to want to satisfy her.

When their lovemaking drew to a close, Keshari nestled spoon fashion in the safe and warm nook that Mars's body created and Mars nestled his face in the Bvlgari fragrance that emanated from Keshari's hair.

"I could very easily fall in love with you, too," she whispered as she fell asleep in his arms.

-17-

Keshari and Mars arrived back in Los Angeles to a media avalanche covering their new romance—*"Larger Than Lyfe Entertainment CEO Ditches Nationwide Talent Search for Caribbean Tryst with ASCAP General Counsel," "Romance in the Air: Most Powerful Woman in the Music Industry Meets Chief of Legal Services at ASCAP,"* and *"ASCAP's General Counsel Wins the Heart of One of America's Most Beautiful and Powerful Women."* Paparazzi photos seemed to be plastered everywhere from the tabloids to television, showing Keshari and Mars exiting their limousine at Los Angeles International Airport, holding hands and sharing a smile as they rushed to catch their flight to Negril. Other photos exposed the two of them on a private stretch of beach outside their hotel in Negril, locked in a passionate kiss. Still other photos revealed Keshari in her tiny, ultra-sexy, Versace dress, being escorted from a limousine into The Jungle nightclub by "her new paramour," Mars Buchanan.

Keshari was positively livid. She could absolutely not

understand why her personal life, her love life would be of such immense interest to complete strangers...to the public...like she was some actress, an Angelina Jolie or somebody, leading a drama-filled life that was just meant for the tabloids. She called David Weisberg, her attorney, to find out what could be done to put an end to the very frustrating situation. She knew that some journalist would eventually get too over-zealous in his reporting and try to reveal more about her than her love life, just as they'd done when she'd first come into the industry.

"It's entertainment and you're in the entertainment industry." David laughed. "Coverage of whatever pieces of a celebrity's personal life that media can get their hands on and that they believe may prove profitable to them is par for the course. You know that."

"I'm not an entertainer!" Keshari snapped. "I'm a fucking record executive."

"You're an exceptionally beautiful record executive... and sole owner of a very successful record label. Add the air of mystery that has surrounded you from the very beginning, particularly with the organized crime rumors, and the public has been clamoring for a detailed story on you for years," David said. "After a three-day trip to Jamaica, you've become a small cash windfall for quite a few tabloid writers and paparazzi, and I'm afraid that, for now, you're gonna have to take the ride. They have not violated your privacy in any way that is a real violation of law."

"Fuck!" Keshari snapped.

"Manage the affairs of the talent search project," David advised. "This will pretty quickly blow over. With the Whitney Houstons and Britney Spearses of the world maintaining constant drama, there will be a new, sensationalized story that bumps you out of the spotlight in no time."

"I certainly hope so," Keshari said. "All of this personalized press coverage is definitely not something that I need right now."

After more than a week, the loss of privacy began to wear on Mars's nerves and patience almost as much as Keshari's. For the first time, Mars considered the potential repercussions that the media circus could have directly on his own affairs. On any given day, phone calls could come through from the East Coast ASCAP offices regarding the intensive media coverage of his new relationship, particularly considering the morals clause in his contract with ASCAP. Mars had been so caught up in his pursuit of Keshari that he had never even taken the time to seriously think and anticipate the degree of media coverage that his new romance with her might receive. He'd worked in the entertainment industry since graduating from law school and, now, he had a far better understanding from personal experience how troubled and eccentric some celebrities became from having to live their lives in a fish bowl, tracked incessantly by media. The media coverage, however, did nothing at all to put a damper on what was blossoming between Keshari and Mars. If anything, it brought them closer. Over the duration of a few days in Caribbean paradise, Keshari had opened her heart to Mars and he had done the same for her. They were falling in love and it was amazing. They were perfect for each other and the positive energy that was created within their new relationship radiated from the both of them and bathed the people around them in its light.

For Keshari, Mars was not only gorgeous, incredibly sexy from the top of his bald head to his feet, he was super-intelligent and driven, the youngest person to ever command the role of general counsel for ASCAP. He was also responsible and funny and sensitive and caring...and positively wicked in bed. Mars brought a level of happiness and peace to her very complicated world that she could not remember having felt since she lost her mother. When Mars wrapped his strong arms around her and kissed her, all of the chaos that crowded her mind seemed to drift away. After Ricky had instructed her to break things off with Mars and focus on running the affairs of The Consortium in his absence, Keshari was literally risking her life to be with Mars... and, when she considered the unbelievable way that he made her feel all of the time, she didn't care.

For Mars, everything about Keshari was to be admired and adored. He'd been drawn to her like a moth to a flame from the moment that he'd accidentally spilled champagne on her. She was the most physically beautiful woman he'd ever set eyes on in his entire life, but that was merely the tip of the iceberg about her. She possessed one of the most shrewd business minds he'd ever had the opportunity to encounter. Then there was the side of her that she kept tucked so carefully away, an unbelievable sweetness mixed with an almost childlike vulnerability. As a powerful executive in the music industry, Mars had certainly been through his share of beautiful, amazing women, but there were qualities about Keshari that were simply extraordinary. It made him want to turn in his "player card" with no regrets. When he stared down into the deep mystery that her green eyes held, he had hopes of the future...with her.

The media, the paparazzi, and the public loved every single second of the two of them together. It was better than romance fiction.

♪ 🎧 ♪

On her way to a morning meeting with a client, Portia stopped at Starbucks in Brentwood for a latte, and then ran across the street to the sidewalk magazine vendor to pick up a *Los Angeles Times* and a stack of copies of the new issue of *Interior Design*. Her firm had been featured in *Interior Design* in a story called "Ultra Modern Meets Africa" that had depicted what she'd done to her very own Beverly Hills loft. The cover of *Entertainment Weekly* caught her eye. *"Love Is in the Air: Record Mogul Keshari Mitchell Connects with ASCAP General Counsel."*

Portia saw bright red as she stared furiously at the tabloid photograph of Mars caught in a passionate lip lock with Keshari Mitchell, CEO of Larger Than Lyfe Entertainment, on a private stretch of beach in Negril, Jamaica. The tropical setting and the two beautiful people in it were perfect, as if it were all an orchestrated scene photographed for a postcard. Keshari was wearing a black, Versace bikini that Portia also owned...and that she intended to burn as soon as she got home...and a shirtless Mars wore white linen trousers rolled up at the ankles that highlighted his suntanned, caramel brown skin. The two looked so madly fucking in love and the press was clearly eating it up. Portia wanted to scream, vomit, and break some shit all at the same time. She could barely keep her thoughts on her work as she went through fabric swatches and paint colors with her wealthy client in preparation for decorating the client's new Hollywood Hills home. She couldn't wait to go to Mars's condo to confront him.

♪ 🎧 ♪

Just after six o'clock that evening, Portia arrived at Mars's condo.

"Shit!" Mars snapped under his breath as he looked through the peephole.

Wearing black Sean John sweatpants and no shirt, he

reluctantly opened the door. He still wore the amazing tan that he'd acquired in Negril. That suntan made Portia fuming mad all over again as she whisked past Mars through his foyer and into the condo's huge living room that she had decorated.

She sat down on the leather sectional, crossed her long legs, and came right to the point. She pulled a copy of *Entertainment Weekly* from her bag and dropped it on the glass cocktail table in front of Mars.

"Do you care to explain this?" Portia asked succinctly.

Mars stared down at the photograph of Keshari and him. The passion between the two of them was practically tangible on the page. The icy silence coming from Portia as she awaited his explanation seemed to stretch on and on. Mars really owed her no explanation, but he tried to piece together the right words to say to her nevertheless.

"Portia...look. I hope that you didn't show up here at my apartment on some sort of jealous tirade. I thought that we had a clear understanding that the two of us are not exclusive. If memory stands correct, it was your idea."

Portia was speechless, even though she'd spent the entire day composing in her mind, frame by frame, precisely how she planned to curse Mars out once she saw him that evening.

Not exclusive? Not exclusive?! she thought now. Was that the best shit that a high-powered attorney could come up with to defend himself?!

"Not exclusive" was what Mars's mouth said now, but

mixed signals were what he'd been serving up to her for nearly two years. When the two of them were seeing each other on a regular basis during the periods when she was in L.A. for a long stretch of time working on a project, Mars was fucking her every other day AND night, then spending the night at her loft a couple of nights every week...EXCLUSIVELY.

When Mars needed a shoulder of support and a listening ear to hear him vent his frustrations about the rigors of his very demanding job and how "ruthless" the "backstabbers" in the industry could be, she'd been there practically like a wife would be, providing him countless words of encouragement and advice, even in instances where she didn't quite agree with him; and she'd done this...EXCLUSIVELY.

What was she?! Some whore to him?! She was good enough for regular fucking, but not quite good enough for a committed, monogamous relationship?!

"I can't see you anymore," Mars said.

The words went straight through Portia's heart like hot daggers. All Portia could see as she sat there, literally choked up on her hurt and anger, were the many nights when she had stood in her kitchen playing the domestic role, cooked extravagant meals and fed this man, massaged his back, listened to his thoughts and dreams while she shared her own thoughts and dreams with him, bathed him, coddled him, brought him chicken soup when he was sick with the flu, showered him with gifts of thousands of dollars' worth of rare, African art, sucked his dick and fucked him in every way and in every place imaginable only to be cast aside as if she were so totally...expendable. She had damned near given her soul to this man and had been patiently waiting for him to overcome his obvious fear of a more committed relationship with her, and now he was giving her the kiss-off for this little, Tracey Edmonds-looking bitch?! What the fuck?!

"Is...is this more than a fling?" was all Portia could muster.

What seemed like an interminable silence passed before Mars answered.

"I'm in love with her," Mars said quietly, shattering Portia's entire world.

A single tear rolled down Portia's cheek and Mars reached out compassionately to wipe it away. Portia smacked his hand away before he could touch her.

It wasn't that Mars didn't care about Portia. He did. Portia was a stunning, vivacious, talented, intelligent, amazing woman. She simply wasn't the woman for him. Ideally, Mars wanted to hold her and reassure her that he would be there for her if she ever needed him. They'd had some good times together and he wanted them to part as friends. But, realistically, Mars knew Portia well enough to know that he would have to make a clean break with her with no future contact whatsoever. There was no middle ground for the two of them and he did not want to inadvertently give Portia some glimmer of hope that there was still a chance for them.

Portia stood up bravely and tucked her Christian Dior clutch under her arm.

"Mars, baby, I wish you the best...of everything," she said as she turned to leave. "Goodbye."

The door closed and Mars found himself dumbfounded but thankful that the whole situation was over and that there had not been an ugly scene. The collected and dignified way that Portia had reacted was not what he'd expected. Drama was much more her style. Drama was what she had initially planned on bringing him that evening and something in his gut told him that things were not over. Mars visualized Portia slipping into his condominium's subterranean garage in the middle of the night while he was out of town and leaving deep, ugly key gouges down the full length of his $140,000 Mercedes, and then flattening its tires as repayment for him breaking things off with her. Several nasty scenarios came to mind that were much more in character for the many-times-driven-to-melodrama Portia that Mars knew than the woman who had so graciously left his apartment.

As Portia slid behind the wheel of her Range Rover and drove away, she solemnly vowed to herself that she would make Mars Buchanan sincerely regret the day that he and Keshari Mitchell had ever gotten together.

-18-

Richard Tresvant's murder trial was well into its third week and the media and the public in Los Angeles were still clamoring for the details of the "reputed gangster charged with the first-degree murder of the high-profile corporate attorney" as much as they had been on day one of the trial. News networks like CNN and CSPAN continued their coverage of the sensational, Los Angeles trial and legal experts on truTV discussed daily the trial's likely outcome and the sordid history of organized crime in Los Angeles all the way back to the Pro-hibition Era.

The prosecution still had the floor and continued questioning its witnesses. Currently on the witness stand was the head of security for the office building where Phinnaeus Bernard III had worked and was murdered.

"Mr. Kowalski, how long have you been director of security for Helzberg Properties?" Steve Cooley, the district attorney, asked.

"Seven years," Stephen Kowalski answered.

"And on the night of March 11, 2005, were you on duty?"

"Yes."

"What were your scheduled work hours on that date?"

"From 10 a.m. until 10 p.m.," Stephen Kowalski responded.

"And were there any other security officers on duty with you during this time frame?" the district attorney questioned.

"Yes, there were four other officers on duty with me, each of them working eight-hour shifts."

"Did you know the victim, Phinnaeus Bernard III, sir?"

"Personally, no," Stephen Kowalski said, "but I was aware that he was a partner at the firm on the thirty-fifth floor. I saw him in passing almost every day."

"Did you see Mr. Bernard on March 11, 2005, the day of his murder?"

"Yes," Stephen Kowalski answered.

"When did you see him?"

"Around lunchtime," Stephen Kowalski said. "He was accompanied by the defendant, Mr. Tresvant."

"And have you ever seen the defendant, Richard Tresvant, at the building before March 11, 2005?"

"Yes," Stephen Kowalski said.

"Lunchtime is probably one of the busiest times of the day at a high-rise the size of 300 South Grand. There is likely to be a tremendous amount of foot traffic during that time. Why would it register in your memory having seen Phinnaeus Bernard and the defendant, Richard Tresvant, during lunchtime, during such a busy time of the day?"

"Because they were arguing, sir."

"Do you know what they were arguing about?"

"No, sir," Stephen Kowalski responded.

"Did you see Mr. Bernard when he returned from lunch?"

"No," Stephen Kowalski answered.

"But you know that he did return from lunch?"

"Yes," Stephen Kowalski answered.

"How do you know?"

"He signed security's after-hours log later that same evening," Stephen Kowalski said.

"So, security maintains a log book in the main lobby to keep a record of all those entering and exiting the building, both before and after regular business hours. Is that correct?"

"Yes, that is correct," Stephen Kowalski said.

Steve Cooley removed from a large, plastic evidence bag the log book that had been present in the main lobby on the night of the murder.

"For the record, this is People's exhibit ten," the district attorney stated.

He opened the log book in front of Stephen Kowalski and flipped to the last pages, locating the entry where Phinnaeus Bernard had signed out for the very last time.

"On the night of March 11, 2005, the night of Phinnaeus Bernard's murder, at what time did Mr. Bernard sign the log book prior to leaving for the night?"

"Nine forty-seven p.m., sir," Stephen Kowalski stated, looking down at the page.

"Was Mr. Bernard accompanied by anyone when he was leaving?"

"I don't recall, sir," Stephen Kowalski stated.

"Who signed the log book immediately prior to and immediately after Mr. Bernard signed out?"

"A 'Sylvia Hendershot' signed the book at 8:27 p.m., almost an hour and a half prior to Mr. Bernard signing out," Stephen Kowalski stated. "A 'Mr. & Mrs. Harry Donnelly' and a 'Richard Driver' all signed out at 10:03 p.m. after Mr. Bernard."

"So, per security's log book," the district attorney said, "it is safe to deduce that Phinnaeus Bernard was alone when he was leaving on the night of his murder. Is that correct?"

"That is correct," Stephen Kowalski replied.

"Do security cameras capture people coming and going from the Helzberg property located at 300 South Grand?" the district attorney asked.

"Yes, of course," Stephen Kowalski answered.

"On March 11, 2005, the day of Phinnaeus Bernard's murder, did security cameras capture Phinnaeus Bernard III leaving his office for the day and heading to the underground garage where he parks?"

"Most likely," Stephen Kowalski responded, "but video footage for the date in question was stolen."

"Stolen?" the district attorney asked incredulously. "Please explain."

"On the night of the murder, LAPD detectives requested

to view security camera footage for the entire day. The tapes for all sectors of the building for the entire day of March 11th were gone. Helzberg Properties also maintains a backup of the security's daily video footage of all sectors of the office building in a password-protected computerized database. The footage for the entire day of March 11, 2005, had been wiped, apparently by some type of computer hacker."

"In your professional opinion," the district attorney stated carefully, "do you believe that the theft of the videotape and hacking of security's computer files were connected to the murder of Phinnaeus Bernard III?"

"Yes," Stephen Kowalski stated succinctly.

"No further questions," Steve Cooley said.

"Mr. Steinberg, are you prepared for cross?" Judge Bartholomew asked.

"Yes," Ricky's lead defense attorney said quickly, approaching the witness.

He cleared his throat.

"Mr. Kowalski, are there any entries in the security log on March 11, 2005, the date of Phinnaeus Bernard's murder, containing my client's, the defendant's signature?"

"No," Stephen Kowalski answered.

"Mr. Kowalski, did you see my client, Richard Tresvant, on the night of March 11, 2005, sir?"

"I don't recall, sir."

"But you can be quite certain that my client, Richard Tresvant, was not accompanying Phinnaeus Bernard as he left his place of business for the evening...immediately prior to his being murdered...per security's after-hours log. Is that correct?"

"Yes, that is correct," Stephen Kowalski responded.

"Now, getting back to the theft of the video surveillance tapes from the security office," Larry Steinberg continued. "Was there any evidence of forced entry into the security office where the tapes are maintained?"

"No," Stephen Kowalski answered, "which makes all of this all the more puzzling."

"So, the theft of the building's security surveillance tapes could have been an inside job, correct?"

Stephen Kowalski hesitated.

"Since the office of the building and the security officers are the only ones who hold keys to the security office, is it plausible to say that someone employed by Helzberg Properties could have removed those tapes?"

"Yes, it is plausible to say that," Stephen Kowalski answered finally.

"No further questions," Larry Steinberg said, turning on his heel and heading back to the defense table.

♪ 🎧 ♪

"Mrs. Hendershot, how long have you been employed by the firm of Carlyle, Brown, Von Klaus & Pennington?" the district attorney asked.

"Six years," Sylvia Hendershot responded.

"And did you work as Phinnaeus Bernard's legal secretary for the entire six years that you've been employed with the firm?"

"Yes," Sylvia Hendershot answered.

"Would you say that you knew Mr. Bernard well?"

"After six years working for him, yes," Sylvia Hendershot said.

"Both professionally and personally?"

"Yes," Sylvia Hendershot said.

"Do you know the defendant, Mr. Richard Lawrence Tresvant?"

"Personally, no," Sylvia Hendershot responded, "but he is a client of the firm."

"How long has Mr. Tresvant been a client of Carlyle, Brown?"

"Up until the murder, Mr. Tresvant was a client of the firm for about two years."

"So, the firm no longer represents Mr. Tresvant?"

"No," Sylvia Hendershot answered.

"Did Phinnaeus Bernard personally handle Mr. Tresvant's legal affairs for the entire time that Mr. Tresvant was a client of the firm?"

"Yes," Sylvia Hendershot replied. "If memory stands correct, a mutual friend of the late Mr. Bernard and Mr. Tresvant brought Mr. Tresvant to the firm."

"Do you know the name of this 'mutual friend'?" the district attorney asked.

"Yes. Walter Bumgaarten."

Rustling and a collective gasp went up in the court-room. The Bumgaarten family was among the "Who's Who" of Los Angeles' old money and aristocracy. It seemed a most strange mix for anyone within that historically known family of bankers, real estate speculators and developers, and philanthropists to be associated in any way with the infamous Richard Tresvant.

"Would you say that Phinnaeus Bernard and Richard Tresvant were friends?"

"Yes," Sylvia Hendershot responded. "They played golf together often. Phinnaeus...Mr. Bernard, had dinner at Mr. Tresvant's home many times. Mr. Bernard was very intrigued by Mr. Tresvant. He said on more than one occasion that Mr. Tresvant was one of the 'shrewdest businessmen he'd ever met in his life.'"

"Was Mr. Bernard aware of Mr. Tresvant having involvement in any kind of illegal activity?"

"I have no idea," Sylvia Hendershot answered.

"Were you aware of Richard Tresvant having involvement in any kind of illegal activity?"

"Of course not," Sylvia Hendershot responded quickly. "With the exception of Mr. Tresvant being a client of the firm, I had no knowledge of him whatsoever."

"On March 11, 2005, did Richard Tresvant visit or make any phone calls to Phinnaeus Bernard at the firm?"

"Yes, he did. Mr. Bernard had a lunch meeting with him that day. Mr. Tresvant called several times that morning and had to reschedule their eleven o'clock meeting for later in the day."

"Did he state why he needed to reschedule?" the district attorney asked.

"He said that his prior meeting was running longer than he'd expected."

"When Mr. Tresvant finally arrived at the firm, how long was he there?"

"Just a few minutes. Mr. Von Klaus, one of the senior partners, stopped and chatted with them for a few minutes. Then the two of them, Mr. Bernard and Mr. Tresvant, left."

"Do you know where the two had lunch?"

"At the Jonathan Club," Sylvia Hendershot said. "I reserved a table for the two of them there the day before."

"Do you know how long the two of them were gone?"

"Not exactly," Sylvia Hendershot said, "but it would be safe to estimate it to be about three hours. Mr. Tresvant arrived after one. I went to lunch myself soon thereafter. I returned and Mr. Bernard was not back. He did return shortly before 5 p.m. He closed himself away in his office and was on the phone until I left around 8:30 p.m. that night."

"Did Mr. Tresvant come back to the office with Mr. Bernard when he returned from lunch?"

"No," Sylvia Hendershot answered.

"Did you see Richard Tresvant again at all that day?"

"No," Sylvia Hendershot said.

"Mr. Stephen Kowalski, head of security at the office building, stated that Mr. Bernard and Mr. Tresvant were arguing as they were leaving for lunch. Do you have any idea what they could have been arguing about?"

"Objection, Your Honor! The district attorney's question calls for speculation," Larry Steinberg hopped up and bellowed from the defense table.

"Mr. Cooley," Judge Bartholomew said, "you'll need to rephrase your question or it will be stricken from the record."

"Did Mr. Bernard seem upset or angry in any way when he returned from lunch?"

"Objection, Your Honor! Still calls for speculation!" Larry Steinberg argued.

"Overruled," Judge Bartholomew responded.

The district attorney repeated the question. "Did Mr. Bernard seem upset or angry in any way when he returned from lunch?"

"Yes," Sylvia Hendershot answered. "He said that if Richard Tresvant called anymore that day to tell him that he'd caught a flight to the San Francisco offices. Then he slammed the door to his office and didn't come out anymore before I left for the night."

"Was Mr. Bernard intending to catch a flight to San Francisco that evening?"

"No," Sylvia Hendershot responded. "Mr. Bernard didn't have any business at all in San Francisco that week."

"No further questions," the district attorney stated.

♪ 🎧 ♪

"Detective Fields, were you the lead detective called to the crime scene at 300 South Grand on March 11, 2005, the night that Phinnaeus Bernard III was murdered?"

"Yes," Detective Fields answered.

"Please describe the murder scene when you arrived."

"There was a 2005 silver Mercedes S500 parked on the third subterranean level of the parking structure at 300 South Grand. The driver's side door was ajar. The victim inside the car was who we determined to be Mr. Phinnaeus Bernard III, a corporate attorney who worked within the building. He was already dead when we arrived at the crime scene. We determined the time of the murder to have occurred between one to two hours prior to our arrival at the crime scene. We believe that it was a professional hit. The shots were very precise, two shots to the chest and one to the head. The shots were likely to have been fired from a gun equipped with a silencer because the caliber of the firearm used in the murder would definitely have been loud enough to be heard and draw immediate attention. Security surveillance tapes that could potentially incriminate the perpetrator or perpetrators of the murder were taken. Then there was the hacking and deletion of security surveillance files from the building's computer system. The whole thing was clearly very carefully and professionally orchestrated."

All the while that Detective Fields provided details of what he and other LAPD officers found upon arrival at the murder scene, color slides of the murder scene were projected onto a large screen at the front of the courtroom. Jurors watched the changing frames of the murder scene with expressions of shock and discomfort. In a well-lit parking garage at an upscale office building in downtown Los Angeles' business district, this prominent attorney had been snuffed off in cold blood. It was the stuff that blockbuster novels and movies were made of.

"What findings led you to identify the defendant, Mr. Richard Lawrence Tresvant, as a suspect in this murder?" the district attorney asked.

"There were substantial prints on the door handles and door frame of the car, as well as in the interior of the car. After completion of an analysis back at the crime lab, we determined that they were the prints of both Mr. Bernard as well as Richard Tresvant, the defendant."

"After determining that Richard Tresvant's fingerprints were at the murder scene, what did you do?"

"Because we were made aware that Mr. Tresvant was a client of the victim's, Mr. Bernard, at Mr. Bernard's law firm, and because we were also informed, by Mr. Bernard's secretary, Ms. Hendershot, that Mr. Bernard and Mr. Tresvant had had lunch together that same day, the day of the murder, we contacted Mr. Tresvant to ask if he would come downtown to answer a few questions."

"Did he agree to do so?" the district attorney asked.

"No," Detective Fields responded. "He was completely uncooperative. He told us to...ahem...'go and fuck ourselves.' Mr. Tresvant and the Los Angeles Police Department have had a rather lengthy and certainly not the most civil history with one another."

"Strike the expletive from the record," Judge Bartholomew instructed the court stenographer.

"What did you do after Mr. Tresvant's refusal to come downtown for questioning?"

"We secured a warrant to search Richard Tresvant's primary residence and offices of business for the murder weapon."

"What were your findings after securing the warrant?"

"We found the murder weapon."

"Where did you find the murder weapon?"

"At Mr. Tresvant's primary residence on Bellagio Terrace in Bel Air, sir. Following ballistics report confirmation, we immediately placed Mr. Tresvant under arrest for the murder of Phinnaeus Bernard III."

"No further questions, Detective Fields," the district attorney said.

-19-

Anyone observing Keshari's life would have to wonder if and when she ever slept and how she was able to dedicate sufficient time to her new romance to sustain it with the almost inhumanly lengthy list of business-related activities and tasks that inundated her typical day. She'd been following Ricky's murder trial as if she was a member of his legal defense team. She kept continuous contact with his attorney and while she was at her office during the day, she kept her television tuned to the local news, truTV, or CNN for regular updates on the trial, which raised a few eyebrows among LTL staff.

Just two days before the launch of "Nationwide Search for a Star," Keshari told Terrence to book her a flight to Palm Beach and have her house and car ready for her arrival in Palm Beach.

"What?!" Terrence said incredulously. "Keshari, it's only two days before the L.A. auditions. You just got back from Jamaica. There is so much on your agenda and you've got a meeting scheduled with the accountants to be updated on the talent search project's current expenses to make sure that it is staying within budget. This trip is a trip that you should absolutely postpone unless it's a life and death emergency."

"Just book the flight, T," Keshari snapped irritably. "I've got business in Miami and it can't be put off until another time."

"Not a problem," Terrence said quickly and left her office.

♪ 🎧 ♪

Terrence had heard the stories. There was no way that he could have worked with Keshari for as long as he had, as closely as he did, without being made aware of the industry rumors regarding who Keshari really was and her alleged high-ranking involvement in organized crime. Did Terrence believe the stories? In the beginning, he'd dismissed them entirely. In entertainment, the media and the so-called "industry insiders" who reported to the media, could take one, tiny tidbit of information, put a spin on it, and blow it entirely out of proportion. He'd seen it time and time again with other entertainers with whom he'd worked or through associates who also worked for well-known figures in the entertainment industry. Over time, though, Terrence had begun to seriously question the validity of some of those rumors. The more time passed and the more closely he worked with his beautiful, mysterious boss, the more he wondered about some of the spur-of-the-moment trips she took, some of the meetings that she took, and some of the people that she knew.

♪ 🎧 ♪

Keshari's flight to Palm Beach was uneventful. A chauffeured car picked her up at the airport and drove her to the exclusive Gulf Stream community of Palm Beach where Keshari owned a $16 million, six-bedroom, contemporary Mediterranean-style home.

Her cell phone rang as the chauffeur carried her bag into the house and set it down in the foyer.

"What are you doing in Palm Beach?" Mars asked.

The tone of his voice indicated clearly that he was irritated with Keshari for leaving town without telling him anything.

"I have an urgent business meeting in the morning," Keshari said. "You know my life, Mars. It goes a mile-a-minute. There are often spur-of-the-moment business meetings on the other side of the country and I'm not always able to provide notification regarding my itinerary to everybody who seeks it."

"Wait a minute, wait a minute," Mars said. "Why are you so defensive? It's me you're talking to."

"I'm not defensive, Mars. I'm tired. I just walked in from the airport and I need to get some sleep. I'll call you tomorrow. I'm flying back into L.A. right after the meeting. Okay?"

Keshari hung up the phone and Mars sat, staring at

the telephone receiver on his end, wondering what exactly was going on with her.

♪ 🎧 ♪

The next morning, as Keshari got ready to leave for her meeting with Enrico Santiago at his home on Jupiter Island, Mars arrived.

"Mars, what in all FUCK are you doing here?!" Keshari snapped.

"What is going on with you?" Mars demanded.

He set his garment bag down and looked around him at the absolutely unbelievable, two-story entry of Keshari's oceanfront, Palm Beach home. It was the first time that he'd been there and it was unfortunate that his impromptu trip was not under better circumstances.

"Mars, you should NOT have come here. I told you that I would be back in L.A. right after my meeting. Why are you blowing a business trip of mine completely out of proportion?!"

Keshari looked amazing in her cream, Valentino pantsuit, but the vibe that came from her was all high stress and, if Mars didn't know better, she seemed to be hiding something as well.

"Keshari, for the very last time, WHAT is going on with you? Why are you being so damned hostile and evasive about this sudden flight to Florida? Did something happen? Does it have anything to do with this meeting that you're headed to? We've maintained a constant, open line of communication, and suddenly you've just shut down. We're in a relationship. I'm concerned and I want to know what's up with you."

"Mars, I can't do this now. I'll be late. My housekeeper will help you get settled and I'll see you when I get back."

Her baby blue Bentley Continental GT convertible sped off up the palm tree-lined drive of her gated home and was gone.

♪ 🎧 ♪

Threaded discreetly among the palm trees and palatial, multimillion-dollar homes of the Florida coast dwells a darker element of power and money that few are cognizant of. This element does not consist of the hardened, profanity-spewing, cigarette-smoking thugs dressed in black as depicted on HBO's *The Sopranos*. These are the polished, golf-playing, grandfatherly multi-millionaires who run reputable, legitimate business enterprises and are major contributors to the arts and long-respected, American charities...and who amass the bulk of their fortunes in organized crime, trafficking literally billions of dollars worth of cocaine, heroin, and other illegal narcotics annually around the U.S., sometimes with some assistance directly from U.S. government, and despite their seemingly harmless, genteel appearances, are far more dangerous than any of the hoods from *The Sopranos*.

Keshari had done her research and could trust the legitimacy of the information that she had acquired underground about the man she was about to meet more than she could trust the news on the front page of the *Los Angeles Times*.

"Keshari Mitchell, it is a pleasure to meet you," Enrico Santiago said graciously as he escorted Keshari into the library of his luxurious, $22 million home on Jupiter Island.

The views from the 180 degrees of windows facing out onto the Atlantic Ocean were magnificent. A wall of first-edition books from Edgar Allan Poe, Mark Twain, and others lined the far wall from the ceiling to the floor. A large koi fountain sat in the center of the huge, marble-floored room. Skylights dotted the entire, twenty-two-foot, cathedral ceiling. The secluded, oceanfront location and the library were the mansion's strongest selling points as far as Keshari was concerned, but she quickly regrouped from the critique of her beautiful surroundings. The Consortium needed a new supplier, someone who could easily furnish $100 million worth of high-purity cocaine from month to month. As well-mannered and refined as the silver-haired Enrico Santiago appeared, he was one of the most powerful criminals in Florida and he definitely possessed the capability to fill The Consortium's needs.

"What can I do for you?" Enrico Santiago asked.

"My organization needs a new, exclusive supplier for

a potentially long-term relationship. More specifically, my organization requires a minimum of 100 keys at 80 percent purity per month at thirty thousand dollars per key and full transport to our receiving locations in Los Angeles at your expense. My organization is prepared to commit to six months today."

"Your organization seeks much on a silver platter, considering your current predicament."

"Despite the current legal troubles that Rick is enduring, the organization remains fully operative and shall continue to be so, even if Rick is convicted."

"I'm not convinced of that. Neither are other organizations, I'm sure. That is how you lost your connections with the Mexicans. Federal law enforcement is watching your every move right now. Be very sure of that. No one wants to be involved with that. It's too risky."

"We have powerful connections in federal law enforcement," Keshari said.

"So do I," Enrico Santiago stated. "However, for every ten federal agents that can be bought, there are two or three federal agents who possess a strong enough code of ethics that they can't be bought at any price and they eat and sleep with the intense desire to completely destroy the livelihoods of people like us and put us behind bars for the rest of our lives."

"Then we should pool our resources and make this far less of a problem," Keshari said.

"Your terms, as they are, are not acceptable, Keshari."

"What would make my terms more amenable to you, Mr. Santiago?"

He looked her over appraisingly before speaking. "Perhaps, if I had the opportunity to fuck the beautiful Keshari Mitchell, we could come to an agreement somewhere extremely close to your terms."

"Mr. Santiago, I came here today and have dealt with you only with the utmost respect. That is the least of what I expect in return."

Enrico Santiago did not respond. He sat, contemplatively staring at her breasts.

"Mr. Santiago, what kind of an arrangement would prove acceptable to the both of us?" Keshari asked. "I have another meeting and I'm confident that this organization will accept my terms."

"The Jamaicans?" Enrico questioned and snickered. "That will be a mess and you know it. I run America's cocaine supply...before the Mexicans, the Jamaicans, or anyone else. The smartest thing that you did was come to me."

"Then tell me what terms are more doable for you," Keshari said again. "Time is of the essence. My organization has a sizeable client base with regular product demands."

Enrico smiled and rubbed his hands together.

"You come here alone and unarmed, as if you have no doubts about what the outcome of this meeting will be. You've got some pair of balls on you, young lady, and that's more than I can say for a lot of these men currently working in our profession. If nothing else, I've got to respect you for that. You're beautiful, you're extremely smart...with an MBA from the Wharton School...you see, I've done my research, too. You have the potential to be far more dangerous and deceptive than the men in this business realize.

"Here are my terms. The product price is thirty-seven... at least until your organization works beyond your current legal troubles. You will pay an additional fifteen percent of the product price each month for transportation."

"That's acceptable," Keshari said, having resolved it in her mind prior to the meeting that concessions would more than likely have to be made, with all of the leverage on the side of the potential supplier.

"And if I should wind up entangled in some uncomfortable situation with federal law," Enrico continued, "you will be the first to die. Comprende?"

"But of course," Keshari replied.

"Very well then. How soon are you seeking delivery?"

"Exactly one month from today," Keshari responded. "One hundred fifty keys to start. Eighty percent purity is non-negotiable."

"These are the delivery points," she stated, placing a list of Consortium-owned residences, warehouses, and businesses in front of him on his very expansive, carved, mahogany desk. "I can initiate transfer of funds prior to my flight back to Los Angeles tonight. The full funds transfer will be finalized upon confirmation of delivery of all segments of the shipment. Funds will be coming from my organization's Grand Cayman account."

Enrico Santiago wrote down details for an account that he held in the Bahamas to which Consortium funds would be paid.

"We will speak again very soon," he said. "Let me show you out."

Keshari got back to her home in the Gulf Stream section of Palm Beach and was far less wound up than she'd been before she'd left earlier that morning. Mars was outside doing laps in the infinity pool. Keshari went out onto the poolside patio, took off her jacket, and tossed it on the chaise beside the pool. She kicked off her sandals and began to take off everything else. Nude, she dove smoothly into the pool as Mars made his turn at the opposite end.

"Hey," Keshari said when Mars arrived back at her end of the pool.

"Hey, yourself," Mars responded.

He noticed that she wasn't wearing a bathing suit. She waded over to Mars and kissed him, her body and her lips drawing him in like an invitation to the very best party.

"I take it that your meeting went well," he said.

"My entire life is about to change," Keshari answered.

-20-

In a caravan of black Cadillac Escalades, Keshari and her crew rolled through Universal Studios' gates for the first day of the Los Angeles auditions in Larger Than Lyfe Entertainment's "Nationwide Search for a Star." The massive lines of auditioners and their families and friends, many of whom had camped out all night to secure a good place in line, whooped with excitement as they watched the caravan of luxury trucks roll past. It was 5 a.m.

An escort awaited the arrival of the Larger Than Lyfe crew and took Keshari and the group of executives and assistants to the soundstage where the auditions would be held. Universal Studios management had tried to anticipate their every need. Fresh coffee, bottled water, scones, fresh fruit and Danishes, legal pads, pens, and telephones had been organized neatly on long conference-style tables at stage left. Connections had been wired for their laptops and PDAs. A panel had been set up where Keshari, Andre DeJesus, Sharonda Richards, and three other executives from LTL's A & R department would critique and select the ten very lucky, very talented finalists from the thousands of hopefuls who were lined up outside to audition over the next week.

Auditions were set to begin at 7 a.m. sharp. Outside, audition coordinators began to issue instructions over megaphones to organize the anxious, noisy crowd. Wristbands containing audition numbers were distributed to the first 1,000 auditioners. Another 1,500 wristbands would be distributed mid-day. A sizeable security team helped to maintain order.

For the first day of auditions, Keshari and her crew wanted to begin establishing a strong and steady routine. They wanted to make full use of the one-week block of time that they had to see and select talent. The goal on each audition day was to audition a minimum of 1,000 people. If time allowed in that grueling time window, they would begin taking auditions from the next block of wristband holders. While two one-hour breaks were to be a part of the crew's daily schedule, Keshari had trimmed the break schedule down to one one-hour break for the first day so that they could build up a momentum in the audition process. No one dared to complain.

Music industry trade papers, *Variety* and *Billboard*, were reporting every tidbit of information as quickly as their staff writers could acquire it and as quickly as Larger Than Lyfe released it. Major publicity ads for "Nationwide Search for a Star" appeared in every consumer publication from *The SOURCE* to *Essence*. Radio disc jockeys from 100.3 The Beat in L.A. to HOT 97 in New

York hyped the talent search throughout the day and, because Keshari had made the very strategic decision to join forces with Cathy Hughes, the most powerful African-American woman in radio, Larger Than Lyfe had negotiated free advertising slots to hype the talent search during the most coveted time slots of the day on Cathy Hughes's Radio One stations.

Expensive commercial promos were running concurrently on MTV, BET, VH1, CBS, NBC, ABC, TV One and VIBE Network. Massive billboards were ordered and displayed on Sunset Boulevard in Hollywood and along several other very well-known thoroughfares in Los Angeles, Miami and New York. Interviews had been requested with both Keshari Mitchell and Cathy Hughes to discuss the much-talked-about new business alliance between two of the most powerful, Black businesswomen in America. The Larger Than Lyfe Entertainment website and the section that had been set up specifically for the talent search project had already received more than a million hits. Two days before the kickoff of the Los Angeles auditions, Keshari made an appearance on "The Steve Harvey Morning Show" via conference call, then on the tremendously popular "Tom Joyner Morning Show." Both radio stations' switchboards were overloaded with calls for the rest of the day with people seeking information about the upcoming, Los Angeles talent search auditions and the other audition cities' auditions.

Television cameras panned the immense crowd. Some

auditioners were spotted rehearsing while family and friends sat atop sleeping bags and blankets or on lawn chairs looking on. Some auditioners got the opportunity to show their stuff when television cameras gave them a few seconds in the spotlight. There was some unbelievable talent out there. Some other auditioners proved that, among the many very promising prospects, there were more than a few very untalented people waiting in line to stand before the CEO of Larger Than Lyfe Entertainment and absolutely waste her time as well as their own.

"Are you ready to do this?" Andre DeJesus asked, gleaming with excitement as he and Keshari sat down next to each other at the judges' panel.

His brainchild was now truly a tangible product that the entire music world was watching.

"With the hefty price tag attached to this project, if I'm not ready for today, I'll be the greatest fucking pretender that you've ever seen."

They both burst into laughter.

With the lights of the television camera directed at the judges' panel and at the marked spot where auditioners would enter and perform, the first auditioner, smiling nervously, took the stage.

-21-

Portia was exceedingly busy lately. Not only was she exclusively designing the interior of an A-list actor's new, Hollywood Hills abode that would be shot for the cover of *Architectural Digest*, she was also receiving very positive reviews and layouts in all of the other noteworthy interior design and architectural magazines. She had contracts and projects coming in from all directions. Her firm was finally receiving the caliber of instant name recognition, particularly among the people who mattered, that she had been working toward. This was a feat that was every real designer's dream and it was a dream that was now her and her firm's reality.

Portia was also extremely busy in another aspect, working on a project that only she knew about. She was immersed in some very intensive research on none other than Keshari Mitchell, president of Larger Than Lyfe Entertainment. The research was her new "pet project" and it received as much time and effort as the business side of her life at her design firm.

What looks too good to be true generally IS, Portia thought, and she had every intention of scouring Keshari Mitchell's closet until she laid her hands on some real skeletons. She wanted to DESTROY that bitch. On the one hand, Portia had no idea why she was doing what she was doing. Mars Buchanan was just a man and she had been involved in romantic relationships before that didn't work out. She had been able to let go and move on. No harm, no foul. But, for some bizarre reason, this particular instance was different. Portia felt as if she had a score to settle. Mars had really hurt her. A huge blow had been dealt to her ego. When Mars chose that bitch over her, and then practically gloated about it by allowing it to be captured on the covers of virtually every entertainment tabloid on the newsstands, it was the kind of slap in the face that was more than a woman like Portia Foster could take. Something like a dam had broken inside Portia and a kind of negative emotional intensity like she'd never felt before seemed to dominate large segments of her every day.

Portia started calling Mars in the middle of the night and she felt certain that he knew who was on the other end of the line as he said hello over and over again, and then hung up in frustration. A couple of times following the happy couple's impromptu trip to Negril, Portia had sat in her car in the park across from Mars's condo community and watched as Keshari's top-of-the-line, black Range Rover cruised through the security gates in the wee hours of the morning. She was, no doubt, on her way to get some of the fine, successful, entertainment attorney's dick that had been stolen away from Portia without a second thought. As soon as Portia had allowed enough time for that bitch to get into Mars's apartment and out of her clothes, Portia went into harassment mode, calling his numbers, both his cell phone and the house phone, disconnecting repeatedly without saying a word. She'd even bought a couple of those prepaid phones and dedicated them specifically to her middle of the night calls. Mars Buchanan would never see anything resembling an orgasm again if she had anything to do with it...and for damned sure not with that Larger Than Lyfe Entertainment bitch. Portia would be livid, furious tears streaming down her face as she made call after ridiculous call for reasons that she could not begin to try to explain to herself, much less to anyone else.

The last time that Portia had placed herself on a "stakeout" mission across the street from Mars's condo, she'd wound up following him to the bitch's house, where he'd gone, probably for dinner, and then stayed the night. She had driven all the way to Palos Verdes behind Mars on the 405 freeway, and then had exited and followed him all the way up Paradiso Drive, stopping just down the hill until the security gate at Keshari's home slid open and Mars's convertible Mercedes pulled inside. Then Portia pulled right up in front to get a better look.

The illuminated mansion could be seen almost fully from the street and Portia instantly wondered who had been hired to do the bitch's decorating. There were armed guards walking the grounds of the mansion throughout the night and Portia wondered what that was all about. Mars was probably not the first man who the bitch had stolen from a relationship and some other woman would probably not be as gracious as Portia had been in letting her man go. Some other woman might have gone as far as threatening the bitch's life. Or perhaps the bitch had screwed some record executive in a business deal and was reaping the repercussions of that. Whatever the case was, the scene was like something straight out of *Scarface*, watching uniformed, armed officers patrolling the grounds all through the night as if they were guarding the White House. The bitch clearly had something to hide.

More than anything, Portia wanted to get a closer look at how the bitch lived. She would love to pay the housekeeper to allow her to come into that bitch's house and get a look around. The moment would be priceless, walking around, fully violating Keshari Mitchell's personal space without her even knowing about it in the same way that that bitch had violated her when she'd stolen away her man. She wanted to see where the bitch worked, get a look into her office, look through her computer files, see what her business endeavors were, see if Mars had sent her any e-mail and see what that e-mail said. She wanted to see where the bitch slept and bathed. She could imagine the bitch's master suite. It was probably something as far-fetched and extravagant as the accommodations that Cleopatra, or the Queen of Sheba, would require. She wanted to see what the bitch ate and the types of clothes she wore. With the kind of money that her record label brought in, she could surely afford to hit all of the major couture houses. Portia wanted to know what exactly had compelled Mars Buchanan to choose that bitch over her. She wanted to know everything there was to know about that bitch before she fucked her up.

As Portia sat there in her car, solemnly watching the beautiful mansion where Keshari Mitchell resided, she wondered to herself what Keshari and Mars were doing alone together inside. She became more and more determined that she was going to get onto the grounds of that mansion and past that bitch's hired henchmen. She had every intention of getting into that bitch's house. She just needed to watch the house for a few more nights to see how its security operated so that she knew precisely how to proceed.

-22-

"R, she says that she's out and her decision is final. She's placed the bulk of her responsibilities in my hands, including completing the upcoming transaction with our new supplier," Marcus Means told Ricky.

"I'm in here facing murder one and this bitch is splashed all over the covers of entertainment tabloids with this pretty-assed attorney that she's hooked up with," Ricky said. "We've gone through three major suppliers in less than a year, like some mismanaged, disorganized, neighborhood YG crime ring. This shit's raggedy and I've got a lot of overpaid motherfuckers on the outside NOT handling my shit!"

Ricky put his head in his hands. Being in jail, the trial, and the possible outcome of the trial, had him stressed enough as it was without Keshari steadily trying to force his hand. She was going to make him do something that he'd regret.

"I'll take care of her, man," Ricky said.

"Is there anything that you need me to do?" Marcus asked.

"Nah, I got it," Ricky responded.

"If I might ask," Marcus pressed, "how do you plan to take care of the Keshari situation?"

Ricky stared at Marcus pointedly for a moment. Marcus was clearly overstepping his bounds.

"Don't worry about it," Ricky said. "Like I said, I got it. On the other hand, after Keshari, you're next in command in this organization. You know what needs to be done. Handle my business and keep me updated...and handle it like your life depends on it, because it does."

"What are your attorneys saying about the case?"

"Man, I pay these motherfuckers eight hundred dollars a fucking hour. They're supposed to be the best legal minds in the fucking country and they're telling me it's fifty-fifty right now for some shit that I didn't do."

"Wow," Marcus said pensively. "Look, I'm gonna break out and I'll get with you again in a few days."

♪ 🎧 ♪

The trial of the *People and the State of California v. Richard Lawrence Tresvant* was in its sixth week and the defense currently had the floor. Nationally renowned attorney Barry Scheck stepped up to the witness stand to question the defense's forensics expert, Adam Crichton of BIOTECH, a privately owned forensics laboratory in Los Angeles. Barry Scheck was probably best known for his role on the "Dream Team" of the infamous O.J. Simpson murder trial. Barry Scheck was currently on retainer with Richard Tresvant. He'd been handpicked by Larry Steinberg, Richard's lead attorney, to work on Richard Tresvant's "Dream Team" because of his phenomenal reputation at winning long-shot, criminal cases with irrefutable DNA evidence. All attorneys present in the room, including Judge Bartholomew and Steve Cooley, the district attorney, held Barry Scheck's legal prowess in high regard.

"Mr. Crichton," Barry Scheck said in his strong, East Coast accent, "please state your background as it pertains to the field of forensics."

"I possess a Bachelor of Science degree in Forensic Science from Pennsylvania State University. I have a Masters degree in Criminalistics from Cal State Sacramento. I worked for ten years as a crime scene investigator for the Federal Bureau of Investigation here in Los Angeles. I founded BIOTECH ten years ago to offer my services to private individuals and enterprises seeking in-depth analysis of criminal evidence for major criminal cases such as this one. I also provide my services on a consulting basis to corporations internationally and to government agencies. My laboratory analyzes biological evidence, trace evidence, impression evidence such as footprints, fingerprints and tire tracks; controlled substances and ballistics. I have served directly as an expert witness in criminal cases for more than twenty years, both during my years with the FBI and through my company, BIOTECH."

"So, it is safe to presume that you are professionally

qualified to discuss analysis of physical evidence taken from the crime scene related to this murder trial. Is that correct, Mr. Crichton?" Barry Scheck asked.

"That is correct, sir."

"To clarify, please provide for me a better understanding of what the field of forensic science is," Barry Scheck said.

"Forensics is the application of a broad spectrum of sciences to answer questions of interest to the legal system, in either a criminal or civil action," Adam Crichton stated. "Essentially, forensics is to law enforcement and solving crimes what imagination, a strong vocabulary, and good grammar are to the fiction writer. One cannot exist without the other. Sometimes crimes are cut and dry, relatively easy to solve. Other times, the crimes are highly sophisticated and require the expertise of several different forensic specialists from areas such as biological evidence, trace evidence, impression evidence, ballistics, and digital forensics. Each forensic specialist takes and carefully reviews each of the tangible pieces of the 'puzzle' of a crime. The majority of physical evidence is taken from the crime scene and from suspects. Sometimes the most minute and seemingly irrelevant physical details can be analyzed and carefully reconstructed into the timeline and turn out to be a most significant factor in solving a criminal case."

"Your laboratory, BIOTECH, was hired by the defense to examine some of the physical evidence in this murder case. Is that correct, Mr. Crichton?"

"That is correct."

"And what specific physical evidence related to this case did your laboratory examine?"

"My laboratory analyzed the murder weapon as well as the fingerprint evidence originally taken from the murder weapon by the Los Angeles Police Department," Mr. Crichton said. "Because it had been established that Mr. Tresvant, the defendant, and Mr. Bernard, the decedent, had an attorney-client relationship, as well as a friendship, and had had lunch on the day of Mr. Bernard's murder, the fingerprints belonging to Mr. Tresvant found on the interior and exterior of the decedent's car, the car from the crime scene, did not hold as much evidentiary weight as the prints which were taken directly from the murder weapon."

"Was the fingerprint evidence temporarily released for analysis to your laboratory by the Los Angeles Police Department determined to be the fingerprints of my client, Richard Lawrence Tresvant?"

"Yes," Adam Crichton answered. "The prints released to BIOTECH by LAPD's forensics lab were determined to be the defendant's, Richard Tresvant's. We also examined the murder weapon and, although there was substantial disintegration, there were partial prints that we could ascertain on the murder weapon to be Richard Tresvant's as well."

"Was there anything unusual about the fingerprint evidence that your laboratory examined?" Barry Scheck asked.

"Yes," Adam Crichton responded.

"And what was that?" Barry Scheck questioned.

"Law enforcement typically uses what is called the 'dry powder method' to take fingerprint evidence from items found at a crime scene. Aluminum powder is applied to the surface of the evidence. The evidence is swept with a brush to adhere the powder to the latent fingerprints to actualize them. Then the actualized fingerprint is printed on gelatin paper. Fingerprint evidence is extremely fragile and may have to be examined by several forensic specialists in preparation for a trial. Over time, physical evidence, like fingerprints, breaks down until it is no longer usable. Butyl paraben is a fingerprint preservative used in the dry powder process that extends the life of actualized prints."

"And, again," Barry Scheck questioned, "what was unusual about the fingerprint evidence that you examined?"

"After extensive analysis of the fingerprint evidence provided by the Los Angeles Police Department, it is the finding of BIOTECH Laboratories that the age of the fingerprint evidence, shown in particular by the aging of butyl paraben on the gelatin papers containing the fingerprint evidence, predates the date of the murder of Phinnaeus Bernard III. My estimation is that this fingerprint evidence predates the date of the murder by as much as one to two months."

Much rustling and movement rose from the courtroom. Judge Bartholomew banged his gavel to regain order.

"Is it your professional belief that the fingerprint evidence provided to your laboratory by LAPD is not evidence taken from the scene of the murder of Phinnaeus Bernard III?" Barry Scheck continued.

"It is my professional opinion that the fingerprint evidence provided by LAPD and analyzed by my laboratory is NOT evidence taken on March 11, 2005, from the crime scene of the murder of Phinnaeus Bernard III. It would be chronologically impossible."

"Do you believe that the evidence that your laboratory analyzed is planted evidence?" Barry Scheck asked.

"One logical conclusion for physical evidence whose age substantially predates the date of the crime, from which the evidence was supposed to have been taken, is that this evidence was planted," Adam Crichton stated.

"Thank you," Barry Scheck stated. "No further questions."

♫ 🎧 ♫

"Sir, please provide the jury and prosecution with a brief summary of your background and credentials," Larry Steinberg stated.

"I possess a Bachelor of Science degree in Psychology from UCLA. I attended the Backster School of Lie Detection in San Diego. I am a certified forensic law enforcement polygraph examiner who is an active member of the American Association of Police Polygraphists. I have testified in criminal cases for both defendants and prosecutors for more than ten years."

"My client, the defendant, submitted to a polygraph test with you following his arrest for the murder of Phinnaeus Bernard III. Is that correct?"

"That is correct," the polygraphist responded.

"I am going to keep things as simple as possible so that members of the jury are not bombarded with too much technical information amidst all of the other extensive details that they will be requested to analyze in deliberations.

"Per the results of the polygraph test that you administered to Richard Tresvant," Larry Steinberg continued, "did Richard Tresvant murder Phinnaeus Bernard III?"

"No," the polygraphist answered.

"Per the results of the polygraph test, did Richard Tresvant have any knowledge of or was he involved in any way in the murder of Phinnaeus Bernard III?"

"No," the polygraphist answered.

"No further questions," Larry Steinberg stated quickly and walked away from the witness stand.

Spectators in the courtroom were now on the edges of their seats. The defense was dropping massive bombshells that would be the continuously running top news story on virtually every Los Angeles television network for the rest of the week.

"Mr. Cooley, are you prepared for cross?" Judge Bartholomew asked the district attorney.

"Absolutely," Steve Cooley said, hopping up from the prosecution table and approaching the witness stand.

"Sir, you state that the results of the polygraph exam administered to the defendant indicated conclusively that Richard Tresvant did not murder Phinnaeus Bernard III and had no knowledge of Phinnaeus Bernard's murder. Aren't there literally thousands of websites on the internet that tell people step-by-step how to fool a lie detector?"

"Objection, Your Honor!" Larry Steinberg snapped. "By California law, polygraph tests are admissible for trial. Questioning the reliability of the polygraph exam is a moot point."

"I'll allow the question," Judge Bartholomew responded.

Larry Steinberg irritably took his seat.

"Please answer the question," Steve Cooley repeated to the polygraphist. "Aren't there literally thousands of websites on the internet that provide people with all the information they need to deceive a lie detector?"

"I'm quite certain that there are," the polygraphist answered, "but I think that the most important factor in the polygraph exam and the reliability of its results is the professional skill of the polygraphist in analyzing those results."

"Nevertheless, a determined person, especially a highly sophisticated criminal or sociopath, can and has successfully faked his or her way through passing a polygraph exam. Isn't that correct?" Steve Cooley asked.

"That is correct, sir," the polygraphist answered.

"And it is very possible that Richard Lawrence Tresvant, the defendant, faked his way through the polygraph exam that leads you to state conclusively as an expert that he did not murder Phinnaeus Bernard III. Isn't that correct?"

"That is correct, sir," the polygraphist answered.

"No further questions," the prosecutor said.

♪ 🎧 ♪

The last defense witness of the day was probably one of the most highly anticipated witnesses to take the stand in the entire trial.

"Mr. Bumgaarten, you are the son of very prominent attorney and real estate developer Victor Bumgaarten. Is that correct?"

"That is correct," Walter Bumgaarten smiled, "but, at this rather late point in my life, I'd like to believe that I've made a substantial name for myself. I am a rather prominent real estate developer in my family's business, just as my father is."

"Absolutely, absolutely," Larry Steinberg responded with a smile.

There were twitters of laughter around the courtroom at Mr. Bumgaarten's humor.

Walter Bumgaarten was an affable man in his early sixties. He had sterling good looks that could most likely be attributed to his Swedish/Nordic lineage. He'd been educated at Yale and abroad. He came from a family of "blue bloods." His family was comprised of well-known members of society, on both the East and the West Coasts. They were well-bred, well-educated real estate moguls and philanthropists. Richard Tresvant, on the other hand, was a "boy from the 'hood" who couldn't for the life of him keep himself from being consistently linked to organized criminal activities and whose sizeable "entrepreneur's" fortune and its origins were constantly in question. The fact that these two men from such vastly different worlds were such good friends had raised more than a few eyebrows long before Richard Tresvant was charged with first-degree murder. Theirs was one of the oddest couplings indeed.

"So, tell me, Mr. Bumgaarten," Larry Steinberg continued, "how did you and Mr. Tresvant, the defendant, meet?"

"We met at a black-tie political fundraiser several years ago," Walter Bumgaarten answered. "He's a brilliant man, brilliant. No formal education beyond high school, but I must say with all frankness that he is a very astute businessman, one of the smartest people I know...certainly smarter than some of my associates possessing family fortunes amassed from oil, degrees from Yale, and a couple of questionably successful runs for the United States Presidency."

There was more laughter in the courtroom.

"And, despite the substantial age difference, would you say that you and Richard Tresvant are friends?" Larry Steinberg asked.

"Yes, absolutely. Richard Tresvant is a very good friend

196 CYNTHIA DIANE THORNTON

of mine...despite the substantial age difference," Walter Bumgaarten replied amiably.

"Have you ever done business with Richard Tresvant?"

"I'm not sure what you mean."

Larry Steinberg clarified his question. "Have you ever contracted in any formal agreement and/or exchanged monies toward any type of business enterprise?"

"No," Walter Bumgaarten stated. "I did refer him to the broker that he used to purchase his current residence in Bel Air. We've had some serious discussions regarding real estate development, as Mr. Tresvant branches much more seriously into that area. As a matter of fact, we were meeting about a real estate development project on the night that...ahem...that Mr. Phinnaeus Bernard III was killed."

"Have you ever heard of Mr. Tresvant having any involvement in organized crime?" Larry Steinberg asked.

"Of course," Walter Bumgaarten answered. "I've heard stories that portrayed Richard like the John Gotti of the West Coast. I put no stock in any of it. I rely upon my personal dealings with the man to form any assessments of his character, and I know that he is an upstanding guy. He did not come from a background like mine, but he certainly upholds many of the same core beliefs that I uphold."

"Do you have any direct knowledge of Richard Tresvant's involvement in any kind of illegal activity?"

"Absolutely not," Walter Bumgaarten answered.

"Mr. Bumgaarten, on the evening of March 11, 2005, you stated that you, Richard Tresvant, Richard Tresvant's attorney, and former Mayor Richard Riordan got together at Mr. Tresvant's Bel Air home for dinner. Is that correct?"

"Yes. We discussed a potential, major, residential development project in Downtown Los Angeles. It was not a formal meeting. We were simply getting together over dinner to toss some ideas and numbers around. I play golf all the time with Dick Riordan and asked him to join us."

"So, there was a strong possibility for you to get directly involved in a business deal with Mr. Tresvant?" Larry Steinberg asked.

"With the downtown condo project? Yes...absolutely."

"And, considering the many stories that you've heard about Mr. Tresvant being linked to organized crime and the questionable source of his wealth, you had no misgivings about entering into a business deal with him?"

"None whatsoever," Walter Bumgaarten responded.

"At approximately what time did you all get together that evening for dinner at Richard Tresvant's home?"

"I'd say that I made it to the house sometime after five," Walter Bumgaarten responded. "Dick Riordan didn't arrive until about seven."

"Was there anyone else present?" Larry Steinberg asked.

"With the exception of the housekeepers and security, no," Walter Bumgaarten responded.

"What transpired over the course of the evening? What did you all do?"

"Richard and I chipped a few golf balls on his back lawn. Dick arrived and we had drinks and dinner. Then we had a few more drinks..."

There were more twitters of laughter from the spectators in the courtroom.

"We discussed the downtown condo development project," Walter Bumgaarten continued. "We tossed around some numbers, and did a bit of networking regarding bankers we each knew who would best be suited to help make this thing happen."

"When would you say that you and Mr. Riordan wrapped up dinner and your meeting and left Mr. Tresvant's Bel Air home that evening of March 11, 2005?" Larry Steinberg asked.

"Ten thirty...10:45...," Walter Bumgaarten answered. "We got quite involved in our discussion. This downtown condo project could be an incredibly lucrative venture with all that's taking place development-wise around the Staples Center right now."

"So, Mr. Bumgaarten, considering that the time window for the murder of Phinnaeus Bernard III has been established to have been between 8 and 10 p.m., would you say that it was possible that Richard Tresvant murdered Phinnaeus Bernard III?"

"Unless he can somehow manage to be in two places at one time," Walter Bumgaarten stated, "it is impossible for him to have murdered Phinnaeus Bernard III because he was at his home during that entire time, meeting with me."

"No further questions," Larry Steinberg said.

Phinnaeus Bernard III's widow burst into tears and had to be taken out of the courtroom.

-23-

"Babygirl, I must say that I am thoroughly, thoroughly impressed. Any man who can manage to take you away from that record label for three entire days and would not take 'no' for an answer when he did it, has got to be a keeper. I can't wait to meet him. I guess somebody's finally taking the advice of her five-months-younger, wiser, finer sister."

Keshari rolled her eyes at her best friend. She and Misha had been kicking back in one of the dressing rooms at Gucci for well over two hours. Keshari sipped a glass of Perrier Jouët while Misha turned this way and that in front of the mirrored wall, admiring her golden, size 6 body in a black number that plunged toward her navel in front and dared to plunge right down past her ass in back. The expensive fabric flowed over her body like liquid.

"Girl, that's the one." Keshari grinned. "Get it and let's get the hell out of here. I have a business meeting to go over the finalized arrangements and expenses for the Atlanta auditions. Not all of us have the desire to dedicate our lives to shopping."

"I work hard, babygirl. I play hard, too...and so should you. Black belt shopping is but one of the rewards for long strings of fourteen-hour workdays."

Misha sauntered over to the door in a black La Perla bra and matching thong and waved to the sales associate to let her know that she was ready. Keshari shook her head. Her friend never did have an ounce of shame.

Since Keshari had missed the New York auditions, she was making it up to her crew by throwing a huge bash to kick off their arrival in Georgia for the Atlanta auditions. She'd hired Misha to put it all together at the Coca-Cola Roxy Theatre, the same venue as the Atlanta auditions. Mars was planning to fly to Atlanta for part of the week and was planning to attend the party. Keshari wanted Mars to meet Misha while he was there.

Jagged Edge was one of the groups booked to perform at the Atlanta kickoff party and, of course, the presence of the music industry's sexiest, thugged-out, R & B twins, Brandon and Brian Casey, required Misha to go out and buy $2,200 worth of man-stealing, baddest-bitch-in-the-room caliber attire. There would be no competition when she went on the prowl that night and the dress that she'd selected guaranteed it.

Misha flopped on the loveseat beside Keshari and slid into her Mizrahi trousers while the sales associate took her platinum American Express card and went out to process the sale.

"Are you happy?" Misha asked. "You look happy."

Keshari smiled. "I'm happy. I'm...very happy."

"You've fallen in love with him, haven't you?"

Keshari was hesitant, feeling almost silly to acknowledge how she felt so soon into her new relationship.

"Girl, you're talkin' to me," Misha quipped, "your sister. You can tell me how you feel. Hell, it's written all over your face."

"Yes," Keshari answered.

"Is he in love with you?" Misha asked.

"Yes," Keshari answered without any doubt.

"Does my brother know?"

"Yeah," Keshari answered. "He's the reason I've got the new Range Rover."

She hesitated for a moment before telling Misha the rest.

"I also told Rick that I wanted out of the organization."

"Oh, damn," Misha said, knowing exactly what was involved and what could potentially happen in trying to walk away from where Keshari stood in the drug game. "Are you okay? Do you need me to talk to that bastard?"

"Yes, I'm okay," Keshari said, "and, no, I don't want you talking to anybody. I don't want you involved in this in any way. I just can't do it anymore and I can't look Mars in the eye and continue lying to him."

"Key, of all the people I know, you deserve to realize some true happiness...and peace of mind. Don't worry about my brother. Fuck my brother's business affairs, too. Take care of YOU and be happy...with Mars."

"I wish it were that simple."

"It IS that simple," Misha said dismissively. "When do I get to meet my soon-to-be brother-in-law?"

"It's not that deep yet," Keshari answered, "but he is coming to Atlanta to meet you and if you embarrass me by interrogating him like you work for the police, I'm going to kick your ass."

♪ 🎧 ♪

Mars was in the underground garage at ASCAP, on his way home to finish packing before his limousine arrived to take him to the airport, when he was approached by a young reporter.

"Mr. Buchanan, how does it feel to be romantically linked to the most powerful woman in the music industry? Is your relationship serious? Have there been discussions of marriage?"

"I have a great admiration for Keshari Mitchell's accomplishments in the music industry. I also possess a great deal of respect for her privacy. I have no further comment."

"It's been rumored in the industry that Keshari Mitchell is connected to one of the most powerful crime organizations in the country. Are you aware of this? Are you involved in her illegal business dealings in any way?"

"Do you want to find yourself and whatever sleazy tabloid you represent knee-deep in litigation?"

"Nah, bro," the young, overzealous reporter responded. "It's not that deep. I'm just doing my job."

"Then get the fuck away from me...and try to find yourself a real job. You call this fucking journalism?!"

Mars slid behind the wheel of his Mercedes and sped away.

-24-

Limousines lined up outside Atlanta's Coca-Cola Roxy as if it was Grammy night at the Shrine Auditorium. Misha, known throughout the entertainment industry, particularly in Los Angeles, for putting together some of entertainment elite's most talked about parties, had flown to Atlanta days before everyone else to orchestrate every single nut and bolt of the night's festivities. With a blank check from Keshari and carte blanche to do whatever she wanted, Misha promised her best friend a Larger Than Lyfe Entertainment party that would be nothing short of spectacular and, from the looks of the night's turnout, Misha had certainly kept her promise. Atlanta was the Los Angeles of the Dirty South. People loved to flaunt their success in every way that they could and without apology, from their world-famous, designer-labeled clothes to the cars that they drove, and even with the people they dated... sporting scantily clad women of mixed ethnic background on their arms like another piece of diamond-encrusted jewelry. The atmosphere both outside and inside the

Roxy was pure excess, money and ego both vying with one another to dominate the evening.

Keshari's limousine pulled up to the front of the music hall and everything seemed to momentarily pause as she stepped from the car before photographers leapt at the opportunity to photograph her with Mars Buchanan. Keshari was dressed like a rock star as she stepped from the car and grabbed Mars's hand. She wore black, beaded, Armani short-shorts that gave full exposure to her killer legs, a matching, beaded bikini top under a black Armani tuxedo jacket, and four-inch Jimmy Choo sandals. A diamond belly chain that was a gift from Mars accentuated a toned stomach that would give Janet Jackson a run for her money. She was definitely a music mogul who operated by her own set of rules.

Mars sported black Armani as well. A single-breasted, black Armani suit with a black, silk knit "wife-beater" underneath. They had to be the hottest-looking couple in the entire music industry and it was becoming abundantly clear that whatever was transpiring between the two of them was not just casual dating. Mars couldn't seem to take his eyes off of Keshari and Keshari appeared to be blossoming right before the eyes of the music industry and the curious public. She still maintained careful distance from the media, but, otherwise, her whole demeanor seemed to have changed, opened up and become much more three-dimensional since her romantic link to the super-handsome, West Coast general counsel for ASCAP.

Jermaine Dupri, who was an ATL native, and his longtime girlfriend, Janet Jackson, along with members of Dupri's SoSoDef record label, arrived. So did rapper Ludacris and his sizeable entourage. Expensively customized Hummers, Mercedes-Benzes, Lincoln Navigators, Porsches, and Ferraris crowded the valet parking lanes. Missy "Misdemeanor" Elliot zoomed up in her trademark Lamborghini. Music video models dressed as minimally as Keshari strutted up the red carpet, trying to project the attitudes of superstars. The twenty finalists who had been selected in Los Angeles and New York were provided with passes and airfare to attend the Atlanta party, and you could read the barely controllable excitement on all of their faces as they were treated with the star quality that they all dreamed of having one day. Paparazzi were having a field day capturing photos of the incoming crowd, but they were kept at bay by very tight security and velvet ropes cordoning off the area.

In two days, the week-long Atlanta auditions would be under way.

♪ 🎧 ♪

Misha could work a room like nobody's business. In the daring, black Gucci dress she'd chosen specifically for that night, she circulated from one side of the Roxy to the other, stopping to chat with party guests and accepting business cards from celebs and other high-profile Atlanta residents who wanted her to coordinate their next party, before she located a quiet corner in the packed party zone just for herself.

Brandon Casey of the R & B group, Jagged Edge, nursing a snifter of Courvoisier, followed her like an obedient puppy, his eyes intent on the switch of her perfect ass. Misha was like the Black version of Samantha on HBO's *Sex and the City*. She was a magnet for men, she conquered them sexually, and then promptly dismissed them when they'd expended their usefulness in her life or had started to grate on her nerves.

She'd done an amazing job with all of the arrangements. Suede sectional seating was scattered all about. Dimmed, lounge lighting and potted palms set a comfortable, "VIP room" ambiance. Cristal, Courvoisier, Hpnotiq, and expensive cigars abounded. Unique, Southern cuisine and appetizers from a renowned Atlanta chef were there for the taking.

The dance floor was full and the music being spun by East Coast deejay Kid Capri was Larger Than Lyfe Entertainment's finest. Keshari gave even Sean Combs a run for his money that night. She didn't spare a dime to make sure that her party at the Roxy was the only place where anybody who was anybody in Atlanta wanted to be.

Keshari made her way through the Roxy, stopping here and there to talk a bit with other music executives and a few hip-hop stars. She located Misha in a secluded corner, kicked back on one of the suede sectionals with her bare feet in Brandon Casey's lap. Misha grinned and hopped up when she saw Keshari approaching. She kissed her best friend on both cheeks, and then looked Mars over appraisingly before introducing them both to Brandon Casey.

"So, you're Mars Buchanan." Misha smiled, taking his hand and planting a kiss on his cheek. "I've heard a lot about you. Very impressive things. You're the youngest general counsel ever to assume the role at ASCAP... never married, no baby's mama drama...you're very easy on the eyes...plus, you've won my sister's heart.

"My sister is a very special woman...and I'm sure you are aware of this already," Misha continued. "The man who hurts her heart should be fearful for his life... because, I assure you, when provoked, I am far more dangerous than I appear."

Misha held eye contact with Mars challengingly. Her intuition was never, ever wrong about men, and she was confident that she would know if Mr. Mars Buchanan was operating on a BS tip. Mars, meanwhile, displayed a somewhat amused expression as if he was fully aware that Misha was sizing him up to give him her seal of approval. Keshari squeezed his hand and glared at Misha. The look she gave Misha told her to stop it...IMMEDIATELY. Misha fanned her off dismissively.

"Tonight, you pass inspection," Misha said saucily, "but be warned, honey. I'm watching you."

Mars laughed and shook his head.

"You are exactly as Keshari described you," he said.

"Oh, really?" Misha said, quickly looking at Keshari with feigned suspicion. "Just what did she say?"

"Only good things." Mars smiled. "Only good things. And I can assure you that Keshari's heart is safe from harm as long as I'm around. I will guard it with my life."

"You'd better." Misha smiled back. "Now, you two get out there on that dance floor and enjoy yourselves. I will get with the two of you later. We can do dinner tomorrow night before I fly back to L.A. As you can see, I've got some unfinished business over here. This man has promised to polish my toes and cook for me."

She grinned back at Brandon Casey teasingly. He had nothing but lust in his eyes.

-25-

Mars flew back to Los Angeles to return to work a couple of days after the Atlanta launch party and it was as if drama had been anxiously awaiting his return. Portia Foster called Mars's office the very same morning that he returned to work.

"I'd like to speak to Mars Buchanan," Portia said. "Would you put me through, please?"

"Who's calling?" Mars's secretary asked.

"Portia Foster."

"I'm sorry, Ms. Foster. Mr. Buchanan is in a meeting. May I take a message?"

"Yes, please tell Mr. Buchanan that I need to speak with him as soon as possible. It's urgent that I speak with him."

"I'll give him the message, Ms. Foster."

Portia waited near her phone for three hours before Mars returned her call.

"My secretary said that you needed to speak to me urgently. What's the problem?"

"We need to talk, Mars. Why don't you stop by my

loft after you leave the office, or I can come to your place."

"There's nothing we need to discuss or see each other about, Portia. I know that you've been calling my apartment in the middle of the night and hanging up. That shit's childish. You need to stop calling me and spend some couch time with a good therapist."

"I'm pregnant," Portia said carefully.

Mars almost dropped the phone.

"Portia, why are you doing this? It's over. I've used a condom virtually every time that the two of us have had sex. Why won't you just let it be over? I'm beginning to regret the day we ever met."

"I didn't exactly plan this, Mars."

"Then this is one helluva coincidence," Mars snapped. "What's the name of the gynecologist who did your pregnancy test?"

"I haven't been to the gynecologist yet," Portia answered. "My periods have always been so sketchy. That's why I started taking birth control pills as a teenager. But I'm nearly three months late."

"Three months?! What the fuck, Portia?! How do you go for three months without having a period and not see that as a HUGE fucking problem?!"

He exhaled in exasperation and switched the phone to his other ear.

"Schedule an appointment with your gynecologist," Mars said. "Call me back and tell me the date and the time and I'll accompany you there."

"You don't believe me?" Portia said darkly.

"To be completely frank," Mars answered, "NO...I don't. Schedule the appointment and we'll have a licensed professional confirm it." He hung up the phone.

"Shit!" he yelled, slamming his fist down on his desk.

While he firmly believed that this was a ploy of Portia's to try to keep him tied to her life, something nagged at him deep in the pit of his stomach. What if she really is pregnant? Mars's life would be tied to melodrama for the rest of his life and to a woman he was coming to despise. And how would Keshari take an unexpected pregnancy slapped right in the middle of their relationship?

Mars's thoughts were interrupted when his secretary rang his office again.

"I have Portia Foster on the line."

"FUCK!" Mars snapped, picking up his extension. "Put her through."

"Mars, I scheduled an appointment with my ob/gyn, Dr. Kardashian, in Santa Monica. It's all set for tomorrow morning at eleven. Is that okay?"

"Yeah," Mars said solemnly.

"Are you okay?" Portia asked with concern.

"I'll pick you up at the loft around ten."

♪ 🎧 ♪

Keshari flew back to Los Angeles as soon as the Atlanta auditions wrapped and it was as if drama had been anxiously awaiting her return. Her black Ferrari convertible pulled into the underground garage at her Century City offices on Avenue of the Stars. The white van doing surveillance at one of the parking meters at the curb outside her building allowed half an hour to pass before radioing the head of their task force. Then Thomas Hencken hopped on an elevator.

"I'd like to see Ms. Keshari Mitchell. Is she in?"

"Do you have an appointment?" the receptionist asked curtly.

"No, I don't," Thomas Hencken answered.

"If you have no appointment, Ms. Mitchell won't be able to see you. I'm sorry. You'll have to come back when you have an appointment."

"I think that Ms. Mitchell will take a moment of her time to see me," Thomas Hencken responded.

"What's your name? What's the purpose of your visit? I might be able to help you."

Thomas Hencken reached into his jacket pocket, and then placed his business card on the desk in front of the receptionist. She frowned for a moment as she read the card, then looked up from it with wide eyes.

"One moment, please," she said, going quickly to Terrence's workspace, Keshari's assistant, not quite sure what to do.

Terrence rang Keshari immediately and informed her who was outside. A moment later, he showed Mr. Hencken into Keshari's office.

"Ms. Mitchell, how are you?"

"I'm fine, but I feel certain that you didn't show up here at my office without an appointment to check on my well-being. Exactly why would a DEA agent have any interest in my record label? Do you rap...sing... produce?"

"I have a few questions I'd like to ask you and I believe that you can be a great help to my current investigation."

"I can't imagine any questions that I would be capable of supplying useful answers to for the Drug Enforcement Agency," Keshari said. "Perhaps there's been some mistake."

"No," Thomas Hencken said. "There's been no mistake at all. You see, you've paid several visits to Mr. Richard Lawrence Tresvant, reputed founder of The Consortium, a Los Angeles-based crime organization, at the Men's Central Jail prior to the start of his murder trial, and I'd like to know more about your relationship with him. I'm also interested in your role in The Consortium's operations."

Keshari narrowed her eyes. "Any questions or concerns that you have should be directed to my attorney, David Weisberg," she said curtly. "I'm not at liberty to answer the questions of any law enforcement officer without proper legal counsel. Surely, you understand this."

"Is that really the way that you want to play this thing through, Ms. Mitchell? I would seriously advise you against such a decision. It could prove quite detrimental to you...and your career and your record label. We've been carefully researching and documenting the movements of key players within The Consortium for eighteen months now. We want Richard Tresvant, but, if you turn this into an unnecessarily dragged-out skirmish between us and your overpaid attorney, we definitely have enough to direct our attentions at you."

"Allow me to reiterate, Mr. ...?"?" Keshari said.

"Hencken," the agent supplied.

"Mr. Hencken, the only basis under which I will allow you to question me is by subpoena or arrest and, even then, I will only consider cooperating with your interrogation in the presence of my attorney." She went to her office's double doors and held them open. "Now, if you will excuse me, I have a meeting. Kindly make sure that you secure an appointment the next time that you decide to pay me a visit."

Thomas Hencken stood to leave. "I thank you for your time, Ms. Mitchell. You'll be hearing from me again very soon."

When Thomas Hencken was gone, Keshari told Terrence to hold all of her phone calls, and then closed up in her office and stayed there for almost two hours. For years, she'd come to take for granted the cushion of safety she had from federal and local law enforcement because of Ricky's strategically formed alliances with people in some of the highest places of the law. Not once had a federal agent ever set foot into the offices of Larger Than Lyfe Entertainment for anything. She'd never been so much as pulled over for a traffic stop, not once. Now the tables had clearly taken a turn.

She shook her head as she stared down at Avenue of the Stars from the ceiling-to-floor windows behind her desk. She already knew that her receptionist had transmitted the story of the visit from the DEA agent halfway around the record label. Then, the people who the receptionist had told had transmitted details regarding the strange visit from the DEA agent all the rest of the way around the Larger Than Lyfe offices.

"David, we need to get together as soon as possible. It's serious," Keshari said, phoning her attorney on his cell phone.

"I'll come up to your house this evening. I'll bring dinner."

-26-

M ars arrived at Portia's Brentwood loft at ten o'clock sharp. Portia came to the door in white linen capris with a matching halter top and a straw sunhat, like the two of them were off for a drive up the coast or something. Mars watched her with irritation and wanted to wring her neck.

She smiled. "Good morning. How are you?"

"Cut the bullshit," Mars snapped darkly. "Let's get this thing over with."

"You say that like it's the end of the world."

"The thought of having a child with you IS like the end of the world."

"You son of a bitch!" Portia said.

Mars didn't respond. He held the passenger door of his Mercedes open and Portia slid angrily into the car.

Mars sat in the reception area of the practically empty doctor's office and sent text messages to Keshari and his secretary on his BlackBerry while Portia went to provide the nurse with blood and urine samples. Mars was trying to find the time in his busy schedule to fly to Miami for a couple of days while Keshari was there for the Miami auditions of her nationwide talent search. He prayed that he was not about to receive any unfortunate news that he was going to have to break to her when he flew out to see her. He hadn't told her a thing about Portia's supposed "predicament" and their doctor's appointment that morning.

Portia returned to the reception area shortly after providing the blood and urine samples to the nurse. She and Mars were told that it would take approximately half an hour before the doctor would provide them with the results.

"There's a Starbucks right down the street," the nurse said to them. "You could go and get yourselves a latté and your results would be ready by the time you get back."

Portia grinned with delight. "That sounds like a terrific idea. Come on, sweetie, let's go."

"Are you out of your mind, woman?" Mars snapped. "I don't want any coffee. We'll wait...here."

Portia rolled her eyes toward the ceiling and shook her head mildly at the nurse as if Mars was merely an expectant father with a strong case of the jitters. She began thumbing through a *Modern Parenthood* magazine.

There had to have been warning signs all over the place over the course of the years that the two of them had dated to indicate to him how delusional and unstable this woman clearly was and Mars had been too busy watching the perfect switch of her ass to get the memo.

Mars's BlackBerry beeped, signaling an incoming text message:

"Hope you've managed 2 get time off for trip. I'll try & see you later tonite. Luv U. –K"

Portia glanced over and skimmed the message display on Mars's BlackBerry and saw the private, little smile on his face.

"How dare you sit here and exchange text messages like a fifteen-year-old with that bitch while we wait for the status of our unborn child!" Portia snarled under her breath.

"Woman...PUH-LEEZE," Mars said loud enough for the nurse at the reception area's check-in window to look up from her paperwork at the two of them.

"The doctor will see you now," the nurse said to them a few moments later.

She escorted them down the hallway to Dr. Kardashian's office, where the forty-something redhead, in a white lab coat and a sizeable Asscher-cut wedding ring, sat at her desk overlooking Santa Monica Boulevard near the Third Street Promenade. She looked from Mars to Portia and smiled warmly. The smile made Mars's heart drop. He thought that it was a smile of congratulations. Portia clearly thought the same thing because she smiled jubilantly back at Dr. Kardashian as if she was the happiest woman in the world.

"The good news," Dr. Kardashian said, "is that you are a very healthy woman, Portia, and can certainly have many babies if you so choose. The unfortunate news is that you are not pregnant now."

"There must be some mistake," Portia said. "I took one of those home pregnancy tests three times and they all came back positive."

"Sometimes home pregnancy tests result in false positives," Dr. Kardashian responded. "A variety of factors cause these tests to fail from time to time. That's why it is always advisable to immediately visit your gynecologist to confirm things after taking a home pregnancy test."

"I don't...I don't understand," Portia stammered in dismay. "Perhaps we should complete the testing again."

Dr. Kardashian shook her head sympathetically. "Portia...you're healthy. If you want to have a child, you simply have to keep trying. There is nothing in your medical history that would act as an obstacle to your getting pregnant. Furthermore, the fun part is in trying to conceive."

She smiled at Portia and Mars as if she were offering consolation to a happy, sexually healthy couple. For the first time, Mars smiled back at her.

"I thank you for your time, Dr. Kardashian," he said, getting up. "Have a good day."

He took Portia by the arm and quickly ushered her out of the row of medical offices and out to the car. When he pulled up at Portia's loft again, he shut off the engine. Portia sat, completely crestfallen, as if the news from Dr. Kardashian was still a complete shock to her.

"You knew damned fucking well that you were not pregnant," Mars said evenly. "I want you to LEAVE...ME...ALONE. Don't call, don't write, don't send e-mail, don't text me, don't show up at my home or workplace ever again. It's OVER! Leave me the FUCK alone. Get some counseling. Get a life. But, if you ever bother me again, I assure you that I will get a restraining order. Now...kindly...get the fuck out of my car without making a scene."

Portia's expression was stoic as she stepped from Mars's Mercedes and headed through the courtyard to her loft. Mars sped away without looking back.

-27-

Keshari looked at the display screen of her vibrating BlackBerry to see who was calling.

"Marcus, what's up?" she said, answering her phone.

"We need to get together. We have quite a bit to talk about."

Keshari rolled her eyes. Why did it seem, lately, like Marcus was always talking within some kind of damned riddle?

"Marcus, surely you've caught it in the media. I'm extremely busy right now. I'm getting ready to fly to Miami as we speak for the fourth leg of auditions in my nationwide talent search project."

"Honey, you got some issues far more pressing than that right here in Los Angeles. Now, would you like me to come to you or are you going to come to me?"

"Are you issuing me orders now, Marcus?" Keshari questioned with annoyance.

"I'll see you at my house at five...and I really don't want to have to come looking for you."

Marcus's end of the line clicked off as he ended his

call. Keshari was furious. She picked up the phone and rang her assistant.

"T., I need you to push my flight back until ten tonight."

"Keshari, you're set at the airport to fly out of here at five. I don't know if I'll be able to get them to push it back on such short notice. We're about to go into a staff meeting."

"T., that's why I've got my own goddamned plane... so that I can switch up my flight times whenever the fuck I need to! And I've got an assistant to make sure that it happens without a single detail being missed!" She took a deep breath so that she did not become completely abusive with Terrence. "T., please push my flight back until eight tonight. Send me a text confirming the change as soon as it's done. We'll let the execs flying with me know in the staff meeting that the flight has to be pushed back."

"Not a problem," Terrence responded and clicked off the extension.

♪ 🎧 ♪

Larger Than Lyfe's "Nationwide Search for a Star" auditions were about to hit Miami. Before the crew loaded onto the record label's private jet and flew into Miami that evening, Keshari called a meeting to review the numbers for the project's budget. She'd been particularly distracted ever since the unexpected visit from the DEA agent. She became even more agitated after the phone call from Marcus Means. She'd been on the phone with her security firm for the greater part of the morning. She'd tripled her security team and hired additional security specialists who were former military intelligence officers, possessing training in stealth, poisons, and explosives. When Terrence saw the figures for the cost of the upgraded security services, he knew that something serious had to be up.

To date, no one had dared discuss the visit from the DEA agent. Not a word went around in LTL's offices or anywhere else, for that matter. The only person with whom Terrence even dared discuss Keshari's peculiar, current activities was his partner, but he felt certain that details would start getting leaked to the media if Keshari continued to behave in the bizarre way that she had been over the last few days in the presence of her staff. The woman was in rare form and Terrence knew that the press and the public would eat it up if they heard about it. "*The Ice Princess of Hip-Hop Finally Has a Chink in Her Armor,*" the headlines would blaze.

"Okay, people," Andre DeJesus said, "I've reviewed several set design layouts for the grand finale show. My group and I have selected the top three and need your final approval, Keshari, on the one we're gonna go with."

He placed the three design boards in front of her and she flipped through them absently.

"We all know that Misha Tierney was contracted to

put together the gift bags for the panel of judges and the top ten finalists. With Misha's connections to top-name vendors through her event planning firm, she's already several items gratis or at less than wholesale. We've got Tiffany & Co., Motorola, Carol's Daughter and Canyon Ranch Spa, just to name a few. These major names are glad to have their names connected to the event. The gift bags are each to have an estimated value of twenty-five thousand dollars."

"Damn!" Marvin Shabazz said, impressed. "That tops the gift bags for the Grammy Awards."

"Current advertising continues to maintain massive public, media, and industry interest in the project," Andre continued, "but we've got to sit down and streamline our marketing and publicity strategies after Miami so that we don't lose momentum and public interest as we get closer to the finale show. As we all know, this project has a pretty wide timeframe and the public has a short attention span. The last thing we want is even a slight dip in public interest."

"Let's talk about the budget," Keshari said.

Andre paused and took a deep breath. For the first time since the start of the staff meeting, his excitement over the plans and accomplished feats for his multi-million-dollar brainchild faltered.

"We are currently seventy-five thousand dollars over budget," Andre said.

Everything happened extremely fast after that. Keshari's

laptop went flying for a definite crash into the wall. Her latté went all over the table and dripped onto the Berber carpet. Executives went hopping away from the table, practically running over each other, as if gunfire had erupted.

"WHAT THE FUCK IS GOING ON HERE?!" Keshari looked at Andre and her two accountants as if they'd been caught embezzling the record label's funds.

No one rushed to provide a response.

"I pretty much give free rein to my executives to make solid decisions for the good of this company. These are not new rules around here. They have always existed.

"I distinctly told you in our very first meeting and I reminded you in every subsequent meeting that 'when it even smells like we're about to go over budget, I better know about it.' Do you remember that, Andre?"

He nodded.

"Do you remember that, Nicolai?"

"Of course, Keshari," Nicolai Livingston replied.

"Very well, then. Here's what's gonna happen. There is a massive figure already allocated to this project...and not a penny more will be put into this project. You guys are gonna have to put your heads together and get us back within budget...NOT ONE PENNY OVER...and you have until we return to L.A. from Miami to get it done," Keshari said.

"Keshari, I'm working as one of the judges at the Miami auditions. There is absolutely no way that I'll be able to do that as well as re-work these budget numbers. It's impossible," Andre said.

"You have never let me down before, Andre, and I know that you won't now. If this problem is not resolved by the time we return from Miami, there will be some terminations of employment."

Andre looked around the room at the other still-startled executives for support.

"I'll help you in any way that I can," Sharonda Richards offered.

The other executives nodded in agreement.

"Alright, what else is on the agenda? What else do I need to know about?" Keshari asked in exasperation.

Terrence was still busy attempting to clean up the sticky mess of Keshari's spilled latté without further agitating Keshari with his movements. He sat down and opened his laptop to pull up his notes.

"You meet with Cassandra Harrington and her son as soon as we return from Miami. It's time to finalize your contract with VIBE Network. Also, Rasheed has requested a meeting when you get back from Miami. His manager called this morning."

"Did he say what it was about?" Keshari asked curiously.

"No," Terrence said, "but it seems like it might be serious."

"Serious?" Keshari said, now giving Terrence her undivided attention. "What makes you say that?"

"That was just what I took from his tone," Terrence responded. "Better yet, you and Rasheed have always had open door communication with each other. You rarely work through his manager. That's mainly why I figured that the matter must be serious."

"Put him down for the first thing available when I return from Miami. Better yet, call him today and tell him that I'll fly him out to Miami if he wants to meet with me there."

"No problem," Terrence responded and quickly typed it into his notes.

"Is there anything else?" Keshari asked.

Everyone present was now still too stunned by Keshari's actions a few moments ago to say or suggest a thing. Keshari maintained a poised and firm control of the operations of Larger Than Lyfe Entertainment that demanded respect because she treated all of her staff with respect, but no one knew how to take this "new" Keshari.

"Okay, then," she said, mental exhaustion clearly wearing away at the very core of her. "I'll see you guys at the airport tonight."

With her broken laptop in her assistant Terrence's hands, she grabbed up her BlackBerry and the set design boards for the finale show and left the conference room while everyone else was left sitting around the conference table wondering what exactly was going on with their boss.

♫ 🎧 ♫

"Babygirl, you've officially got more extremely volatile shit on your hands than you've ever dealt with in your life. You're not gonna be able to continue going about your days, playing executive, and leading a relatively uneventful double life with this one. The moment that DEA agent walked into your office in search of information, the entire game changed. So, what's your plan?" Marcus asked.

"What the fuck do you mean, what's my plan?" Keshari snapped. "I plan to do exactly what I told you that I would do; separate myself COMPLETELY from this organization."

"Girl, do you realize that you are so close to having a price put on your head that you can bank on not making it to see the winner of your nationwide talent search?" Marcus chuckled and shook his head. "I always told Rick that no matter how smart you are, you were NEVER cut out for this business."

"Marcus, I have negotiated terms, safely moved and distributed more cocaine than any woman and most men in the United States."

"I sure hope that you didn't tell that to the DEA agent who paid you a visit," Marcus said.

"Fuck you!" Keshari snapped.

"Keshari, are you taking any of this seriously? No, better yet, have you lost your fucking mind?! You go about your day-to-day affairs as if you're completely oblivious to what's happening. You've even gone and gotten yourself involved in some romantic relationship that's plastered on the cover of every entertainment tabloid in every major city in the U.S. You follow this trial nonchalantly as if you don't fully comprehend the ramifications of Rick being sent to prison. So, again, I ask, are you taking any of this seriously?"

"To be completely honest, the only thing that I've really been doing is everything in my power to begin to try to live a normal life," Keshari responded. "The only way for me to leave this business, Marcus, is for me to leave this business, stop handling The Consortium's affairs, walk away from all of it, and never look back."

Marcus shook his head and rolled his eyes. He was becoming extremely irritated by Keshari's stupidity. "You do realize that the only reason you're not dead already has to do with the history you have with Rick."

"Yes, I'm well aware of that," Keshari said seriously. "I also know that I will have to take more precautions than I ever have to protect myself, but I have to do this. I can't live with myself another day, leading my life as a member of The Consortium."

"Keshari, we're operating at a disadvantage here and we have never been in a position like this before. The changes in suppliers, Rick's murder charges, the visit from the DEA agent...and, for now, at least, I've managed to keep out of the pipelines information about your determined efforts to walk away from your role in this organization. Word gets around in our world a lot faster than it gets around anywhere else. Sharks smell blood in the water and rush to attack. A billion-dollar, Black-owned enterprise is in serious jeopardy right now. You owe it to The Consortium, you owe it to Rick, to help preserve what we've built."

The two of them sat in the living room of Marcus's tenth-floor oceanfront apartment with its magnificent view of Santa Monica and the Pacific Ocean.

"Rick put you through college and then paid for your very prestigious MBA from the Wharton School," Marcus continued. "He even provided you with the initial funding to start up your record label...and this is how you repay him?"

"All that's going on right now, Marcus...maybe it's a sign to all of us that it's time for things to change. Better yet, maybe it's just like you said. Perhaps I was never cut out for this business."

"This is more than just about The Consortium, Keshari. The Mexicans, our new supplier in Miami, the Colombians... These organizations span generations with power that reaches out farther than The Consortium. DEA inquiries are not acceptable to them, under any circumstances, and they believe in silencing every witness that federal law enforcement might even think about subpoenaing before a grand jury. They don't give a fuck about history."

"You know that I know all of what you're saying," Keshari responded.

"You know that The Consortium will no longer protect you if you walk."

"I know that, too," Keshari said, "and, still, I cannot do this anymore."

"You're on your own now, Keshari," Marcus said solemnly, "and there are dire consequences in this business for disloyalty."

-28-

L arger Than Lyfe's private jet landed at Miami International Airport. Two limousines awaited the group. One took the LTL executives to their block of hotel rooms at the Mandarin Oriental Miami. The second limousine loaded Keshari's Louis Vuitton luggage into the trunk to deliver Keshari to her luxurious, Mediterranean-style home in Palm Beach. The house was twice the size of her mansion in Palos Verdes and twice as extravagant.

Palm Beach was an ultra-exclusive community comprised of mainly White, "old money" residents who were still quite resistant to accepting rich, Black residents into their ultra-elitist, little microcosm, no matter how wealthy they were. This made Keshari all the more determined to purchase the $12.5 million home that she had fallen in love with at first sight. She could have easily purchased or built the home of her dreams on Star Island, another ultra-exclusive, Florida community that welcomed very affluent, celebrity types like Rosie O'Donnell and Sean "Diddy" Combs, but she'd owned the Palm

Beach residence for more than a year now and her neighbors, for the most part, were amicable.

Keshari had sat by herself on the plane for the entire trip. She tried to sleep but couldn't, so she kept her eyes closed so that she wouldn't be bothered. Almost everyone kept a safe distance anyway, after her blow-up earlier at the staff meeting. The last thing any of them wanted more than a mile up in the air was a verbal or physical assault that they couldn't fully get away from.

Keshari's security team had arrived the day before to get settled and view the property. They'd already reviewed the blueprints of the property prior to flying out of Los Angeles and they prepped Keshari as soon as she arrived. The housekeepers unpacked her things in the master suite while Keshari took a bath. Then she curled up with a cashmere throw on a chaise longue on the master suite's balcony and went to sleep. Even while she slept, her mind could not stop analyzing her situation over and over again and planning her next steps.

♩ 🎧 ♩

Mars's limousine arrived at Keshari's mansion late that night and Mars found Keshari wide awake in the library reviewing fabric swatches and design sketches for her upcoming apparel line, "The Plush Collection." The woman was like a locomotive, Mars thought. She moved smoothly from one, intensive project to another all day every day, flew back and forth across the country almost every week, worked out with a physical trainer whenever she could fit her in, rarely ever slept, and still managed to be the most beautiful woman he'd ever laid eyes on.

She had a long, project table set up next to her desk, where she could spread out the fabric swatches and sketches and organize them into groups. She had the telephone receiver to her ear and she was speaking to someone in Italian. She rolled back and forth in her desk chair between her desk and the project table while reviewing on her laptop photographs of models wearing samples of the prospective pieces for her apparel line.

She waved to Mars and blew him a kiss as he came in and sat down. "The Plush Collection" had been a goal of hers for some time and she was finally laying the groundwork to bring her hip-hop-to-couture line to market. She was so excited about the ideas that were coming to fruition and she was zealously managing every aspect of the development of this brainchild by herself. She loved high-end clothing and accessories almost as much as she loved music and she'd become something of a fashion trendsetter in the industry. "The Plush Collection" was destined to become yet another endeavor of hers that was larger than life.

Keshari tossed one idea after another at the designer on the phone, and then discussed taking a trip to Milan to view more fabrics and a few runway shows for insight.

242 CYNTHIA DIANE THORNTON

Mars pulled off his suit jacket and tossed it across the arm of the library's leather sofa. He went over and spun Keshari around in her desk chair to face him.

"I didn't fly all the way here to watch you work," he said.

"In a minute, sweetie," Keshari whispered, placing her hand over the receiver's mouthpiece.

She smiled up at Mars distractedly, and then turned back to her laptop and phone call. Mars spun her chair around again, knelt in front of her, and kissed her though her satin pajama pants. Keshari smiled and attempted to shoo him away. Mars reached under her top, untied the drawstring of her pajama pants, and pulled them off.

"WHAT ARE YOU DOING?!" she mouthed at Mars as he smiled up at her mischievously.

He buried his face between her thighs and found what he was seeking.

"Woo-o-o-o!" Keshari yelped as she felt Mars's tongue exploring her intimately.

"I'll have to call you back," she said to the person on the other end of the line. "You are a very bad man," she told Mars, wagging a finger at him.

With freshly polished, pink toes dangling over Mars's shoulders, she put her head back and allowed her gorgeous man to have his way with her.

♫ 🎧 ♫

The kickoff of the Miami auditions at the Broward Center for the Performing Arts in Fort Lauderdale received as huge a turnout as the Los Angeles, New York, and Atlanta auditions. News cameras panned the huge crowd of young hopefuls. Many of them had camped out outside the performing arts center like they had in Los Angeles. All of them wanted to secure one of the highly coveted, numbered wristbands that guaranteed them a place in the auditions.

The local FOX news station did an exclusive interview with Keshari to discuss the nationwide talent search. Keshari put on her public relations face and talked candidly about how pleased she was at the amazing talent that her record label had discovered in the audition cities they'd hit so far and how excited and assured she was that Larger Than Lyfe would discover some equally amazing talent in Miami.

The interviewer pleaded with Keshari for the name of a celebrity or two who would sit on the celebrity panel of judges at the televised grand finale show. Keshari smiled demurely and stayed mum. The celebrity panel of judges was not being revealed to anyone. It would be a complete surprise that would not be revealed until the night of the grand finale event.

The interviewer changed the subject.

"You've been keeping company with the very handsome general counsel for ASCAP. I know that he accompanied you to the Atlanta auditions and very reliable sources tell me that he flew into Miami late the other night. Are things serious? Any wedding bells in the near future?"

"The nationwide talent search and other projects demand my complete focus," Keshari responded. "I barely have time to sleep, much less establish and maintain a love life."

"Oh, come on," the interviewer cajoled. "I know that you're not attempting to convince me and the public that you're not in love. You're GLOWING, for God's sake."

"It's the Miami humidity," Keshari responded coyly.

♪ 🎧 ♪

On day two of the Miami auditions, a very, very special discovery was made. Sharonda Richards and Andre DeJesus had been carefully observing the incoming crowd of auditioners from the television monitors set up around the judges' panel. Although Keshari was also present as a member of the panel of judges, she'd been preoccupied on her laptop for the greater part of the morning, trading communications with her attorney.

A twenty-year-old female singer took the stage wearing a flowing, Asian-inspired sundress and high-heeled sandals. She was stunning, an amalgamation of cultures... half-Black, half-Korean, with warm, flawless, brown skin and a cascade of silky, raven curls. Physically, she looked a lot like Keshari and almost everyone commented on that. Her voice was PHENOMENAL. It was an intoxicating mix of smoky, sultry, with a streetwise edge and a hint of the angelic. She sang a song that she had written herself and her whole aura exuded star quality that could not be denied.

The New Millennium music industry is roughly 70 percent image and about 30 percent true talent. Only a handful of artists possess the kind of transcendent creativity in production and writing and vocal ability and range as singers that makes the music industry and public music enthusiasts just KNOW that music was what these artists were MADE to do. The rest of the industry are illusions very carefully concocted from strategic marketing plans, state-of-the-art recording studio technology, and whatever is most popular in the music industry at the time.

A significant goal that Keshari intended to accomplish with her label's nationwide talent search was to firmly establish its R & B and jazz genres by filling its repertoire with fresh, amazingly talented, new R & B and jazz artists. Keshari was a lover of MUSIC, not just hip-hop, and one of her long-range plans had always been to have all of the Black music genres under her label's umbrella and she wanted to fully start realizing that goal with a female R & B singer possessing the kind of magnetism and crossover quality to make millions for her record label.

Larger Than Lyfe had been searching for quite some time for a young, beautiful, highly talented female to groom to become a worldwide superstar, its R & B-hip-hop princess. Beyoncé Knowles was one thing. What Larger Than Lyfe had in mind was even greater. Prior to the nationwide talent search project, LTL's A & R team traveled the country, hitting nightclubs on the tips of others. They'd listened to hundreds of demos and viewed stacks and stacks of photos with accompanying CDs of models-slash-singers. They'd attended high school and college talent events. Not once had they found the female who possessed the distinctive qualities that they were looking for...until now.

The moment that she took the stage, Sharonda Richards was in awe. She leaned over and tapped Andre DeJesus, but he was already on the same vibe. He leaned over and whispered to Keshari. Keshari had already stopped what she was doing and was watching the young woman with interest.

"She's the one," Andre said.

"I know," Keshari replied.

All of the judges seated at the panel leaned together in a huddle. They were about to make the very first exception to the rules of the audition process and the entire nationwide talent search project since the project commenced. The young lady's name was "Ntozake," a Swahili name that means "she who comes with her own things." She was named after the famous, Black poet-activist Ntozake Shange. She was a military brat. She was extremely talented and her background was inter-esting without their PR department having to create a bio for her.

Keshari Mitchell and Larger Than Lyfe Entertainment wanted to extend to her an invitation to bypass the entire audition process, come to Los Angeles, and go into their studios to record for them. She'd get the opportunity to flex her writing chops, she'd work with some of the country's best producers, and LTL would give her project the kind of attention and promotion that was usually reserved for megastars.

"Tell me," Keshari said. "How would you like to come to Los Angeles and record an album for our label?"

"I'm not sure I understand your question," Ntozake responded. "Are you asking me how I'd feel to be the winner of the nationwide talent search?"

"No," Keshari said. "We'd like you to forgo the talent search altogether and sign with Larger Than Lyfe immediately."

Ntozake's screams and tears of delirious delight were surely confirmation enough of her acceptance of their astounding offer. The local news got wind of the story later in the day and covered the story for the remainder of the Miami auditions.

♪ 🎧 ♪

Mars had only been able to spend a day with Keshari right before the Miami auditions kicked off because he had to fly back to Los Angeles to be in court, but he returned to Palm Beach the night that the Miami auditions wrapped. He planned to fly back to L.A. with Keshari and her crew on the Larger Than Lyfe Entertainment jet.

Keshari was unusually quiet now that the excitement of the auditions and a multitude of press coverage were past. Mars simply believed that she was exhausted and needed a little time to fully decompress. He had no idea that there was so, so much more weighing on her mind than fatigue. The two had dinner on the terrace, swam naked in the middle of the night in the infinity pool, and curled up in the master bedroom suite in the wee hours of the morning to watch a movie.

"What's on your mind?" Mars asked her. "You've been so quiet and you seem tense."

The two were lying in a pile of pillows on the floor in front of the huge, wall-mounted plasma television. She pulled Mars's arms around her tighter as they spooned, half-watching *Love and Basketball*.

"I feel like, at any moment, I'm gonna wake up and ALL of this...even you...will have just been a dream."

Mars chuckled. "As long as you're not talking about a nightmare when you say that."

Keshari was serious. "Mars," she said softly, "I love you. There is so much that I want to say to you. There is so much that I need to say to you, but the timing is always off. Over what's only been a very brief period, we've had an *incredible* time together. I feel as if I've known you all my life. But there is still so much about me that you don't know...and, right now, my life is on the verge of spiraling completely out of control."

"Why don't you take some time off?" Mars suggested. "You have a more than competent staff to manage your record company's operations in your absence while you take some personal time for yourself to regroup. I know that this talent search...flying from city to city week after week...has got to be wearing you out, and your mind and your body are trying to tell you that they need a break."

"Mars, it's more than that."

"Then, what is it?" Mars asked.

"You are the best thing that's ever happened to me and I'm probably...no...most likely...going to lose you."

The telephone rang and postponed their discussion. The call was from Los Angeles. There'd been some sort of security breach at Keshari's mansion.

-29-

Portia was sickly obsessed and a part of her absolutely knew it, but she'd come to a point where she couldn't seem to stop herself from doing what she was doing, even if she wanted to. She'd always been something of a "drama queen" and she was definitely no stranger to the "Naomi Campbell syndrome" when she was provoked. The pregnancy stunt absolutely took the cake, but what she had been getting herself into lately was extreme, even for her. Almost every day, Portia had been orchestrating her hectic work schedule around her driving up to spy on Keshari Mitchell's Palos Verdes mansion.

If it was daytime, she would sit up the street from the entrance to the bitch's house and watch the comings and goings of delivery trucks, pool cleaners, gardeners, security officers, Keshari Mitchell's employees from her record label, Misha Tierney, the party promoter, Mars, and the bitch herself. She'd even begun to notice who she believed to be paparazzi in an unmarked van photographing, and sometimes videotaping, movement on Keshari's enclosed property.

If it was nighttime, Portia would often boldly sit directly across the street from the mansion's driveway, ducking down in her car seat and waiting until the bitch came speeding up the street in one of her fleet of six-figure-price-tagged cars. She'd watch the bitch get out of her car and go into her beautiful home. A couple of times, she saw Keshari running on the lawn, tossing a tennis ball at her two massive Rottweilers.

Portia had no earthly idea what she was hoping to accomplish after weeks of "surveillance" outside Keshari Mitchell's mansion. The whole problem with Portia's situation was that Mars was not her man. He never had been. Portia and Mars had dated off and on for some time and exclusivity was not something that existed even once between the two of them. Portia had wanted an exclusive relationship with Mars, but Mars had made it pretty clear that he didn't want anything resembling a serious relationship, so Portia acted as if she didn't want anything serious either. Then Mars went and got himself involved with that Keshari Mitchell bitch and it was serious from day one and, well, GOD-DAMMIT...that's why Portia was parked outside that bitch's house right now! The hurt and the anger of Mars unceremoniously dumping her so that he could give that bitch exclusivity was as fresh in her mind and heart as if it had happened only moments before and Portia was now strangely fixated on doing damage to the bitch who had walked up out of nowhere and assumed HER position. Portia just hadn't firmly decided yet what that "damage" would be.

From a sane person's point of view, nothing would come from what Portia was doing except a lot of wasted time and trouble, particularly if she got caught, and it kept her from moving on with her life. But Portia was not working from a very sane place these days. She knew that the bitch was out of town again. She was in Miami for another leg of auditions in her nationwide talent search project. Portia caught the details regarding the Miami auditions on the E! channel on the day the bitch left. Portia watched the limousine arrive and load up her luggage to take her to the airport.

The armed guards who were typically present were not patrolling the grounds. Security seemed to be lighter on the property whenever the bitch was traveling and Portia was going to use that as an opportunity to sneak past those remote control gates and onto the property.

Portia had timed it all perfectly. The timing mechanism on the remote control gates took about fifteen seconds to completely close the gates. As soon as a FedEx delivery truck was pulling out of the gates, Portia literally ran from her parked car and straight inside the closing gates.

The little piece that was left of the rational side of Portia was screaming at the top of its lungs, "Why are you doing this?! What is this going to accomplish?!" The side of Portia that had just gotten onto Keshari Mitchell's private property and was about to take a close look around at how that bitch lived gave the "rational" side a slug in the face and kept Portia focused on their far better plan. "Hurt the bitch!" it said, a twisted, horned, little devil sitting on her shoulder and angrily serving up horrific advice. "She's got your man!"

Armed with a black backpack containing a couple of cans of black spray paint, a loaded .22 handgun, a digital camera, her cell phone, and a handheld copying device, and dressed in black sweats and black running shoes as if she was participating in a caper from *Mission Impossible*, Portia hopped behind a hedge and took a deep breath, amazed that she was actually inside. She looked around and thought for a moment and figured that she could scamper across the lawn and make it into the house through the open solarium doors. Little did she know that high-powered, security cameras were capturing her every move and, while the bulk of the security team who generally walked the grounds seemed to be off duty, the regular security who manned the guard office and patrolled the property twenty-four hours a day, seven days a week were definitely on duty.

Before Miss "Mission Impossible" could even swing into action, two of the armed security guards exited the guard office and chased her across the grounds to apprehend her. Sometimes a person never really realizes how stupid she's being until her actions leave her looking like "Public Idiot Number One." Portia Foster was placed under arrest by the Torrance Police Department and placed in the back of a squad car as she wilded out like Zsa Zsa Gabor, kicking and screaming profanities as the squad car drove away with her inside.

The media made it over to the Torrance Police Department in record time to capture the unfolding story. They even secured Portia Foster's brazen-looking mug shot photo and plastered it all over the local news.

Keshari was still in Palm Beach, having just wrapped the Miami auditions, when she received the call from her security company in Los Angeles, alerting her of the security breach and arrest. Keshari had no idea who Portia Foster was. Because of the immediate media coverage that made it all the way to Miami, she was promptly provided with a complete background of the woman who'd slipped onto her property with the clear intention of vandalizing it and possibly doing her harm.

"Ex-Girlfriend of ASCAP's West Coast General Counsel Arrested for Stalking," a local, Miami news station reported.

-30-

Keshari and Mars flew back to Los Angeles together out of Miami and were hounded by the press as soon as their plane touched the ground. Reporters questioned Keshari about Portia Foster and whether or not she and Portia had ever met. The media wanted to know if Keshari was responsible for Mars and Portia's breakup. The press posed the same questions to Mars, and then asked if Keshari recently finding out about Portia Foster had hurt his and Keshari's relationship in any way. The press asked Mars if he was aware of Portia having any history of mental illness. They asked if Mars and Keshari were afraid that Portia would do something to try to harm the two of them after her release from police custody. Then reporters went way-y-y off into left field by asking if Mars and Keshari were getting married. It was all very intrusive and more than a little ridiculous.

Portia was released from jail on bail, pending her court date, and the media immediately accosted her as well. Keshari's attorney acquired temporary restraining orders for both Keshari and Mars and they were served to Portia the moment she exited the Torrance Police Department following her release. Portia was not allowed to come within 1,000 feet of Keshari or Mars or either of their workplaces and their residences. Portia was both embarrassed and livid.

Portia's design firm received calls from morning until night. A couple of big-name clients called urgently with the desire to immediately cancel their projects and terminate their contracts. Reporters pumped Portia's employees for information regarding their boss. They also called and called in vain, attempting to speak directly to Portia Foster herself. They wanted to know about Portia's past romantic relationship with Mars Buchanan and they wanted to see if Portia Foster was as crazy as she currently seemed. A couple of extra-resourceful reporters contacted a few well-known models to see if they could obtain a bit of "dish" regarding Portia Foster's history back in her fashion runway days. Perhaps she'd been something of a nut job back then and there were some peculiar stories to be passed on to the public.

Paparazzi snapped photos of Portia, no matter where she was or what she was doing, and they seemed most inclined to try to take the photos of Portia that were unbecoming and that would lead the public to believe that she was, in fact, unstable. Portia finally decided, at the advice of her attorney, to assign her pending projects to one of her senior interior designers and go into hiding until her court dates and until the nasty publicity surrounding her died down.

♪ 🎧 ♫

While Portia's twisted, little saga had her own life in temporary unravel, it seemed to render Mars and Keshari's relationship stronger than ever. Mars told Keshari all about Portia Foster and how he had terminated all dealings with her directly after his and Keshari's trip to Negril. He told Keshari that Portia was a little melodramatic, but that she had never done anything as long as he'd known her, like what she had done recently to get herself arrested. Mars mentioned nothing at all to Keshari about Portia's faked pregnancy.

Mars went on to tell Keshari that there had never been an exclusive relationship between Portia and him, even though he knew that that was precisely what she wanted...which was another reason that he'd broken things off with her. He didn't want to lead her on. Keshari took it all in, with few questions and no arguments, anger or suspicion. If anything, Keshari seemed mildly amused at the crazy woman slipping onto her property for whatever reason that she had. She'd set aside the withdrawn, distracted, and agitated state she'd been in in Miami. She strategized her movements privately and managed to keep it all together so that she didn't worry Mars. She and Mars never finished the conversation that they'd been engaged in prior to the call from Keshari's security company in Los Angeles. Mars broached the subject and Keshari quickly brushed it off.

-31-

It was the day before Keshari would be flying out of Los Angeles for the kick-off of Larger Than Lyfe's talent search auditions in Detroit, the seventh audition city. It was also the day one of closing arguments in Richard Tresvant's murder trial. Mars had taken the day off to hang out with Keshari before she left for Detroit and he flew to San Francisco for the rest of the week for a music conference. Keshari had promised Mars before he arrived that morning that she would not do a single, work-related thing or take a single, work-related call. They were going to veg out all day, order take-out, and get some much-needed R & R. Keshari was curled up in a white, Juicy Couture sweatsuit watching television in the solarium, eating a big bag of Doritos, when Mars arrived.

"You've gotten yourself addicted to this murder trial like three-quarters of the rest of Los Angeles. I cannot believe you TiVo it."

Keshari chuckled, but, as the day went on, seemed to be taking in the ongoing trial a lot more seriously than the typical, interested viewer. Mars watched the subtle cues in her body language and she seemed to be watching almost as if she had some vested interest in the trial and its outcome.

"Do you know him?" Mars asked curiously.

"Who?" Keshari said.

"Richard Tresvant...the gangster..."

"Yeah," Keshari responded. "I know him."

Mars didn't say anything.

"I'm gonna tell you something that not a whole lot of people know...and it's just between the two of us, okay?"

"Okay," Mars said. He was now apprehensive.

"Richard Tresvant is Misha's biological brother."

"SAY WHAT?!" Mars said in complete surprise.

"Yeah," Keshari said. "She changed her last name because of him. Her last name is not really Tierney. It's Tresvant. She wants no connection or association to him whatsoever."

"Damn," Mars said, eying the television screen and immediately noticing the strong, physical resemblance between Misha and Richard Tresvant. "How well do you know him?"

Keshari was quiet for a few moments. As much as Mars was trying to be cool about it, she could see the anxiety building in his eyes.

"I know him very well, Mars. A long, long time ago, I was romantically involved with him."

Mars didn't ask any more questions. A flash of what

his best friend, Jason Payne, had said to him when Mars first told him about Keshari went through his mind. He also thought of the wise, old adage, "Don't ask the question if you are not prepared to handle the answer."

♪ 🎧 ♪

Steve Cooley, district attorney for Los Angeles County, approached the juror box. His salt-and-pepper hair was freshly cut. The navy, pinstripe suit he wore was new.

"Ladies and gentlemen," he said, "justice is in grave danger...and, right now, it is your duty as citizens to help save it.

"Phinnaeus Bernard III was a very shrewd, corporate attorney. He graduated from USC and went on to graduate from the Yale School of Law. He joined the very prestigious law firm of Carlyle, Brown, Von Klaus & Pennington right out of law school and he was on the fast track to become a partner from the start. He married his college sweetheart, Bunny. They went on to have two beautiful children and they've resided in their Brentwood neighborhood for more than twenty-five years. They have always been liked and respected by most. The Bernard family has always been an upstanding asset to the Los Angeles community.

"I felt it necessary to remind the jurors of these significant details because they have been downplayed by all of the other sensationalized drama of this trial...

mainly the defendant's sensationalized drama. A good family has been irreparably damaged by murder...and they need justice.

"Richard Lawrence Tresvant, the defendant, was a client of Phinnaeus Bernard III at the law firm of Carlyle, Brown, Von Klaus and Pennington. As Mr. Tresvant's attorney, Phinnaeus Bernard set up corporations for Mr. Tresvant and advised Richard Tresvant on tax shelters for his personal income as well as for the revenues of his corporations.

"Richard Tresvant is an interesting character. He possesses no formal education beyond high school, yet he is a millionaire many times over... not that such a feat is an impossibility...but Richard Tresvant also has a rap sheet that includes charges for some very heinous crimes and markedly few convictions that could stretch right out the doors of this courtroom. He's been accused of everything from racketeering, drug trafficking, extortion, aggravated assault, and even murder...all before we even get to our current murder trial...and he's managed virtually every time to walk away, a free man, when very compelling evidence was stacked against him.

"Another very interesting thing about Richard Tresvant is that powerful, wealthy, upstanding men are absolutely mesmerized by him. You heard Walter Bumgaarten's testimony. He said that Richard Tresvant is one of the most astute businessmen he's ever met in his life. He said the words with unabashed admiration.

Walter Bumgaarten's family could very easily be called the Second Camelot, yet Walter Bumgaarten is close, personal friends with Richard Tresvant, whose reputation has always been less than savory.

"The People believe that Phinnaeus Bernard III was mesmerized by Richard Tresvant in the same way that Walter Bumgaarten and other prominent, Los Angeles businessmen who are personal friends of Richard Tresvant are mesmerized by him. Most of us, to varying degrees, are intoxicated by the mysterious allure of gangsters. *The Godfather*, *GoodFellas*, *Scarface*, are all blockbuster movies glamorizing the lives of gangsters and most of us ravenously collect them in our video collections to watch on movie night again and again. Some of us are drawn to danger like moths to the proverbial flame. Richard Ramirez, infamous, convicted serial killer, has a lengthy list of female admirers writing to him, desiring to visit him, some of them proposing marriage to him, while he sits behind bars, unrepentant for his unimaginably horrific crimes. It boggles the mind, but this is the reality.

"The People believe that Phinnaeus Bernard, as Richard Tresvant's attorney, got to know more and more about Richard Tresvant, both on a professional level as well as a personal one. They played golf together. Phinnaeus Bernard introduced Richard Tresvant to established politicians and judges and other prominent figures he knew who might prove instrumental to Richard Tresvant in some way. The People believe that

Phinnaeus Bernard got more involved in Richard Tresvant's business affairs than merely the set-up of corporations and providing tax shelter advice. He was MESMERIZED by Richard Tresvant and the dangerously mysterious allure connected to him. The People believe that the chief objective of the set-up of corporations for Richard Tresvant was to launder Richard Tresvant's drug money and diversify his dealings into completely legitimate enterprises. Over the course of his dealings with Richard Tresvant, Phinnaeus Bernard more than likely got a taste of the underworld in which Richard Tresvant operates. The People believe that Phinnaeus Bernard eventually had second thoughts about what he'd gotten himself into. Perhaps something happened that was more than he could handle. Phinnaeus Bernard had a meeting with the other partners of his firm a short time before his murder to discuss transferring Richard Tresvant's files to another attorney within the firm. He also asked the other partners to strongly consider returning Richard Tresvant's retainer to him and terminating the firm's legal services to him.

"Once he got word of it, Richard Tresvant must have viewed this move by Phinnaeus Bernard as a definite betrayal. He'd allowed Phinnaeus Bernard into his world. He'd allowed Phinnaeus Bernard to be privy to details of his business operations. Phinnaeus Bernard held information about Richard Tresvant that could, most assuredly, get Richard Tresvant locked up for the rest of his life and, then, Phinnaeus Bernard suddenly had a flash of conscience and wanted nothing more to do with him. All of you have certainly watched at least one gangster movie, or you've heard enough stories about the Mafia or some other organized crime operation, to know how betrayals are handled by gangsters.

"Something must be done about criminals with pockets deep enough to get away with the crimes that they commit. Something must be done about criminals with pockets deep enough to intimidate witnesses and jurors and bribe law enforcement and judges and, like a magician, make guilt be turned to innocence with a wave of dirty money.

"On March 11, 2005, Richard Tresvant had a meeting and lunch with his attorney, Phinnaeus Bernard III. The head of security at the office building where Phinnaeus Bernard worked testified that Richard Tresvant and Phinnaeus Bernard were clearly arguing when they left the building for lunch that day. Phinnaeus Bernard returned to work later that afternoon and continued to work late into the evening. The office building's security log indicates Phinnaeus Bernard signed out for the day at 9:47 p.m. and his family never saw him alive again. Phinnaeus Bernard III was murdered, execution-style, in his car before he even left the parking garage at his place of business. Richard Lawrence Tresvant murdered Phinnaeus Bernard III. The murder weapon with Richard Tresvant's prints all over it was found in Richard Tresvant's Bel Air home.

"Richard Tresvant's ride of slickly slipping through the hands of justice needs to end HERE and NOW. The People ask that you, the jurors, find Richard Lawrence Tresvant guilty of the first-degree murder of Phinnaeus Bernard III."

♪ 🎧 ♪

The following day was dedicated to the defense's closing argument. Larry Steinberg paced in front of the jurors' gallery and made eye contact with each of the jurors individually for a few seconds before he proceeded.

"The prosecution has trumped up a case based on relentless speculation, circumstantial evidence, complete and utter nonsense, and outright fabrication.

"There must be justice for the murder of Phinnaeus Bernard III. None of us will disagree with this. However, wrongfully convicting a man for first-degree murder based on falsified, physical evidence and a prior criminal record that has nothing at all to do with this case is an INJUSTICE...an absolute injustice.

"An anonymous phone call to the police department is what led LAPD to secure a warrant and find the murder weapon that killed Phinnaeus Bernard III at Richard Tresvant's Bel Air home. To this day, we have yet to determine exactly who made the anonymous call from a phone booth on Century Boulevard in South Central Los Angeles. We know that this anonymous person sounded like a male...and that's about it. Perhaps this person was connected in some way to Phinnaeus Bernard's murder. Perhaps this person framed Richard Tresvant for murder. How did this person know to direct police to Richard Tresvant's home to find the murder weapon? How did this person know anything about Richard Tresvant in the first place, to even connect him to Phinnaeus Bernard? There are enough questions surrounding this phantom informant who has conveniently disappeared like he never existed to build a mountain of reasonable doubt.

"Now...I've watched enough television, from *CSI* to *Law and Order* to big-budget, psychological thrillers at the movie theaters, to know that, if you want to commit a murder and get away with it, you're probably going to want to wear gloves. You don't want your prints anywhere near the crime scene and you definitely don't want your prints anywhere near the murder weapon. You'll also want to get rid of the murder weapon immediately after commission of the crime. You certainly won't want to take it home with you like some sort of a keepsake or souvenir.

"Throughout this trial, the prosecution has painted Richard Tresvant as this 'highly sophisticated criminal' who repeatedly slips out of the grasp of justice because of his organized crime money and witness intimidation. Yet, if we are to believe the reenactment presented by the prosecution, this 'highly sophisticated criminal' clearly dropped the ball on the night that he allegedly murdered Phinnaeus Bernard. If we are to believe the reenactment presented by the prosecution, Richard Tresvant laid out a trail of bread crumbs after, allegedly, murdering Phinnaeus Bernard that led directly back to him and, ultimately, incriminated him—he met with Phinnaeus Bernard on the day of the murder and had lunch with him, he and Phinnaeus Bernard are seen allegedly arguing as they leave for lunch on the day of their meeting, Phinnaeus Bernard returns to work after lunch and is, later that same evening, murdered execution-style in his office building's parking structure, a large quantity of cocaine and one hundred thousand dollars cash are found by detectives in Phinnaeus Bernard's car trunk that the killer conveniently left behind, and then...the pièce de résistance...the murder weapon is conveniently found at Richard Tresvant's home after an anonymous phone call to police. Nothing about the flaming trail evidence revealed in this crime indicates that a 'highly sophisticated criminal' was involved. Better yet, if Richard Tresvant is even half the man that the prosecution proclaims him to be, why wouldn't he simply hire someone to carry out the job of executing Phinnaeus Bernard, thereby keeping his own hands clean?

"Ladies and gentlemen of the jury, Richard Lawrence Tresvant is NOT guilty of the first-degree murder of Phinnaeus Bernard III. Richard Tresvant has been FRAMED! Richard Tresvant submitted to two polygraph exams, one administered by a polygraphist hired by the defense and a second administered by the polygraphist selected by the district attorney of Los Angeles County. Richard Tresvant passed BOTH polygraph exams.

"The most glaringly suspect evidence in this entire trial is the fingerprint evidence taken from the murder weapon. We brought in an expert forensics witness, formerly employed with the FBI, to examine the fingerprints on the murder weapon. The forensics expert determined that the age of the fingerprints on the murder weapon substantially predated the date of the murder, thereby giving validity to the defense's claim that Richard Tresvant was set up, framed for the murder of Phinnaeus Bernard III and certainly adding to the mountain of evidence already existing that establishes REASONABLE DOUBT in this case.

"Ladies and gentlemen of the jury, for you to convict Richard Tresvant for the first-degree murder of Phinnaeus Bernard III, the evidence presented against him must REMOVE ALL DOUBT that there is some other person still walking around free who is actually responsible for the commission of this crime. If the evidence presented over the course of this trial raises and leaves far more questions unanswered than inarguable facts, reasonable doubt is established. As it stands, there is a lengthy list of factors establishing classic examples of reasonable doubt in this case and, where there is such a substantial level of reasonable doubt as is apparent in this case, you have no other option except to acquit the defendant. The defense implores each and every one of you to find Richard Lawrence Tresvant 'not guilty' of the first-degree murder of Phinnaeus Bernard III."

-32-

Timing conflicts between the nationwide talent search project and Rasheed the Refugee's touring schedule had repeatedly kept Keshari and Rasheed from meeting, per his request, for weeks. The two were finally able to sit down and have lunch together on the sectional in Keshari's office right before she and her crew flew to Houston, two cities away from wrapping up the talent search's audition phase. Terrence had ordered Mr. Chow's for the two of them. Keshari uncorked a bottle of pinot grigio for herself and Rasheed poured Pellegrino over ice. Rasheed seemed to be in a very serious frame of mind that day, but he managed to kick back casually and make small talk with Keshari about the business, about their lives. Over time, they had become good friends as well as business associates. Rasheed held a great deal of respect for Keshari and she held tremendous respect for him.

"A lot's been going on in your life lately," Rasheed said.

"Yeah," Keshari said. "This talent search is absolutely wearing me out."

"You've got much transpiring in your life outside the record label," Rasheed said.

"Very true," Keshari responded without elaborating.

"I'm leaving the label," Rasheed said. "My contract is up in six months and I've opted not to renew. I'm also requesting release from the remaining six months of my current contract and I'd like to purchase the masters for all of the songs that I produced."

"Say what?!" Keshari said, snapping up in her seat in complete shock.

"Word has it that a price is now on your head. Are you aware of that?" Rasheed asked.

"Yeah," Keshari answered seriously, "but I can't stop the wheels of my life from turning. I've got a business to run...and, for the time being, at least, I've got a life to live."

"You know I love you," Rasheed said. "You are my sister and you always will be, but it's gotten too dangerous to be around you...and I'm headed in a different direction with my life and my music anyway. I'm taking greater control of my intellectual property and I'm laying the groundwork as we speak for my own label."

Tears filled Keshari's eyes and spilled down her cheeks.

"Maybe you need to take a break and go somewhere for awhile," Rasheed suggested, "until things calm down or until you can reach some sort of compromise with these people."

"I can't go anywhere for awhile, Ra. I'm an unapologetic workaholic. You may as well tell me to slit my wrists."

"You can't keep doing what you're doing, Keshari, like nothing is seriously wrong. You're like a moving target at this record label every day...no matter how specialized your security is. You're endangering your staff.

"Look...," Rasheed went on, "I never judged you for what you did and I always knew what you were involved in. I've got people who were involved in the game. I've got some people who are still involved in the game. You know like I know that the Mexicans will walk right into this record label and kill you if you don't find some way to make this whole thing right. You've got DEA breathing down your neck and you think that you can just continue to pretend and try to carry on some semblance of a regular life and ignore the rest? Your whole staff knows about the DEA agent showing up here. Before long, this whole mess is going to blow up in your face."

"You were the very first artist I signed to my label," Keshari said nostalgically, changing the subject. "You brought me my very first platinum plaque. You were my very first superstar...and now the whole game's changing...in so many ways."

"Yeah," Rasheed said, squeezing her hand and staring at her seriously.

"Whatever you want," Keshari said. "I'll get with my attorney. We'll touch bases with you and your people to finalize."

"Get out of here for awhile, Keshari. I mean that. I don't want to turn on the news and hear that you've been killed. You know the game. These people are not fucking around with you."

"I know," Keshari responded, "and, as much as it looks like it, I am not asleep at the wheel. I've got this thing under control. My entire life's changing and what's taking place right now is the 'storm,' so to speak, before major transformation."

-33-

A week passed and the sequestered jurors continued to deliberate. The deliberations were ugly. Jurors were practically at each other's throats, trading ugly words, and then going into complete silence, unable to reach unanimity on the verdict. Los Angeles news stations and news stations in other major cities around the country now covered the trial with the same, around-the-clock fervor as they had on the first day of the trial when Richard Tresvant was escorted into the courthouse, surrounded by law enforcement like a high-profile, political figure. On CNN and truTV, attorneys wielded their legal expertise regarding the likely outcome of the verdict. None of them had any idea that the ferocious arguments taking place behind closed doors among the jurors would easily be almost as hot a story as the notorious defendant and the trial itself.

On more than one occasion, one juror threatened to request a meeting with the judge to discuss what was transpiring in the deliberations room. After two weeks of being no closer to a verdict than they had been on the day that deliberations started, quarters that were entirely too close and disagreements that had grown increasingly personal, had them all at their breaking points. One Black and one White juror were about to come to fisticuffs over their conflicting opinions. They literally had to be physically separated by two other jurors. This information somehow found its way outside to the media and media quickly inserted the race card into what was already madness.

"I know this Richard Tresvant character," the Black juror said. "I grew up in the neighborhood where he's done his dirt and where he still probably owns crackhouses. I've watched an entire community change for the worse because of scum like him. FUCK A REASONABLE DOUBT! I vote guilty!"

"We took an oath to examine the evidence and testimony of this case...ALL OF IT...and render a fair and IMPARTIAL verdict BASED UPON THE EVIDENCE!" Sally Goldenblatt, the jury's foreman, reminded all of them. "This is a man's life! Despite what he's allegedly done in the past, despite what has been said about who he is and what he's gotten away with, the real murderer is probably walking the streets right now because a few of you have decided to become vigilantes, instead of doing your civic duty! If we cannot come to the resolve RIGHT NOW to do what we each took an oath to do, I am going to go to the judge myself!"

There was silence as each of the jurors' consciences seemed to weigh what Sally Goldenblatt had said. They were tired. They all wanted to go home. A couple of them couldn't wait to put as much distance as possible between themselves and a couple of the other jurors they'd come to despise over the course of the trial and more than two weeks' worth of completely unsuccessful deliberations. They all reached the agreement that they needed to immediately set aside their personal feelings about the defendant and get seriously down to the business of deciding the right verdict.

♪ 🎧 ♪

After three-and-a-half weeks and Judge Bartholomew not having to intercede, the jury had reached a verdict. Members of the national and local media were lined up outside the courthouse in Downtown Los Angeles, almost as they had been for the verdict on the infamous O.J. Simpson murder trial.

Richard Tresvant was brought into the courtroom in black Hugo Boss, surrounded by his throng of attorneys, his assistants, and his attorneys' assistants. The Bernard family sat together in the gallery right behind the prosecution table. Phinnaeus Bernard's only son watched Richard Tresvant with venom and disgust. Phinnaeus Bernard's widow had not been able to sleep at all the night before. She couldn't even bring herself to look in Richard Tresvant's direction when he was brought into the courtroom.

"Madam Foreman," Judge Bartholomew said to Sally Goldenblatt, "has the jury reached a verdict?"

"The jury has, Your Honor."

She carefully unfolded the verdict form and read it with a strong, loud voice for all to hear. "We, the jury, find the defendant, Richard Lawrence Tresvant, guilty of first-degree murder."

For a moment, the courtroom was completely silent like the eerie silence that precedes a very destructive storm. Then, all hell broke loose.

"Agh-h-h-h-h!!! I didn't do this! I didn't do it! I'm not going to jail for something that I didn't do!"

Ricky hopped up from the defense table and began throwing laptops, legal pads, the water pitcher, anything and everything that he could lay his hands on. It was an all-out melee, a cyclone of chaos in the tight area of "dream team" attorneys and their out-of-control client. Bailiffs rushed to restrain Richard Tresvant and try to gain some semblance of order in the courtroom. Spectators, the ones who had not hopped up and made an immediate run for the door to get out of harm's way in the volatile situation, watched the chaos in horror. Judge Bartholomew banged his gavel furiously to no avail. Phinnaeus Bernard's wife, who had been seated quietly and with dignity with the rest of her family in the gallery directly behind the prosecution table since the first day of the trial, burst into tears. Family members tried to console her.

♪ 🎧 ♪

Keshari had just wrapped four days of auditions in Philadelphia when the verdict came down on Ricky's murder trial. She and her crew were all gathering in the hotel lobby at the Rittenhouse Hotel in Philadelphia. Their limousines were being loaded with all of their luggage and equipment, preparing to take them to the airport to fly back to Los Angeles.

Terrence was scrolling through the local, Los Angeles news on his BlackBerry when he caught the breaking news regarding Richard Tresvant's murder trial. Terrence, like everybody else, had gotten himself addicted to the drama and had been following Richard Tresvant's trial the way people had glued themselves to television sets, newspapers and the internet to watch every detail unfold in the O.J. Simpson murder trial.

"Whoa-a-a-a!" Terrence said. "That gangster guy, Richard Tresvant, was just found guilty of first-degree murder."

Keshari's legs seemed to turn to jelly under her as she passed out.

-34-

A few stories floated around in the entertainment tabloids that Keshari Mitchell might be pregnant after her collapse in the lobby at the Rittenhouse Hotel in Philadelphia.

"I really just don't understand it. I'm not an entertainer. I own a record label. I'm an executive. Why the fuck does the media seem so determined to turn my life into some kind of reality show?!"

Keshari was livid, but, with all else that was going on with her, she had to let the media nonsense go. She should have long ago become accustomed to regular invasions of her privacy by the media. Entertainment media had been relentless in their attempts to get an exclusive story on Keshari's very private personal life since the day she'd set foot into the music industry. They wanted to deliver the goods on some of the rumors floating around about her, along with some good photos to confirm their stories. Thus far, Keshari consistently operated under the radar with only the exposures to the press that she herself orchestrated typically at the advisements of her public relations team. So, thus far, media had yet to be successful at getting what they really wanted, so they concocted stories from the photographs that paparazzi supplied and prayed that they didn't encounter a run-in with Keshari's attorney, and the public ate it all up greedily, not really caring whether what they were seeing and reading was the truth or not.

"I just want to go someplace away from all of this for a few days, enjoy some privacy...some relaxation...someplace really exotic, in the middle of nowhere, where paparazzi can't even get to me before I go to work on this grand finale show," Keshari said.

"Then, let's do it," Mars said, planting a kiss on her forehead. "Let's go away for a few days...someplace exotic and private. Find a replacement for your spot in the last audition city and let's just go... whatever you want to do...wherever you want to go."

Keshari owned a yacht, a seventy-eight-foot, $4.5 million Hargrave Custom Yacht named "Larger Than Lyfe," that she kept in Florida and rarely got the opportunity to use. She had Terrence organize a crew, and then she and Mars flew off to Miami with strict instructions to Terrence that he, "unfortunately, knew nothing about Keshari's whereabouts." She and Mars were going to sail to the Caribbean island of Antigua, do some shopping, explore the island, have a lot of sex, not do a single, work-related thing for the next three days, and just decompress.

The very same night that the Larger Than Lyfe jet lifted off to whisk Keshari and Mars off to Miami, a cluster of photographers and writers hopped another flight, trailing the powerful, attractive, music industry couple on their little adventure.

♪ 🎧 ♪

The first photos to reach Los Angeles newsstands and television entertainment news depicted Keshari sunning in a white bikini on the upper deck of "Larger Than Lyfe" as they sailed into English Harbor, the internationally known, premier yachting port of Antigua. A shirtless Mars, in black cargo shorts, smoothed sunscreen on Keshari's back while she lay face down, looking almost as if she was taking a nap. The money-maker shot came when a very lucky photographer in a hired helicopter captured Mars leaning in and planting a kiss on Keshari's rear end as he continued to apply sunscreen. Misha laughed her ass off two days later when she saw the photograph on the cover of the *National Enquirer*.

-35-

The three days on Keshari's ultra-luxurious yacht off the coast of Antigua had been absolutely amazing. At the most unexpected moments during his day now, all Mars could do was envision every curve of Keshari's luscious body, every place he had touched, the sound of her voice. He could barely concentrate when he was working. He'd sat in a board meeting, the words of the ASCAP executive trailing off into nothingness as he thought of the three days he'd spent on the water and exploring parts of Antigua with Keshari. He couldn't remember having been happier in his life. More than once, he thought about the fact that he needed to get with a very good jeweler sometime soon. He'd been seriously thinking about asking Keshari to be his wife.

♫ 🎧 ♫

The Los Angeles DEA was getting extreme pressure from their Washington, D.C. headquarters to come up with a solid case against The Consortium very soon to take before a grand jury or not a penny more would be allocated to the special task force's ever-increasing budget. DEA brass in Washington were, after nearly two years, drawing the conclusion that the special task force was ineffective, turning up only inconsequential triumphs in an operation that was beginning to reek of a profound waste of man hours and money.

Dissension and low morale were on the rise among the agents. Two agents had lost their lives attempting to go deep undercover into The Consortium. Many of the agents had begun to vocalize their disagreement with the tactics being used. They believed that pursuing the people who reported to Richard Tresvant, instead of going after Richard Tresvant himself, put Richard Tresvant more on guard than ever and made it all the more difficult to connect him to the crimes he'd committed and virtually impossible to convict him of the lengthy list of heinous crimes that he'd committed.

Thomas Hencken, head of the special task force, was adamant that the only sure way that DEA or any other law enforcement agency would be successful at indicting and convicting Richard Tresvant was to take down the key people that Richard Tresvant set up all around him to shield him and do his dirty work. Richard Tresvant had so many people in his employ, doing everything from witness intimidation to murder to keep his hands clean, that the only way to get to him would be to take these people down. For that reason, Thomas Hencken remained concentrated on Keshari Mitchell, The Consortium's second in command, Richard Tresvant's protégé, who Richard Tresvant had fully trained himself for organized crime.

Thomas Hencken firmly believed that Keshari Mitchell held the most inside information about The Consortium and would be the easiest to compel to cooperate. Over the course of researching all of The Consortium's key players, Keshari Mitchell was the strangest bedfellow of them all. She did not fit the profile of a career criminal. She did not fit the sociopathic, narcissistic personality profile of any of the people who surrounded Richard Tresvant. Due to a set of unfortunate circumstances following the death of her mother years before, Keshari had, for the most part, been lured into The Consortium and Richard Tresvant's intricate web of manipulation and criminality during a period when she was romantically involved with him, when she was little more than a child, and when she was enduring a great deal of emotional turmoil.

Years later, Keshari Mitchell was now a very public figure with much to lose. She owned a multimillion-dollar record label that she'd built from the ground up herself, and she was fiercely dedicated to its operations. The DEA had checked out the legitimacy of Larger Than Lyfe's business activities since its inception and the company was not a front for the laundering of The

Consortium's drug money in any way. Larger Than Lyfe's original start-up capital had come from a confusing mix of dummy corporations that were eventually traced back to Richard Tresvant's attorney, Phinnaeus Bernard III, but Larger Than Lyfe Entertainment's operations after its start-up funding had always been clean. Keshari Mitchell would not want her record label's operations intercepted in any way or the company's overall reputation damaged by a massive, DEA investigation, seizure of her company's records, and the strong potential of a grand jury indictment.

Most recently, Keshari Mitchell had been repeatedly linked romantically in the media to ASCAP entertainment attorney, Mars Buchanan. The DEA ran a complete background check on Mars Buchanan and turned up nothing...no criminal record...not even a negative credit profile. The DEA was confident that Mars Buchanan was not connected in any way to the business operations of The Consortium. Thomas Hencken was even more confident that Mars Buchanan possessed zero knowledge of his new paramour's affiliation with The Consortium, but all of that was about to change. If the DEA had to throw a wrench into Keshari's personal and professional life, shake things up, and make her extremely uncomfortable to push her into cooperating, that was precisely what they'd do. Her testimony before a grand jury was absolutely instrumental to a special task force operation that was teetering close to collapse.

♪ 🎧 ♪

Thomas Hencken arrived at ASCAP's Los Angeles offices and checked the directory in the office building's busy lobby. He rode the elevator up, displayed his badge, and asked the receptionist if he could see Mars Buchanan. Mars came out to the reception area himself, wearing a bewildered expression on his face.

Drug Enforcement Agency? Mars thought. *What could the DEA possibly want to speak to me about?*

"Mr.?"

"Hencken," the DEA agent supplied.

"Why don't you come on into my office," Mars said.

Mars closed the door and Thomas Hencken took a seat in one of the leather chairs in front of Mars's desk. He passed one of his business cards across to Mars.

"What can I do for you?" Mars asked.

"You are currently involved with Keshari Mitchell?"

"Yes, I am," Mars answered, "but I can't imagine why that would be of even the remotest interest to the DEA."

"Do you have any dealings with Ms. Mitchell's business affairs?"

"In what way?" Mars asked. "I'm general counsel for the American Society of Authors, Composers, and Publishers. Directly and indirectly, I have a connection to the business affairs of many record labels."

"Well, allow me to tell you why I'm here," Thomas Hencken said. "I head a special task force, a branch of the DEA, responsible for the investigation, indictment, conviction and dismantling of operations of major, West Coast narcotics traffickers and distributors. The DEA possesses substantial evidence that leads us to believe that your girlfriend, Keshari Mitchell, is currently heading, in Richard Lawrence Tresvant's absence, one of the most notorious, organized crime rings in the United States...The Consortium...responsible for the distribution and sale of hundreds of millions of dollars of Colombian and Mexican cocaine. Do you have any affiliations with this organization?"

Mars laughed. "This is ridiculous. Is this some sort of joke? I have an extremely busy day today and if you cannot lay out some legitimate reason...quickly...why you are here taking up my time...without a warrant...I'm going to have to ask you to leave."

"I can assure you, Mr. Buchanan, this is not a joke," Thomas Hencken said. "Perhaps you really have no idea what your girlfriend does...outside the operation of her record label, that is. We've been carefully combing your background and, thus far, you've come up clean, but I can assure you that Keshari Mitchell is currently in charge of a multibillion-dollar criminal enterprise while her longtime boyfriend, Richard Tresvant, battles to overturn his recent, first-degree murder conviction."

Mars didn't respond, but he was shell-shocked by the information. He thought of the conversation that he'd had with Keshari not long ago when he'd asked her why she was so riveted to Richard Tresvant's murder trial. Then he thought of the conversation he'd had with his best friend, Jason Payne, right after he and Keshari first met.

"She works ALL the time...at her record label. She travels ALL the time...on the business of her record label. She had to select a replacement so that we could go away for a few days. We just returned from Antigua. Whenever our schedules allow a small stretch of time, she's with me. There has to be some mistake. How could she possibly run some major 'drug' empire?"

"I take it that you had no knowledge, until now, of Keshari Mitchell's criminal background," Thomas Hencken said.

"Criminal background?" Mars said. "Of course not! I'm still having grave doubts about the legitimacy of anything that you're telling me right now. Furthermore, what exactly does all of this have to do with me?"

"Keshari Mitchell is closer to you emotionally than she is to anyone else right now," Thomas Hencken stated. "She trusts you, she is vulnerable to you, and I believe that you could persuade her to testify about Richard Tresvant and The Consortium's operations in front of a grand jury for the DEA. We know that she is not a career criminal. We have absolute reason to believe that Ms. Mitchell is working to completely extricate herself from the business affairs of The Consortium as we speak...which places her in a grave amount of danger...

as well as you. We can help her to completely separate herself from The Consortium. If you can persuade her to cooperate with us, I assure you that the DEA will provide her full, legal immunity and physical protection."

Mars's head was pounding. "Mr. Hencken, I can't help you. I don't know anything about any of this, I have absolutely zero desire to be involved in your investigation in any way, and Keshari Mitchell and I won't be seeing each other anymore."

"Why don't I stop by again in a few days," Thomas Hencken stated, "after you've had some time to clear your head and think about this?"

"Mr. Hencken, should you feel the need to visit my workplace again for any reason whatsoever, I strongly suggest that you bring a warrant with you."

-36-

Mars sat staring absently down at the DEA agent's business card until he wasn't aware how much time had passed. He was hurt. He was confused. He was frustrated. He was mad. Then he didn't want to believe that any of it was true. His heart had him clouded in a state of denial. Logic made him pick up the phone and call Keshari's office. Her assistant told him that Keshari's plane had not arrived back from Chicago, where she had a meeting with Cathy Hughes that day. Mars wanted to immediately confront Keshari and he wanted her to deny everything and he wanted to believe her when she did. He wanted to be able to disregard the visit from Thomas Hencken and never have to think about it again. It was much too bad that life didn't work out that way.

Mars tried Keshari's cell phone and got her voice-mail. He hung up without leaving a message. There were so, so many questions, but a mind that was typically very strong and highly analytical kept drawing a blank, as if it was trying to block the whole mess out.

Mars called Keshari's cell phone again and still got no answer. He called Terrence back at Keshari's Century City offices and asked him to please get a message to Keshari as soon as he could, asking Keshari to call him. Around four o'clock, as Mars stepped into the elevator, leaving his office for the day, Keshari finally returned his call.

"Hi, baby," she said. "Terrence told me to call you right away...that it was urgent. What's the matter?"

"I need to see you tonight. We need to talk. Stop by my place on your way home, when your plane gets in."

"Mars, I'm exhausted. Can't it wait until tomorrow? I've been on and off a plane for what feels like the greater part of my life. I've had meetings all week regarding the production schedule of the finale show, and I am mentally and physically burned out now. I need a hot bath and my bed before I completely disintegrate. Is this really serious? What's wrong?"

"Yes...this is really serious and I need you to come by tonight as soon as you land."

Mars's tone seemed cold, lacking the intimacy that had become so much a part of all of their interactions. It made Keshari very uneasy.

"Mars, WHAT IS WRONG? Give me some idea of why you're acting like this. Did I do something? Has something happened to you? Why are you being so evasive, if the matter is so urgent?"

"Look, I'm pulling out into rush-hour traffic. I'll see you tonight," Mars said and hung up.

♪ 🎧 ♪

It wasn't until 11:30 that night when Keshari arrived at Mars's Marina Del Rey condo and let herself in. The apartment was dark. The housekeeper had left for the day. Mars sat outside on the terrace drinking a Heineken. Keshari saw the deep, serious expression on his face as he stared out at the man-made lake in the darkness. She bent down and kissed him on the forehead. Mars seemed to almost draw away from her. She frowned at his strange reaction.

"You wanna tell me what's on your mind?" Keshari asked quietly, sitting down at the end of the chaise longue beside Mars.

He looked at her. She'd been to Chicago twice that week to meet with Cathy Hughes and her son regarding the televised, grand finale show for her nationwide talent search project. Between flights back and forth to Chicago, she held production meetings with her staff at her Century City offices, reviewing set designs, looking at footage taken from each of the audition cities, and signing contracts for promotion, sponsorship and expenses while still reviewing and managing the regular, day-to-day affairs of her record label and roster of artists. All of this was on her plate and she looked stunning, with flawless, brown skin, a body to die for, not a hair out of place, and dressed casually in suede, Roberto Cavalli jeans and a cashmere T-shirt like she could handle the weight of the world without breaking a sweat. He loved this woman and she said that she loved him and he had had no reason to ever doubt it. He had been seriously considering asking this woman to marry him. Now it may be that he did not know this beautiful woman who sat beside him with his heart in her hands at all.

"Someone came to see me today...to ask me a few questions...and to try to persuade me to get you to cooperate with his investigation," Mars said, looking straight ahead of him out into the darkness. "Do you know who Thomas Hencken is?"

The words hit Keshari like a slap in the face.

"Thomas Hencken told me things today that absolutely blew my mind," Mars went on. "Drug trafficking... organized crime...Richard Lawrence Tresvant, the guy from the high-profile murder trial, and...and you. He came to see me to talk to me and to ask me questions about YOU. I told the man to get the fuck out of my office. I thought that it was some kind of sick prank."

Keshari didn't say a word. She was wishing for a lot of things that would not alter her current predicament one bit. She wished that she and Mars had finished their conversation in Miami. She wished that she'd made the time to talk to him when they were on her yacht alone together off the coast of Antigua. The very last thing that she had ever wanted was for him to find out from someone else all that she had failed to tell him for months.

"I want you to reassure me right now that all that this man said to me today was a big, big mistake...some ridiculous misunderstanding because you, at one time, had romantic ties to Richard Tresvant," Mars said. "Tell me that it's all a lie and that my head is really, really fucked up right now over nothing."

"Mars, you wanna know something? The reason that I have adamantly refused to get involved in a serious, romantic relationship for years is because my life is so complicated."

"'Complicated'?" Mars said incredulously. "What kind of shit is that?! Infidelity is some 'complicated' shit to have to deal with in a relationship. Financial problems can complicate a relationship. This shit right here is in a league of its own!"

Keshari didn't respond.

"Are you a member of this 'Consortium'?" Mars asked.

"Not anymore," Keshari answered quietly.

"'Not anymore,'" Mars said. "Hmmm…That's interesting. So, how long has it been since you separated yourself from this organization?"

"I firmly decided that I wanted out before I ever met you," Keshari answered.

Mars was overwhelmed by a mix of intense emotions. He buried his head in his hands. "So, you're telling me that you have been responsible for importing massive quantities of cocaine into this country and then putting it into communities around the country where your people are literally destroyed?"

Keshari could not respond.

"How have you managed to operate in a major crime ring for years while holding the very public position as president and CEO of a successful, major record label? It doesn't make sense."

"It happens more often than you think, Mars," Keshari said. "Every major criminal enterprise invests in completely legitimate business enterprises. Every major criminal enterprise operates in conjunction with some completely legal, publicly known company or financial institution to launder its money. Remember MCA? There were a number of years when the label was said to have been almost completely Mafia-run. My label is completely legitimate and it always has been. It has no connection to The Consortium in any way. When I first came into the industry and the success started to come pretty fast, I became the 'focus-of-the-moment' for the media. Rumors circulated about me. The press wanted to present stories surrounding those rumors to the public. My attorney took care of it. The fact that my affiliations were not just a rumor took care of the rest."

Mars shook his head as if he was trying to shake off the complete madness of what he was hearing.

"Have you ever killed anyone?" Mars asked.

Keshari looked down at the ground. Her failure to answer was answer.

"Who ARE you?" Mars asked incredulously, tears filling his eyes. "WHAT are you?"

"Mars, years ago, I made some horrible, horrible decisions in my life. My life is different now...and a large part of that has to do with you. I am exactly who you thought I was before that DEA agent came to see you."

"No, you're NOT!" Mars snapped angrily. "Everything about you is a lie...at least, everything that you've revealed or completely failed to reveal to me! You are a beautiful illusion barely disguising a perverse level of... EVIL and CRIMINALITY!"

Keshari was hurt to her core at his angry words.

"Mars...this amazing man fell in love with me. I fell in love with him. I WANTED what we have. I didn't want to lose what we have. How exactly was I supposed to tell you about that part of my life? 'Mars, I was once one of the most powerful drug traffickers on the West Coast...but I'm not anymore.' There was NEVER going to be an ideal time to tell you something like that. I have never been in love with anyone in my life the way that I am with you, and if I had to take the biggest risk in the world to experience with you what I've never had the opportunity to experience before, that was the risk that I was willing to take, until I figured out the right way and the right time to tell you."

The silence that followed seemed deafening and interminable.

"Get out," Mars said.

He went into his dark apartment, into his bedroom, and slammed the door. Keshari rushed in after him.

"Mars, WAIT!" Keshari said to his locked door. "There

is so, so much that you don't understand. We've opened discussion on this issue. Please...let's finish it. That is not my life anymore! I'm risking my life to walk away from that life! Please...just open the door."

The response to her plea was silence. Keshari stood at Mars's locked door for what seemed like forever, hoping that Mars would open the door. He never did.

"I love you," she whispered.

Heartbroken tears spilled down Keshari's cheeks as she picked up her purse, left the keys to Mars's apartment on the cocktail table, and hurried out while DEA agents captured her tearful departure on film.

-37-

The following week was misery. Keshari cried for days. Then she was furious with herself for having gotten involved with Mars in the first place. Then she cried all over again, missing him, thinking of him, loving him. Then she had to try to regroup, remembering the gravity of her situation overall.

Media commented that there may be trouble in paradise for music's power couple. The press constantly worked to convey celebrities' lives to the public like some kind of reality soap opera. There were few insiders offering up juicy information to tabloid writers to confirm or deny the Keshari and Mars situation, however. Most of the people surrounding Keshari and Mars didn't really know what was going on and the few who did would not dare betray their privacy.

Mars took a couple of days off work and stayed in his condo with the blinds drawn. A man known for his suave, all's-under-control demeanor was at his breaking point. Anger, sadness, hurt, resentment, disgust, and judgment at the choices Keshari had made in her life drowned out everything else around him and he needed a little time to get his head back together. He also didn't want to run into another reporter in the garage of his office building, hounding him with questions.

Mars had been deluding himself from the very beginning, from the day that he'd told his best friend about Keshari, and his friend had warned him to be careful, he knew that he had almost intentionally gone into a state of denial. When Keshari gave confirmation to the truth of the words of the DEA agent, in an instant, something shattered that night like glass between the two of them. Mars was absolutely in love with Keshari and it was a feeling that he could not simply turn off. Never in his life had he ever fallen for a woman the way that he had for Keshari, but he didn't know if they would ever be able to repair what was now broken between the two of them, especially now that he knew what he knew.

Meanwhile, "Nationwide Search for a Star" continued to move. The televised grand finale series would be a week-long event promising to showcase some of the hottest, unsigned talent in the country and some of the biggest names in music would be judging the contest and choosing the winner. Keshari had budget and production meetings every other day to distract her from her broken heart, and then she sat in the studio to hear LTL's newest, rising star producer, Mack-A-Do-Shuz, put the finishing touches on sure-to-go-platinum tracks. At the office, she appeared to be bravely holding it all together. Almost everyone at LTL knew about her break-up with Mars, but felt certain that the two would quickly get back together, and only a few shared in hushed whispers why the two had broken up. Keshari went home in the evenings and dropped her brave facade and felt like she might fall apart.

♫ 🎧 ♫

Exactly one week and a day after Keshari's break-up with Mars, Keshari headed home early. Since first thing that morning, she'd been on the set of a video shoot for her label's group, C-Walk, because, as usual, the group were posing a problem to themselves and everyone around them. For three days, C-Walk had been coming onto the set drunk, reeking of marijuana, with their parasitic entourage in tow. Their management was little more than one of their homies from the 'hood. He had no experience managing their budgets and even less experience managing their ridiculous behavior. C-Walk found it difficult to take constructive criticism from anyone and they refused most advice offered to them by professionals. What was supposed to be a three-day video shoot for their new single, "Stripper Song," was now running overtime as well as over budget. C-Walk showed up late, practically coerced video models to provide sexual favors for them and their entourage, and then could not seem to follow the guidance of the video's director at all. Before everyone working on the video got pissed enough to walk, the director called Keshari to ask her to immediately intercede.

Keshari's presence on the set had definitely improved working conditions and the crew was finally back on timeline to wrap the shoot before dark. Nevertheless, Keshari was thoroughly prepared to drop the group from her label. They were far more trouble than they were worth and their first CD had barely sold 300,000 units. When she got home late that afternoon, she was still pissed at having had to waste valuable time baby-sitting one of her label's artists. She made a stiff drink, and then threw herself into bed before the sun even set.

♪ 🎧 ♫

One of the regular guards at Keshari's residence was starting his vacation that evening and another security officer would be temporarily taking his place. The security officer arrived with his special clearance documents from the security firm hired to protect Keshari and her residence. The gate at the entrance to the mansion slid open and the new officer drove the short distance up the drive to park and report to the property's security office.

Samuel Perkins, head of security, sat in the security office sipping a cup of coffee and chatting with Donald Schweitzmann, one of the senior officers. Sam Perkins watched several monitors linked to the property's numerous cameras, always keeping an eye out for intruders.

"Hi, I'm Tim Harris," the new officer said. "Reporting for assignment."

Sam Perkins looked over Tim Harris's clearance forms, cross-referenced them to the ones that had been faxed to him earlier, and then escorted Tim Harris outside to give him a walk-through of the grounds and to go over procedures with him. Tim was introduced to the other regular guards who patrolled the property during the evening. Then he was shown the area of the grounds that would be under his watch.

The evening was cool and Tim Harris wore his company-issued jacket. He carried his company-registered .9 mm Baretta in a holster on his hip. He wore a second gun in a shoulder holster. He strolled across the terrace outside the mansion's solarium and admired the quiet opulence of the record mogul's residence. He stared up at the balcony and the open, French doors leading into the bedroom of the woman they were hired to protect. Her bedroom was dark, but he knew that she was home. He headed back down onto the grounds and stood his post. Sam Perkins radioed him.

"Everything okay?"

"I'm fine," Tim answered. "Just admiring the beautiful property."

"Keep your eyes open," Sam Perkins said. "I'll radio you again around break time."

Tim stood his post, walking back and forth toward the cliffs that composed the area that he patrolled. He could just make out the lights of Catalina Island in the distance. The security that Keshari Mitchell maintained was very expensive, running her upward of almost $100,000 each month, depending upon her schedule, itinerary and level of security that she required. Something serious must have transpired recently because, at the current time, Keshari Mitchell maintained the highest level of security and maintained it around the clock. Most officers hired to protect Keshari Mitchell were former police officers and FBI agents or had been members of highly trained, special units in the military. Tim Harris himself was a former Navy SEAL who had just joined the security firm hired to protect Keshari Mitchell and her home.

Tim walked the perimeter of his patrol area a few times, and then diverted his path and headed up the stone steps leading to the balcony outside Keshari Mitchell's bedroom. Keshari's Rottweilers, "Marcus Garvey" and "Hannibal," immediately started to growl as Tim approached. Tim reached into his jacket pocket for a handful of steak treats he'd picked up at the pet center. He tossed the treats off down the steps and the two massive, purebred dogs bounded off to get them.

Poised in the doorway, Tim Harris watched as Keshari Mitchell slept. The covers were pulled up, practically covering her face. He'd seen many photographs of her and she was exceptionally beautiful. What Tim Harris was about to do was purely part of a business transaction. This mission was not personal. He was not some sort of stalker.

Tim screwed the silencer onto the gun from his shoulder holster. An expert marksman, he took a shot and Samuel Perkins, who'd been carefully watching his movements, took a shot at the very same time. Tim Harris's shot landed in the pillows directly next to Keshari's head. The head of security's bullet landed in the side of Tim Harris's neck. Tim Harris fell to the ground. Keshari snapped up in her bed.

The head of security quickly radioed the police department. Then he radioed the other security officers and told them to secure and lock down the premises. They had an emergency.

Keshari looked at the pillows beside her and the mess of down filling that protruded from the pillows' gaping holes. An almost successful attempt had just been made on her life. The bile rose in her throat and she rushed into the bathroom to throw up.

♪ 🎧 ♪

When Keshari came out of the bathroom, her mansion was the chaotic venue of police cars and television crews attempting to get as close as they could to the dramatic scene of death and a nearly accomplished hit.

Misha rushed as fast as she could to be at her best friend's side. Keshari broke down and cried in her arms.

"It's all falling apart," Keshari sobbed. "It's all falling apart."

"Get it all out," Misha soothed, stroking Keshari's hair

and holding her best friend tight. "I'm here for you, girl, as long as you need me."

Misha knew that her brother had ordered the hit on Keshari and the wheels of Misha's mind were already turning, plotting the appropriate way to use what she had on Ricky. David Weisberg, Keshari's attorney, also rushed to be at Keshari's side. The police wanted to question Keshari, and David Weisberg assured the investigators that Keshari would cooperate fully with all of their questioning later in the day. She was simply too distraught, he said, to be of any real help to them now.

The coroner's office took Tim Harris's body away and crime scene investigators worked with Keshari's security team to hash out the details of what had occurred that evening. The president of the security company quickly arrived on the scene. He apologized profusely to Keshari and her attorney for what had happened, and then got with Samuel Perkins and the rest of the security team to supply whatever information was needed to the crime scene investigators and to secure details regarding what had happened for himself.

Misha wanted to pack a bag for Keshari and book a cottage for her at the Beverly Hills Hotel so that she didn't have to face the chaos and drama currently going down at her house. Keshari, however, assured her that she would be okay and needed to stay put. There were a number of things that she needed to discuss with her attorney. She walked Misha out to her car, amidst the circus-like atmosphere, and Misha promised that she would be back to check on her a little later in the day. Then Keshari and David Weisberg went into Keshari's large, formal dining room and closed the double doors to talk.

-38-

Things were getting HOT in L.A.!!! Before the public could even digest the nearly successful hit on Keshari's life, breaking news on every Los Angeles station reported that Richard Lawrence Tresvant had been killed in an apparent stabbing at San Quentin Prison in northern California, where he was awaiting a new trial on appeal for the first-degree murder of his attorney, Phinnaeus Bernard III.

Keshari, the epitome of the workaholic and trying hard to maintain appearances despite all that was going on, heard the news from her attorney and nearly passed out in her office. All the while, she had been thinking that Rick had been the one who had ordered the nearly successful attempt on her life. In fact, he had placed a price on her head, but Tim Harris had nothing to do with it.

Before Keshari could even wrap her mind around Richard Tresvant's murder and who might be responsible for it, the absolutely unthinkable happened. Los Angeles Police Department officers burst into her offices and

314 CYNTHIA DIANE THORNTON

placed Keshari under arrest for conspiracy to commit murder/murder-for-hire in conjunction with the prison murder of Richard Lawrence Tresvant.

It was absolute chaos at Larger Than Lyfe Entertainment as LTL's staff and the media got wind of the story.

♪ 🎧 ♪

Keshari sat in a holding cell for ten hours while her attorney wrangled to secure her release and news crews surrounded Parker Center in downtown Los Angeles, working to capture the breaking story. Ironically, Judge Phelton Bartholomew, who'd been the judge in Richard Tresvant's murder trial, presided at Keshari's bail hearing. The D.A., basking in the spotlight of what promised to be another highly sensational case, demanded vehemently that the court deny bail to Keshari Mitchell because, with her money and power, she was most certainly a flight risk. David Weisberg vehemently argued in Keshari's defense. He argued that Keshari Mitchell was sole owner of a major record label, Larger Than Lyfe Entertainment, and she directly managed, every single day, the operations of the record label that she'd built from the ground up. She had no criminal record whatsoever. She had much too much at stake to pick up and run away. She was no more a flight risk than the district attorney himself, David Weisberg contended.

Keshari's bail was finally set at $1 million, an outrageous amount which David Weisberg instantly got on the phone to acquire before he even exited the courtroom. Thomas Hencken was sitting at the rear of the courtroom when David Weisberg was walking out. He nodded to David Weisberg. David Weisberg did not acknowledge the gesture.

"Are you okay?" David Weisberg asked as his Mercedes sped away from Parker Center.

"Yeah, I'm okay," Keshari said.

She said no more for the rest of the drive to her house and David left her to her thoughts.

♪ 🎧 ♫

Mars was watching the madness transpiring in Keshari's world and all around her. He watched news story after news story unfold and Keshari's typically very private life was dissected and speculated upon and raked over the coals by complete strangers in the media for the public's entertainment. More than anything, he wanted to drop everything and go to her, be there for her...at least, until some of the turmoil around her died down. But he didn't go. Something held him back firmly and left him torn by guilt and mixed emotions, knowing that the woman he still loved was going through it and he was not there to support her.

He called Misha and asked her if Keshari was okay.

"Why don't you call her and find out for yourself?" Misha responded.

"I thought about it...you know, I was going to...but things are really difficult right now since...,"Mars said.

"Look," Misha said. "She's okay. She just arrived home from Parker Center a little while ago. She's quiet. She's understandably under a lot of stress. She's more than likely suffered some sort of a shock, but...for the most part...she's okay. I'll make sure of that."

"I'm really glad you're there for her," was all that Mars could manage to say.

"I would have thought that YOU, the only man she's ever been able to truly be herself with, the man she's in love with, would be able to set aside what she did in the past, set aside your personal feelings about what she's done, and be there for her when she needs you most. Keshari had nothing at all to do with Richard Tresvant's murder, Mars. Nothing."

"Misha, I'm trying. I really, really am. But I can't be there for her in the way that she needs until my mind has gotten to a place where I stop judging her and being angry with her. It wouldn't be fair to her to step back into her life with all that she has going on until I get beyond that."

"Fuck it," Misha said. "I'm headed up to the house now. I'm spending the night there. I'll let her know that you're thinking of her."

Misha hung up.

-39-

Misha,

You remember how I used to spend the night at your house and we would polish our toes and do each other's hair while watching Midnight Love on BET, eating a big plate of nachos and talking about the men we were going to marry? I was gonna marry Kenny Greene of the R & B group, INTRO, and you were gonna marry "Treach" of Naughty By Nature. I truly miss those days. Everything was so much simpler then.

You and I have been like peanut butter and jelly for as long as I can remember. You are my sister and, even though we are not bonded by blood, you have always been the most important person in the entire world to me.

On a lot of levels, the two of us have led some pretty damned charmed lives. We've done most of the things we used to fantasize about doing. You're the BADDEST events coordinator in the entire country and I just know that you're gonna wind up orchestrating the details for the first Black President's inaugural ball or something else completely major. I've done alright myself. I started my own record label that turned out to be successful beyond my wildest imaginings. Then, relatively recently, I fell in love. WOW...love...it changes EVERY-THING. Too bad the good things don't last forever.

Misha, I've done a lot of shit that I greatly, greatly regret and all of it is finally catching up to me. I'm in too deep now and it's drowning me and I simply cannot go on.

Please don't hate me. Please forgive me for leaving you. Please remember all of the things that were so remarkably good about our friendship. Your confidence, your spunk, your style and the way that you have always lived life so FULLY have always been qualities about you that I have both envied and admired. If there is such a thing as an afterlife or rein-carnation, I'd still want you to be my very BEST friend, my sister, all over again.

I LOVE YOU, Misha.

Keshari handwrote the letter on her signature, pink parchment stationery, and then sealed it in its matching, parchment envelope. She cried like a baby as she composed what she wanted to say to Misha on the page.

Few women were fortunate enough over the course of their lifetimes to share laughs, tears, successes, and fears with a sisterfriend who was as SPECIAL as Misha Tierney was. Misha knew every dirty deed that Keshari had ever committed and loved her anyway, never judging her, always wanting the very best for her. Misha Tierney was the kind of friend who would go to hell and back for Keshari without ever questioning it and without ever expecting repayment for it.

Keshari poured herself a snifter of Courvoisier to steady her nerves, and then took out a few more blank pages of her stationery to write her next letter.

My Dearest Mars,

How and where do I begin?

If you had known everything that there was to know about me in the beginning, the two of us would never have gotten together...and, then, because so much of my life was such a mystery to you, it ended up tearing us apart. Life is a trip like that.

Who would ever have thought that God would be so kind to someone like me and send me someone like you? You're like the finest, smoothest, Belgian milk chocolate, the best champagne, the winning lottery numbers, and making love while it rains...the kind of man that EVERY woman dreams about. I feel like my adult life TRULY began on the night that I met you...and it ended on the night that I lost you. There has never been an ounce of doubt in my mind that YOU were "The One."

Some people go their entire lives and never meet that one person who was made just for them. I feel honored to have stared into your beautiful, brown eyes, held your hand, heard the masculine resonance of your voice tell me your dreams, been your friend, and your lover.

I so wish that things could have been different. I wish that I had had the courage to tell you what you had to hear from someone else. I wish that there could have been more time for the two of us. But there never, ever seems to be enough time to truly savor the extraordinarily SPECIAL things.

By the time you receive this letter and whatever happens has happened and so many questions and anger and, possibly, sadness hang in the air, please know without a doubt that I did not do this because of you nor because we broke up. My troubles were much greater than losing you and my troubles certainly existed long before you came. I've done too much to go back and correct things and I'm in too deep now to go on.

Mars Buchanan, I loved you and I still love you IN-FINITELY. You are an AMAZING man. From the moment you first kissed me, my love for you has consumed me like the heat of a flame.

As Erykah Badu says, "Maybe in my next lifetime"...we can pick up where we left off. Please forgive me for what I have done and when, if ever, you think of me, think of Negril. It was the very best time of my life.

Keshari

-40-

Misha had given Keshari all the fucking space that she intended to give her. Enough was e-goddamned-nough! Misha knew that Keshari had been going through a tremendous amount over the past few weeks, particularly following her arrest for conspiracy to commit the recent murder of Richard Tresvant. The very last time that the two of them had actually spoken was the same day that Keshari had been released on bail following her arrest. Misha had driven up to Keshari's home to offer emotional support to her best friend for as long as she needed. Keshari told Misha that she was going to take a few days to herself, to re-group and get her head together. She sent Misha home that night and promised to get in touch with her soon.

An entire week had passed and Misha still hadn't heard so much as a peep from Keshari. Media crews, who were still stacked up outside Keshari's mansion, knew more about her best friend's current condition than Misha did and the annoying housekeeper had clearly been instructed to intercept all of Keshari's phone calls.

Although the housekeeper could barely speak English, she quickly cranked out that "Mees Meetchell es unavailable," and then hung up on Misha. Misha tried calling Keshari's cell phone and only got her voicemail. She was too furious to even leave a message. Misha called Terrence, Keshari's assistant, and he couldn't be of much help either. Keshari was working from home, dealt with him via e-mail, her fax machine, and messenger service and wasn't really entertaining any calls from anyone...even Cathy Hughes.

Misha decided to bypass the futile phone calls altogether. She was going straight to Keshari's house and she was not leaving until she saw Keshari, made sure that she was okay, and gave her a piece of her mind.

Misha got dressed and was preparing to leave when a messenger rang her doorbell. Misha quickly signed for the envelope and ripped it open. It was a letter from Keshari. She read it as quickly as she could while juggling files from her office, her purse, sunglasses, cell phone and keys.

"OH, MY GOD!" Misha screamed, realizing what was being conveyed in Keshari's letter to her.

She dropped everything she held on the floor and went racing frantically out to her car.

♪ 🎧 ♪

Mars was in his office when his secretary came to his door, escorting a messenger carrying a letter that could only be signed for by Mars Buchanan himself. Mars opened the messenger envelope and instantly recognized the pink parchment stationery. He closed the door to his office and sat down to carefully read Keshari's first communication to him since their break-up. His secretary had no idea what was going on as he went running for the elevator. A moment later, his Mercedes was speeding at 100 miles per hour up the 405 freeway toward Keshari's Palos Verdes mansion.

♫ 🎧 ♫

Mars arrived at Keshari's house to a scene of utter chaos. Police cars lined the street and police officers contended with the television news crews arriving on the scene as they attempted to capture a breaking story and the police attempted to bring order to the chaos. Mars could barely get through the pandemonium as he pulled up outside the mansion's gates. A reporter recognized him and was instantly in his face.

"Get the FUCK away from me!" Mars yelled, rolling up his window.

Sam Perkins, head of security at Keshari's residence, opened the gates and Mars's car pulled quickly inside.

"Mr. Perkins, what's going on?" Mars asked anxiously, hopping out of the car.

Sam Perkins bowed his head and Mars took off running up the drive.

Misha Tierney was standing on the lawn just off the

drive in front of the house. She was being consoled by a police officer. Mars went to her and she collapsed in sobs in his arms. Cold, frozen fear took hold of Mars's heart.

"What's happened, Misha?" Mars asked, hugging her and attempting to console her.

"She's...she's...she's...dead," Misha garbled through her uncontrollable sobs. "She's GONE!"

Misha had arrived at Keshari's mansion that morning, directly after receiving Keshari's letter, and had demanded to be let in. The access codes to the gate sealing off the house's entrance had all been changed, so Misha was unable to just let herself in. The security officer manning the entrance curtly informed Misha that Ms. Mitchell was not receiving any visitors that day and Misha promptly commenced to curse him out. She had stirred up such a ruckus, verbally castrating the security officer with a stream of profanities, that he had quickly radioed Sam Perkins for assistance. Sam Perkins came to the scene from the rear of the property and took control of the heated situation. Because Sam Perkins knew that Misha Tierney was Keshari's best friend, he immediately called the house and told the housekeeper to let Keshari know that Misha was there. Misha explained to him that the situation was an emergency and that Keshari may have done something to harm herself. Sam Perkins tried to explain to her, as calmly as he could, why he couldn't allow her to go on up to the house as he typically did. Keshari had issued very specific instructions and there were to be NO EXCEPTIONS. When the housekeeper went up to Keshari's bedroom suite to tell her that the security office was on the line, she found an unconscious Keshari in her robe, on the bathroom floor with a nearly empty bottle of sleeping pills splayed out on the bathroom counter. The housekeeper went into hysterics and came back to the phone, babbling in a mixture of her native Spanish and broken English. Sam Perkins opened the gates for Misha and the two of them rushed up to the house, Sam Perkins radioing "9-1-1" as they went.

Misha found Keshari unconscious on her bathroom floor. Misha checked and Keshari was not breathing. Sam Perkins quickly began to administer CPR while they waited for paramedics. Everything that was happening seemed surreal. Misha felt as if she was floating in the middle of a nightmare. She held Keshari's hand and sobbed, almost hysterically, as Sam Perkins continued CPR and chest compressions. Misha begged God not to let this happen. She begged Keshari to wake up.

Emergency medical technicians burst into the room and began to work on Keshari. They worked on Keshari for what seemed like hours. A police officer escorted a distraught Misha downstairs and out onto the mansion's lawn so that she could get some air and allow the paramedics to continue trying to revive her best friend. When they brought Keshari out of the house on a stretcher with a sheet pulled over her face, Misha screamed inconsolably, running toward the stretcher, and had to be restrained.

When Mars arrived, the ambulance with Keshari inside had just left. When Misha tearfully told him that Keshari was gone, Mars couldn't bring himself to believe her. His entire body went ice cold and he stood paralyzed, the chaos all around him suddenly seeming far away.

"This is not happening...this is not happening...this is NOT happening," Mars said over and over again, in confusion and disbelief.

♪ 🎧 ♪

Thomas Hencken's office received the call regarding Keshari Mitchell's collapse in her home just after emergency units were dispatched to her residence. Thomas Hencken quickly loaded two cars with DEA agents and rushed to Palos Verdes, arriving just after the ambulance had sped away with Keshari inside, sirens blaring, for South Bay Hospital.

Thomas Hencken's mind was reeling. The news was not at all what he'd expected. He'd been preparing to pay Keshari another visit to show her some of the evidence that the DEA was continuing to mount against her to take before a grand jury, still convinced that she would break down and provide the testimony that he needed. Although the evidence was still mostly circumstantial, it included an intricate maze of dummy corporations that had funded the start-up of Larger Than Lyfe Entertainment. This peculiar string of business enterprises had eventually led back to Phinnaeus Bernard III, Richard Tresvant's murdered attorney. There were also photographs of Keshari Mitchell outside two known cocaine processing houses reputedly owned by The Consortium, one of which had been raided by the Los Angeles Police Department. Now this woman that the task force had been relying upon to give a two-year-old investigation on life support new life was gone and Washington was not going to give the task force another dime, and Thomas Hencken knew that he had a lot of blame to take for most of it.

When Thomas Hencken regrouped from the initial shock, his gut instincts quickly went into overdrive. Something kept telling him that there was something amiss about Keshari Mitchell's untimely death. Thomas Hencken was not fooled. Over the course of his career, he'd seen it all. Behind celebrity, wealth, power and a prestigious, Wharton MBA, Keshari had very successfully managed to keep hidden for years a double life that involved major crime. That was not to be overlooked. She may not have fit the profile of the kind of criminal that typically surrounded Richard Tresvant. She may have had some kind of epiphany of conscience that had compelled her to separate from The Consortium. But no one, particularly a woman, held a controlling position in a major, organized drug ring without possessing a Machiavellian level of cunning and strategy accompanied by nerves of steel. That kind of person would not swallow a bottle of pills and call it quits on life because of, what amounted to people like them, a few, relatively minor legal problems. That kind of person kept local and federal law enforcement on their payroll. That kind of person had a wealth of connections and virtually unlimited financial resources at hand to fake her own death.

A suicide would free Keshari Mitchell from persecution by The Consortium and anyone else who might put a price on her head. A suicide would free Keshari Mitchell from being subpoenaed to testify in front of a grand jury about the operations of The Consortium and its client list and suppliers. A suicide would certainly keep Keshari Mitchell from having to face the recent murder-for-hire charges against her. A faked suicide was very plausible and, considering Keshari Mitchell's current circumstances, easily believed.

Thomas Hencken got on the phone to secure the warrants necessary to view Keshari's body at the coroner's office and mortuary. It required more than a few strings to be pulled and he had to call in a lot of favors all the way to Washington, D.C. Unfortunately, things took yet another turn for the worst when he arrived at the coroner's office the next day and Keshari Mitchell's body had been quickly moved to a mortuary by her attorney for immediate cremation. The pathologist allowed the DEA agents to review the paperwork containing Keshari Mitchell's cause of death as well as the contents from her stomach pump provided by the paramedics. Keshari's apparent cause of death was an acute overdose of secobarbital.

Thomas Hencken was livid. The special task force was being dismantled, agents were being assigned to other cases and Thomas Hencken's superiors in Washington, D.C. called him and demanded a meeting. In Washington's eyes, as well as in the eyes of many of the task force's agents, the special task force simply had not made enough progress to continue putting good money after bad. Two agents had lost their lives. The convictions that had been made through the work of the special task force agents were at the bottom of The Consortium's hierarchy. Thomas Hencken strongly believed that there might be some DEA agents in The Consortium's pocket. Such was often the case in America's "war on drugs." Criminals were often two or more steps ahead of law enforcement. Major criminals' pockets were almost always deeper than law enforcement task force budgets. When law enforcement budgets were depleted, they were forced to move on, whether or not they had accomplished their mission; and even if they had accomplished their mission, there was always a new criminal organization at the ready to assume position wherever the prior organization had left off. Drug trafficking in the United States was a trillion-dollar enterprise and sometimes it was made crystal clear to law enforcement that trying to eradicate its operation was akin to trying to take on a missile launcher with a peashooter. There was simply too much money and corruption involved to realistically foresee any REAL progress.

But Thomas Hencken was determined that he would not let go.

-41-

Security was extremely tight. Police and news helicopters flew overhead. Live television news crews captured the Who's Who of the entertainment industry arriving in limousines and forming a lengthy procession of respectful mourners heading up the stone steps and into St. Thomas Cathedral on Figueroa. Keshari's mother was deceased. So was the grandmother who had tried to care for her following Keshari's mother's passing. Keshari had no real family to speak of except for Misha, although the two of them were not related by blood. Most of the funeral's attendees were nothing more than business associates of Keshari's, some of them were total strangers, and many of them had the most selfish of ulterior motives for coming. Keshari's funeral, like a Def Jam party thrown by Russell Simmons himself, was just another place where everybody who was anybody needed to be. Fans of the Larger Than Lyfe Entertainment record label and Larger Than Lyfe's roster of superstar artists watched the procession behind barricades on the opposite sides of the street outside St.

Thomas Cathedral. Many of them snapped photographs with their cell phones, digital cameras, and disposable cameras. All of them craned their necks to take in the celebrity faces that dotted the crowd of mourners.

The front pages of all of Los Angeles' newspapers and tabloids had been dedicated to Keshari Mitchell, reporting the details of her career, the mystery and the rumors that had constantly surrounded her life, and the questions that now surrounded her death. An exquisite, huge, hand-carved, mahogany urn that had been imported from Egypt, topped by an enormous spray of white roses, was carried into St. Thomas Cathedral by Andre DeJesus, Terrence Henderson, Shaquille O'Neal and Rasheed the Refugee, the pallbearers. The female "Jane Doe" who had been quickly cremated and transferred into the urn that was supposed to contain Keshari's remains was receiving a VIP send-off instead of a pauper's grave.

Misha Tierney was escorted into a side door by her handsome, New York Knicks fiancé and a throng of security. Dressed in black Chanel and huge, black, Christian Dior sunglasses, Misha was but a shell of her usual, beautiful, well-known to be outspoken self. She had been under heavy sedation since the fateful day that she'd discovered Keshari's body on the bathroom floor of Keshari's master suite. She had been so distraught days after Keshari's death that everyone felt certain that she was having some sort of nervous breakdown. Her assistant had had to cancel two large projects of hers because Misha was in no condition to do anything.

Misha had been the obvious choice to give the eulogy at Keshari's funeral, but, because of her current mental state, Andre DeJesus had stepped in to give the eulogy instead.

♪ 🎧 ♪

Mars adamantly refused to go to the church to attend Keshari's funeral. He refused to sit in the same room where Keshari's remains were in a box and then ride to a cemetery to watch that box being placed into a mausoleum. That was too much for him to take. He'd had to take a brief leave from work because of what the shock of Keshari's death had done to his head. He lost the mental and physical ability and desire to function, professionally or otherwise.

Even though he had not spoken to Keshari since the night that he'd confirmed the truth of the federal agent's story about Keshari's link to organized crime, Mars still loved Keshari as deeply as when he'd fallen in love with her in Negril. He had always known that, one day, he would overcome his hurt and anger and judgment at Keshari's violation of their trust. He had always known deep down that, eventually, he would have forgiven her. His heart would have compelled him to forgive her and, if Keshari would have had him, the two of them would probably have reconciled...her past in the past, all cards on the table, the future bright. Now all of that was nothing more than wishful thinking, possibilities that would

334 CYNTHIA DIANE THORNTON

always be nothing more than possibilities, time that could never be recaptured, and a chain of events that could never be changed.

Since the day that the entire music industry was shocked and saddened by the news of Keshari's suicide, Mars had lay in a disheveled mess on a chaise longue on his terrace. He hadn't shaven. He hadn't eaten. He hadn't even taken off the suit he'd worn on the day he'd gone rushing up to Keshari's house, only to find out that she was gone. The mix of emotions that had dominated his thoughts since their break-up were quickly replaced by profound guilt and grief.

Mars's best friend, Jason Payne, came to Mars's condo repeatedly to check on his grieving brother. Mars wouldn't let him in. He didn't want to see nor be around anyone. Mars's mother and sister had been watching coverage on the news in New York and called Mars to let him know that they were flying to L.A. to be with him. Mars had his answering service tell them not to worry, that he was okay and just needed to be by himself for a while.

The one time that Mars did finally answer his phone himself, Portia Foster had the temerity to be on the other end of the line. Her voice, filled with sympathy, said that she was calling Mars to make sure that he was okay, that she'd been so worried about him since Keshari's... well, since her...uhm...passing, and that she'd like to come by and bring him some food, a little "care package" to help him to feel better.

"You crazy BITCH!" Mars yelled before slamming down the phone. "Why couldn't it have been YOU?!"

He lay in a drunken stupor on the chaise longue that had become his bed on his terrace. He should have passed out from alcohol poisoning after all of the liquor that he'd consumed. He sent his housekeeper on a two-week, paid vacation to her native Mexico to visit family. Between bottles of Patrón tequila and Heineken, Mars questioned the very meaning of life.

In his restless sleep, Keshari came to Mars in his dreams. Wearing a $40,000 sable coat with nothing underneath except the platinum-and-diamond belly chain that Mars had purchased as a gift for her at Raffinity, Keshari curled up on the chaise longue beside him, kicking off high-heeled sandals, her red toes tickling his legs, and whispered in his ear, "See...I'm still here." She planted soft, seductive kisses on his neck and he smiled, her every touch taking him to special places. He couldn't control himself as he took her aggressively on top of that sable coat, her perfect, brown legs wrapped around his waist.

"See...I'm still here," she murmured over and over again in his ear, arching her back, making him come faster than he wanted to.

When he climaxed, it was like an explosion that snapped him awake. He looked all around him at the dimly lit terrace. Keshari was gone. Mars was all alone. He started to cry. Keshari was gone forever.

-42-

David Weisberg's messenger service hand-delivered requests for the presence of the entire list of Keshari's heirs at his firm's offices exactly one week after Keshari's funeral. Misha was away on a trip to the Caribbean with her fiancé. The handsome player for the New York Knicks believed that a change of scenery would be just the thing to help Misha overcome the debilitating grief that she'd suffered after losing her best friend.

David Weisberg secured the particulars of Misha's travel arrangements from her fiancé's assistant and hired a messenger service in Trinidad to hand-deliver the notification regarding the reading of Keshari's will. Misha handled the situation extremely well. With her fiancé at her side, she shed more tears, but she resolved herself to the fact that it was time to get back to the business of living her life. She had a business to run and her own wedding to plan and the distribution of Keshari's assets would help to bring some closure to one of the most painful situations of her life.

Mars was still on leave from ASCAP and notification was delivered to his condo. He was drunk, disheveled, and completely out of himself when the messenger rang his doorbell. He tossed the notification regarding the reading of the will over the railing of his terrace and told himself that he would not go.

On the afternoon of the reading of the will, all of the heirs who'd received notification were assembled in the main conference room at David Weisberg's offices. Misha appeared to be getting back to her old self. She wafted into the room on a cloud of Viktor & Rolf's Flowerbomb perfume, dressed to kill in charcoal gray Gucci and wearing the tan that she'd acquired in Trinidad very well. Her handsome fiancé had accompanied her for moral support. Andre DeJesus, Sharonda Richards, and Terrence Henderson all sat together. Everyone was present with the exception of Mars Buchanan.

David Weisberg sent his secretary over to Mars's condo. They'd tried calling repeatedly and had only received his answering service. They contacted the management office and explained the urgency of their situation and asked if someone could send security to check to see if Mars's car was in the garage. It was. David Weisberg's secretary was furious at having been assigned such a task. She had no idea what to expect from this Mars Buchanan. If he had no interest in appearing for the reading of that female mobster's will, that was certainly his prerogative.

The secretary rang the bell and received no answer. She rang it again and still received no response. Just as she walked off down the hall back toward the bank of elevators, Mars leaned out his door.

"Yeah. What's up?" he grumbled.

Mars Buchanan was clearly a very attractive man, even though it was pretty evident that he had been working diligently over what appeared to be more than a week's time to let himself go to absolute shit. He was unshaven, with a healthy film of stubble on his face and on his usually bald head. His clothes were a mess. He wore the wrinkled trousers that belonged to a very expensive, Italian suit and a white wife beater T-shirt that looked as if he'd vomited on it.

"I'm here from the offices of David Weisberg, Keshari Mitchell's attorney," the secretary stated as evenly as she could, attempting to hold her breath from the stench of Mars. "The reading of Keshari Mitchell's will is today and Ms. Mitchell made very clear specifications that Mr. Weisberg could not proceed with the reading of the will until every heir, including you, was present at Mr. Weisberg's office. Everyone is assembled right now in Mr. Weisberg's office...except for you. How long will it take you to get dressed?"

"I'm not going to the reading of any will," Mars slurred. Then he proceeded to cry. "I loved her so...much," he said, sounding like a broken, little boy.

The secretary pushed past him into his apartment and

found her way to Mars's kitchen. She put on a pot of coffee, and then rushed off to his bedroom to locate fresh clothes for him to wear. She also started a hot shower for him.

"What the fuck are you doing?" Mars grumbled, watching the strange secretary making her way, uninvited, through his apartment. "Who ARE you?"

"I already told you that, Mr. Buchanan," the secretary responded. "Now...how quickly do you think that you can manage to go in there and wash the funk off you and get shaved? I've got hot coffee right here to get you on your way. Here...drink some."

She held the cup up to his lips maternally, and then pushed him toward his bedroom. It took more than an hour for the coffee to start doing its job and for Mars to get showered and shaved.

David Weisberg called the secretary on her cell phone. "CELESTE!" he snapped. "What the fuck is the hold-up?!"

"Mr. Buchanan is really quite a mess, David. I'm helping him to pull himself together. We'll be back at your office in about an hour."

The other heirs had been waiting in the conference room as patiently as they could, making small talk and occasionally checking their watches. David Weisberg offered to have one of the other secretaries call Chin Chin and order lunch. While the heirs were beginning to become restless, they weren't hungry and all of them courteously declined the offer. Andre DeJesus made comments about other appointments on his schedule for that day. David held up a hand to reassure all of them.

"Keshari was very specific about wanting each and every one of you present before I proceed with the reading. My secretary is on her way back to the office as we speak. For those of you who have other engagements today, I would advise you now to make the necessary calls or texts to reschedule."

Moments later, the double doors of the conference room opened and Mars Buchanan made his appearance, seemingly with some assistance from David Weisberg's secretary, Celeste. In black wool trousers and a black, V-neck, cashmere sweater that rippled around every carefully chiseled muscle of his biceps, he was enough to cause everyone in the room to pause their thoughts. This was the gorgeous specimen of a man who Keshari Mitchell could not help falling in love with.

He wore dark, Gucci sunglasses, but Celeste suggested that he remove them. When he did, his eyes had a difficult time adjusting to the bright light of the conference room. His eyes were swollen and red from more than a week of crying and drinking. Misha's heart immediately went out to him, and she patted the seat beside her for him to come and sit down. Everyone in the room watched him and felt the unbelievable sadness and grief emanating from him. It was clear that Keshari Mitchell's untimely death had unraveled him emotionally.

David Weisberg immediately began the reading. The first portion of the will was all of the inconsequential legalese that is included in every professionally prepared last will and testament by a testator with substantial holdings. David Weisberg read through all of it as quickly as he could.

"...and, therefore," David Weisberg read, having reached the actual distribution of assets, "I leave the most significant portion of my estate, Larger Than Lyfe Entertainment, to my best friend, my sister, Misha Michelle Tierney. Misha Tierney will hold eighty percent ownership of Larger Than Lyfe Entertainment with the remaining twenty percent being broken down as follows: ten percent to Andre DeJesus and ten percent to Sharonda Richards, both of whom are current employees of Larger Than Lyfe Entertainment. If any of the new owners should choose to relinquish or sell all or any portion of their ownership shares of Larger Than Lyfe Entertainment, these shares can only be offered for sale to Mars Buchanan or David Weisberg, my attorney, and an escrow account has been established for the buy-back of these shares should the need present itself. As the new holders of a percentage of ownership of Larger Than Lyfe Entertainment, Andre DeJesus and Sharonda Richards shall also take on new job titles. Both of them shall be named respectively 'senior vice president of operations'...

"As the new 'president and chief executive officer' of Larger Than Lyfe Entertainment, Misha Tierney shall perform in precisely the same capacity as I did. She holds majority in the decision-making of every facet of Larger Than Lyfe Entertainment operations. Hers is the exclusive signature on all checks and contracts designating budgets and allocating funds from Larger Than Lyfe Entertainment revenues. Because Misha Tierney possesses little experience in the management of the business affairs of a major record company, Andre DeJesus and Sharonda Richards, as the new senior vice presidents of operations, as well as new shareholders in ownership of Larger Than Lyfe Entertainment, possess a vested interest and shall be responsible for educating Misha in all facets of this music industry as well as all facets of the day-to-day operations of Larger Than Lyfe Entertainment...

"...to the warmest, kindest, most honest, most special man that I've ever met in my life, I must, first, say thank you for loving me. Words cannot begin to convey how much you meant to me. To you, I leave my mansion in Palm Beach, Florida. The mansion and its grounds have a current market value of $16.2 million. You can, of course, do with the property whatever you so choose. If you decide to keep the property, a special fund has been set up for complete upkeep of the mansion's grounds, for security, property taxes, and payroll of the mansion's servant staff for the next five years. I hope that you treasure this gift because I truly treasured the time that we spent there together..."

Mars became wracked with sobs. Misha hugged him

and tried to console him, feeling his pain, tears coursing down her own cheeks as she watched the horrible struggle that he'd been having with his emotions since the day that Keshari had left them. They'd loved her so much. Yet, clearly, it had not been enough.

"...to my assistant, Terrence Dwight Henderson, who consistently went above and beyond the responsibilities of his job title to satisfy me. He became a brother and a dear friend to me and I bequeath the cash sum of two million dollars."

There was an instant catching of breath around the room. Terrence started to cry. His partner rubbed his back consolingly and handed Terrence his handkerchief to dry his tears. Keshari had just turned her executive assistant into a millionaire.

Marvin Shabazz was designated as the new "director of artists and repertoire." The Palos Verdes mansion was to be sold and the proceeds split among organizations that were important to Keshari. The AIDS Research Foundation, Susan B. Komen Cancer Foundation, and several substance abuse outreach and recovery programs in Southern California were specifically referenced. There was more than one million dollars' worth of jewelry, which had been left to Misha. Keshari left the yacht to Mars. Keshari had six, luxury automobiles that would be sold and the proceeds used to pay outstanding creditors. Keshari also had substantial stock holdings that, curiously, were not mentioned in the will. Funds in Keshari's personal bank accounts would be used to pay all of her outstanding creditors. The furnishings and substantial artwork in both of Keshari's homes were left to Mars Buchanan.

The media, having gotten wind of the reading of the will a couple of days before, swarmed the small group of heirs as soon as they exited David Weisberg's offices. The heirs quickly got into their respective cars and sped away. When the news aired locally later that evening, media had somehow found out how Keshari Mitchell's estate had been distributed and reporters began to speculate about whether or not a very inexperienced Misha Tierney, while a prominent and very successful party promoter and events planner, would be able to fill Keshari Mitchell's sizeable shoes in the music business.

-43-

Keshari had held her staff to the highest professional standards and her staff continued to demand the highest professional standards of themselves after Keshari's passing. The entire staff at Larger Than Lyfe Entertainment worked around the clock to help Misha become fully acclimated with day-to-day procedure at the busy record label.

Cassandra Harrington of VIBE Network was flown in from Chicago for her and Misha to be formally introduced. Cassandra Harrington was saddened by the tragic loss of such a young, unbelievably intelligent, personable and indomitable force in music. She knew Misha's work as an events planner and she wished Misha well in her new role as president and CEO of Larger Than Lyfe Entertainment.

The record label was moving full steam ahead toward the multimillion-dollar, televised, nationwide talent search grand finale. Everyone was extremely excited. Just as Keshari had envisioned, the nationwide talent search was bringing massive exposure to Cassandra

Harrington's VIBE Network as well as to Larger Than Lyfe Entertainment and the two, powerful, Black women who controlled these two, major business enterprises.

The LTL staff crunched a lot of overtime with Misha and Andre DeJesus at the helm to wrap up all remaining details and produce an event that they knew Keshari would smile down from heaven and be immensely proud of. The media was anxious to cover the event as inside information leaked to them promised that the week-long event would be spectacular. Other music industry heads were anxious to see the outcome of the very expensive event as they considered doing similar projects themselves.

♪ 🎧 ♪

A dynamic, pyrotechnic show and an unbelievable theme that was a hip-hop track that segued into R & B and then jazz opened Larger Than Lyfe Entertainment's "Nationwide Search for a Star." For nearly a month, expensive billboards, TV commercials, magazine and newspaper ads, as well as radio and internet advertising, had dominated the airwaves, building massive public interest for a spectacular week of not-yet-signed music talent and an absolutely spectacular opening night at Kodak Theatre in Culver City, California.

Tickets to the event were the hottest tickets on the market and had been listed for astronomical amounts on eBay for weeks. Keshari's death, the scandal immediately preceding her death, the scandalous stories that followed her death, and even the current media speculation that Keshari was still alive and had merely faked her death to avoid federal prosecution and a successful attempt on her life by gangsters, were just some of the factors that combined to make "Nationwide Search for a Star" a bigger music event than even the Grammy Awards. And, with entertainment's hottest party promoter and events planner at the helm, the after-parties surrounding the week-long event promised to be the venues where everybody who was anybody wanted to be as well.

Twenty, beautiful, scantily clad, female dancers and a troupe of Bronx, New York break dancers took the stage and hyped the opening of the show to the thumping bass lines of the theme and the kind of lyricism that had placed Larger Than Lyfe Entertainment at the top of the music industry food chain. The audience inside the packed theater could not contain their excitement. There were screams and smiles and fans holding up posters to show their support for their favorite contestants as the live television cameras panned the seating areas.

Ten-foot video screens on either side of the stage began to run concert footage of Larger Than Lyfe's line-up of platinum-selling artists. The crowd went wild as footage of Rasheed the Refugee's show in Japan was shown. There was something incredibly sexy in hearing Rasheed the Refugee rap in Japanese.

Video highlights of footage from each of the ten audition cities drew both hysterical laughter and cheers of appreciation from the audience. There were blooper moments as the completely talentless howled out their fifteen minutes of fame and there was some amazing talent discovered in the ten audition cities who would likely score a record deal at some label, even if they were not signed at Larger Than Lyfe.

Misha had messengered tickets for the grand finale opening night to Mars's office at ASCAP. She hoped that Mars would come to see the last major project that Keshari had worked on before she passed. Because Mars was still on leave from ASCAP, his secretary sent the tickets to Mars's condo. Misha looked out into the audience from backstage and spotted Mars on the front row. She blew him a kiss and he smiled.

Then the lights dimmed and the video screens each displayed gigantic photographs of Keshari Mitchell. There was thunderous applause and a standing ovation for the recently fallen record mogul. Clips of various industry executives, producers, and recording artists talked about their personal and professional experiences with Keshari. Keshari's old house and the Leimert Park neighborhood where she'd grown up was shown. Professors at UCLA and Pennsylvania's Wharton School of Business spoke proudly of Keshari Mitchell and the remarkable student that she had been. They'd all known that one day she would be incredibly successful because of her profound intelligence and unbelievable drive.

Members of Larger Than Lyfe staff were interviewed and talked about Keshari Mitchell as a leader. She was no-nonsense, extremely driven, demanding only the very best from her team, but she was also fair, she actively listened to their input and she used all of their strengths as often as she could to achieve the tremendous success that Larger Than Lyfe Entertainment had achieved. The editor of *Vogue* magazine was interviewed and talked of the exotically beautiful, driven, amazingly successful, intensely private woman with the kind of style that seemed a part of her genetic makeup. Keshari Mitchell merged hip-hop and couture magnificently and made even the "ladies who lunch" take note of the way that she put fabulous, designer pieces together.

Then, Misha Tierney, new president and CEO of Larger Than Lyfe, took the stage, strutting confidently in red Dolce & Gabbana and red Jimmy Choo sandals as only Misha Tierney could.

"Keshari was my sister...she was my very best friend," Misha said, standing center stage, her eyes filled with tears of both pride and sadness. "I've known Keshari ever since the two of us were thirteen years old and, even back then, she had a passionate love for music, especially hip-hop. Larger Than Lyfe Entertainment was Keshari's greatest dream come true. She put everything that she had into this record label and she was always looking to make history. Larger Than Lyfe's 'Nationwide Search for a Star' has already made history. More than 100,000 people participated in the audition process. Tonight's finale show will make ratings history... on an African-American television network, TV One, owned by another phenomenal woman, Cathy Hughes."

The audience applauded.

"We've got some unbelievable talent here tonight and we've got the very best in the music industry here composing our panel of judges to select the newest superstar for the Larger Than Lyfe Entertainment roster."

There were screams and cheers from the excited audience.

"Before we introduce our panel of judges and tonight's spectacular line-up of finalists, let me bring out our emcee, one of the funniest, smoothest, finest brothas in today's comedy arena. Here's my chocolate teddy bear... CEDRIC THE ENTERTAINER!"

Outkast's "So Fresh, So Clean" played as Cedric the Entertainer came out onto the stage and made much ado kissing the drop-dead gorgeous Misha on both cheeks, and then spinning her around to get a better look at the Dolce & Gabbana dress that went all the way to there at the back and made an asymmetrical slash across her bodacious cleavage in front. He fanned himself like he might overheat as he watched Misha strut offstage.

"That girl is lucky that I'm married," he said, "'cuz I would take her from that lil' ole boy she's engaged to and she'd forget about him like he played third string for the L.A. Clippers."

He was hilarious and the audience went wild for him.

Cedric the Entertainer promptly took over as a master of ceremonies and introduced the panel of judges. LL Cool J, Russell Simmons, Sean "Diddy" Combs, Sylvia Rhone of Elektra Entertainment fame, Jay-Z, Marvin Shabazz and Sharonda Richards all smiled and waved to the audience of screaming fans.

"We love you, Jay-Z!!!" a band of silicone-breasted fans holding signs squealed from the tenthrow.

"I love y'all, too." Jay-Z smiled modestly, looking over at LL Cool J, and exchanging an all-knowing chuckle.

The troupe of sixty finalists took the stage and the grand finale competition was underway.

-44-

I t was two days after the wrap of the week-long, televised, grand finale miniseries of Larger Than Lyfe Entertainment's "Nationwide Search for a Star" and Misha was so glad to see a bit of calm come into the record label. She was exhausted. She had a couple of press interviews that afternoon to discuss what was upcoming for the winner of the talent search, and what some of her future plans were for the record label, particularly since Larger Than Lyfe was delving into the genres of R & B and jazz. After that, she was going to take a ride out to the studio in North Hollywood to take a listen to the label's new artist, Ntozake. The word was that the tracks for this extremely talented, young, twenty-something's first CD were coming together impeccably well. Her vocals were lush with an urban edge to them and there had already been comments around the label that she bore a strong, physical resemblance to Keshari Mitchell. Larger Than Lyfe was putting together a package for her that would render her the record label's new premier artist, taking the place of

Rasheed the Refugee, who had left the label shortly before Keshari's death.

After Misha left the studio in North Hollywood, she planned to take a long weekend to catch up on sleep and some of the projects at Misha Tierney, her events planning company. Misha's preparations to leave were abruptly intercepted by a most unexpected visitor. Marcus Means bypassed the receptionist, walked into Misha's office and took a seat in front of her desk.

"Ms. Tierney, would you like me to phone security?" the receptionist said over Misha's intercom.

"No, it's okay," Misha said, puzzled at Marcus Means's abrupt presence in her office. "Hold all of my calls."

She clicked off the intercom.

"Marcus Means," Misha said, "not even in the farthest recesses of my mind can I imagine why you are here."

Marcus smiled. "Same ole Misha. You and that gorgeous mouth of yours."

"Why are you here and what do you want?" Misha snapped, her patience quickly leaving her. "I'm not in the dope game. I don't owe you any money. I truly hope that you're not looking to get a record deal, so to what do I owe the displeasure of your goddamned company?!"

"I see that you are settling very nicely into your new role as CEO. You had a lot of naysayers in the industry betting against you. It's good to see that you're working so hard to prove them all wrong."

"So, that's why you stopped by...to give me some positive reinforcement?"

"I have a proposition for you," Marcus responded. "I guess you might call it an offer that you can't exactly refuse."

"You wanna bet?" Misha said.

"Wait," Marcus said. "Take a listen to what I'm about to tell you and, perhaps, you'll weigh your feisty, little snaps a lot more carefully."

Misha crossed her legs and sat back in her chair.

"Somewhere along the way, in the ongoing saga of the past few weeks, media has formulated the conspiracy theory that Keshari is still alive. Can you believe that shit? Just like Tupac Shakur."

"No. That shit is patently ridiculous," Misha said, "which is why I pay it absolutely no mind. Is that why you're here? To discuss conspiracy theories?"

"I think you know me better than that," Marcus responded. "I have more than a theoretical reason to believe that your best friend is still alive and has pulled off an intricate, little ruse in which YOU were an active participant. What if someone located your friend and finished what Tim Harris failed to finish?"

"Get the fuck out of my office right now!" Misha snapped.

Marcus Means didn't even consider budging.

"Here's my proposal," Marcus said. "I'm going to need ten percent of Larger Than Lyfe's revenues every month until further notice. In return for this ten percent, I make the promise to you that your best friend will remain safe wherever she is, wherever she goes, and I will not divulge her and your little secret to the authorities."

"You sick son of a bitch!" Misha snapped, furious tears splashing down her cheeks. "Keshari is gone! GONE! And I don't give a fuck what you believe to the contrary. I will not dispense one penny of Larger Than Lyfe revenues to you, or anything like you, and you can take that shit to the authorities!"

"Misha, when your brother was charged and tried for the first-degree murder of Phinnaeus Bernard III, did you ever wonder if he might be telling the truth and that he had nothing at all to do with his attorney's murder, just like he said? I mean, think about it. Rick took two sets of polygraph exams and passed them both. In all these years, Rick never got caught up with any murder charge that could stick...and now he's dead."

"You know what I think?" Misha said irritably. "I think that I couldn't give a fuck about Richard Tresvant's murder trial. If he finally went to prison for a murder he did not commit, it sounds like the karma of a man who got away with far more heinous shit FOR YEARS! Now, why the fuck are you still here?! Do I need to have security remove you?"

Marcus stared at Misha pensively, and then shook his head sympathetically.

"I know what it is. You still blame your brother for your mother's death. You still hold so much anger about it. Unfortunately, that has nothing to do with me. Ten percent. You have twenty-four hours to decide how you want to go about this. I'll be back at the same time tomorrow...and I don't think you'd be foolish enough to stand me up."

"Do whatever the fuck you think that you can get away with," Misha responded. "I will NEVER give you one penny from ANY source. I don't have any business with you and I never have. You won't be strong-arming me for shit! Come back at the same time tomorrow if you want. You can be assured that my answer will be the same."

-45-

A six-hour flight out of Los Angeles International Airport and Darian Boudreaux landed in São Paulo, Brazil. Because it was not a vacation, but an abrupt, one-way departure from the life she knew into the unknown, all she felt was numb, unable to fully process the lights, the hustle, bustle and excitement of the airport in the major, foreign city that she'd just stepped into. Neither sadness nor fear had hit her yet, just numbness through every fiber of her being.

A limousine driver loaded her luggage and delivered her to Hotel Intercontinental in downtown São Paulo. Less than thirty-six hours before, she had still been Keshari Mitchell, pulling off the greatest stunt and fraud of her life, her very own suicide. From the paramedics who had arrived on the scene, worked on her valiantly, and pronounced her dead, and then quickly transported her lifeless body away from the scene, to the first police dispatched to the scene, to the pathologist at the coroner's office who had falsified the paperwork confirming her death, including a falsified death certificate, and then provided an actual body to represent her at the mortuary, to the mortuary who had knowingly cremated a Jane Doe and represented it on even more falsified paperwork as Keshari Mitchell, to the authentic passport, birth certificate, social security card and other legal documents issued for her new identity, everyone had had a price, Keshari had met their price and they all had willingly participated in the intricate plot that had liberated her from her former life.

She sat in the living room of her luxurious hotel suite and stared at her new passport for more than an hour. "Darian Boudreaux," born in New Orleans, Louisiana, on January 27, 1979. For the moment, she was safe. There was no way to be sure how long the safety she had at that moment would last. For all intents and purposes, she was deceased. But there had been numerous people involved who had been paid and who had assisted her and her attorney in carrying out her suicide. Eventually, and there was absolutely no way to be sure when someone would talk. The thing about paying for silence was that it could not really be bought and if you gave it a blank check, it would never prove to be enough. The only way that silence was assured was if the persons who held her secret ceased to exist. Going in that direction only opened up a whole new set of problems.

Darian looked all around her at the chic and modern furnishings of her hotel suite. Even after the colossal sum that she'd incurred to do what she'd done, she was still a very rich woman. But all of the luxuries all around her seemed to hold a very blatant emptiness to them now. All of it was just so much expensive stuff. The people who had once surrounded her and had been her friends and business associates and advisors and confidantes were no longer people to whom she could turn for advice and support. When Keshari Mitchell ceased to exist, every single person in her life ceased to exist as well. For the very first time since the ambulance had taken her away to South Bay Hospital and the coroner had formally pronounced her dead and her attorney had quickly spirited her away from the hospital unbeknownst to media and she took the six-hour flight to Brazil, it now began to sink in for her how truly alone she now was and that it would be this way for a very long time. Darian knew that her thoughts would seriously entertain again and again, probably for the rest of her life, whether she had made the right decision.

♪ 🎧 ♪

The first couple of weeks after Darian's arrival at São Paulo's Hotel Intercontinental, she stayed in bed practically the entire day like someone battling a serious depression. She barely ate. She didn't go out. She thought about Mars a lot. She missed him so, so much. She thought about Misha...her sister...the very best friend that anyone could have. She thought of David Weisberg, her attorney, who knew absolutely everything about her life...The Consortium and all. Over time, David Weisberg had become a father figure to her and tears filled his eyes as he hugged Keshari for the very last time in an underground parking garage in downtown Los Angeles and she slid into a limousine in disguise, headed to the airport, exiting the life of Keshari Mitchell and about to become Darian Boudreaux.

Intricate planning had been put into getting Keshari away from her former life. Virtually no planning had been given to what she would do and become once she entered her new life. Formulating a game plan for what Darian Boudreaux would do with the "blank slate" that was the rest of her life would become the project to occupy her days and nights in the unfamiliar territory of her new home, Brazil, over the days and weeks to come. But she didn't know how long she would be able to live like this. She truly didn't know how long.

Her eyes welled with tears as, once again, she felt the vast expanse of aloneness that surrounded her. When she finally pulled herself together, she pulled out her new laptop, logged into her new Internet account, and began to review Stateside news stories.

There was coverage of Keshari's funeral. There was sensationalized coverage of the reading of Keshari's will and the distribution of millions of dollars' worth of assets. There were numerous good reviews on the nationwide talent search finale and the amazing job that Misha

Tierney had done in bringing all of the final details together for the week-long event, which had been the last major project that Keshari Mitchell had worked on at her record label prior to her death. And there was substantial coverage and photos of all of the entertainment names that had come out for the much-talked-about after-parties connected with the show.

Darian smiled with pride. She had always known that her best friend would be able to carry it off.

Darian ordered dinner, a humongous, loaded cheeseburger and french fries and a bottle of wine and a slice of cheesecake with fresh berries, a calorie-ridden, extra-extravagant splurge that she never indulged in as her former self. As she savored her decadent meal like a child, she went back to her laptop and commenced to order music and books for herself. For years, she had worked eighteen-hour days, driven to succeed, and had never had the opportunity to sit back and read simply for the leisure of it and enjoy music without it, ultimately, having something to do with her business. She ordered everything that Me'Shell N'Degeocello had ever done. There was something incredibly mesmerizing and deep and sexy about the woman and her music. She ordered Slum Village and a lot of Cam'Ron, Tori Amos, Earth, Wind & Fire, Anita Baker, Sade, Sarah McLachlan and Rasheed the Refugee. She ordered software so that she could immerse herself in the Portuguese language, which was the predominant language of Brazil. She called the concierge and expressed to him that she wanted to take a tour of São Paulo and wanted the best, English-speaking tour available. The concierge called her back a short time later and let her know that he had scheduled her on a three-hour bus tour of São Paulo and the surrounding area the following day.

When Darian fell asleep that night, after having taken up activities to busy herself and to make her more comfortable in her new environment, she dreamed of Keshari and Mars. The two of them were lying on the upper deck of her yacht, "Larger Than Lyfe," in the moonlight, wrapped in a blanket together just talking.

"Do you believe in redemption?" Keshari asked Mars.

"Yeah, I do," Mars answered matter-of-factly.

"Do you believe that, after all that I've done, there's a possibility of redemption for me?"

He kissed the tip of her nose reassuringly and, just as he was about to answer her question, he was gone and only the darkness of the hotel suite's bedroom surrounded her.

Darian turned over and tried to fall asleep again.

-46-

Hours turned to days, days turned to weeks, and more than a month had passed since Keshari Mitchell's death. Darian was becoming stir crazy and the touristy-type things that she had been doing to occupy her time had just about run out of gas. She began to orchestrate plans to lease a yacht and travel along the coast of the beautiful, Brazilian nation, stopping at ports so that she could see some of the exotic cities she'd always heard about but never had the time to explore like Ipanema, Copacabana, Salvador de Bahia, and Pão de Açúcar, which translates to "Sugar Loaf" in English, and was said to be entirely too beautiful to be real. She also considered traveling to Switzerland, where she had money in the Bank of Switzerland. She also thought of various nations in Africa that she'd like to visit. She knew that the change of venue would definitely, if only temporarily, brighten her state of mind.

Time was, also, now making it a necessity for Darian to start planning to make a move. She'd now been at the Hotel Intercontinental for more than a month and, until she had undergone her physical transformation, there was always the risk of recognition...even if it was only a very small risk in such a densely populated nation like Brazil.

With the need to begin making moves in mind, Darian touched bases with one of the contacts her attorney, David·Weisberg, had provided to her. The contact was a world-renowned, plastic surgeon who would completely alter Keshari Mitchell's physical identity all the way down to her dental work so that she could fully assume her new identity as Darian Boudreaux. The surgeon gave Darian a full tour of his surgical facilities, showed her photographs of some of his previous work, discussed each of the procedures that she would be having, and then showed her pictures of the beautiful, secluded piece of real estate near Ipanema where she could very comfortably recuperate. Darian would have to commit herself to remaining in Brazil for at least one year in order to complete the several rounds of surgeries and for recovery and healing. The surgeries were very drastic, very high-risk, and expensive, and the surgeon had a pretty substantial list of clients who had elected to completely alter their physical identities and who federal law enforcement, in a number of nations, would surely be interested in knowing about.

Keshari expressed to the surgeon that she'd like to take a few more weeks before she scheduled a firm date to commence the work. While the physical transformation had always been a part of the plan in the intricate scheme to fake her death, she had much to think about, especially in terms of the dangers involved in the surgeries. She also thought of Mars over and over again. Late at night when she couldn't sleep, as was often the case, she would sit, staring out her huge, living room windows, and miss Mars's touch. She missed his arms around her. She missed the intoxicating smell of him, that perfect, masculine scent that left her thinking of him even when he wasn't there. She missed his lips, his voice. She missed him making love to her. She missed how they talked about everything...well, almost everything...and the way that he just GOT her. She missed Mars so much that she was frequently left in tears, sometimes sobbing as if there was no tomorrow, thinking how she had had to, literally, terminate that part of her life.

For the fourth time that month, she strode through São Paulo's Museum of Modern Art that she had come to love so much, where she was surrounded by Marc Chagall, Pablo Picasso, José Antonio da Silva and Emiliano Di Cavalcanti. While browsing in the museum's gift shop, she was overcome by the strangest impulse. She purchased a set of postcards depicting vibrant photographs of Brazil's most famous landmarks. She took one of the postcards and, using a typewriter provided by the hotel, addressed it to Mars's condo and typed the message, *"I miss you...SO much."* No signature.

She rode a taxi to the post office and sent off the postcard that very same day. For some reason, she felt better after mailing the card. The overwhelming loneliness that she had been feeling seemed to dissipate just a little bit.

-47-

When Misha messengered Mars a pair of tickets to Larger Than Lyfe's "Nationwide Search for a Star" opening night along with a handwritten note, telling him how much it would mean to her if he came, Mars had been extremely reluctant to commit himself. He rationalized repeatedly that he wasn't ready to be around people. The day before the event, Mars had a change of heart. Misha had been so kind to him since the reading of the will...before that even. She'd called several times just to check on his well-being. She'd sent him flowers multiple times and a Ghiradelli chocolate basket and Mrs. Fields cookies to cheer him up, always with handwritten notes containing words of encouragement and little prayers to try and help him feel better. She was reaching out to offer comfort to him as only a friend would.

Mars went to the show's opening night and truly enjoyed himself. He'd even dropped into the after-party at Skybar for a little while. Now, a month later, he was trying to reestablish a groove for himself. He sat on his terrace and began to go through the overflowing bin filled with his mail that the office of the building at his luxury, condominium community had graciously been holding for him. He called his best friend, Jason Payne, who he hadn't seen in ages and told him that he wanted to get together and play some ball. He was also getting ready to get back into the swing of things at ASCAP and talked to his secretary several times that week to begin coordinating his work and travel schedule.

In his burgeoning mail stack, Mars came across a postcard depicting Rio de Janeiro and its Corcovado Mountain with the huge, Christ the Redeemer statue for which Rio de Janeiro was most famous. The brief message from the sender said, *"I miss you...SO much."*

The postcard slipped from Mars's fingers and fell to the ground. He sat there for a few moments as if someone had just sucker-punched him. It, for whatever reason, left him dazed and confused. With all of the speculation by the media, he couldn't help asking himself the question: Was there any possibility that Keshari might be alive? Was there any possibility that there was truth to the media speculation?

NO! he finally told himself. It was a malicious joke, just as he was starting to come out of his debilitating grief. Undoubtedly, it was Portia Foster, pissed at him for blowing her off yet again when she'd reached out to him immediately following Keshari's death. He dropped the postcard on the cocktail table, grabbed his keys and his gym bag and went to meet his friend at the athletic club.

He came home that night accompanied by a beautiful, Black and Korean sista that he'd met sipping mochachino on the patio at Magic Johnson's Starbucks in Ladera Heights. She had the most interesting name, Ntozake, like the Black poet, and she looked a lot like Keshari. He didn't ask a lot about her. She told him that she was a singer/songwriter and that she was working on a CD. In broad and slightly evasive terms, Mars told her that he was an attorney. In all honesty, he didn't want to know anything about her and, that night, she didn't appear to be very interested in getting to know him in any great detail either. There was a strong, physical attraction between the two of them and that was pretty much all that needed to be said. It had been a long time since Mars had had a one-night stand, even though the entertainment industry was the quintessential smorgasbord for them. For a time toward the beginning of Mars's legal career, when the money started to get a lot longer and he was feeling his ego and himself like most of the other men in the industry, he'd been only too happy to indulge in them...no strings, no emotions, no complications. Things were different for him now, mentally and emotionally. One-night stands were not really his thing anymore. But with Keshari gone, his emotions were currently a "no man's land" and a one-night stand was perfectly acceptable.

Mars lit candles, he put a sample of everything good in the jazz and neo-soul genres on his CD changer, poured Ntozake a glass of wine, and then fucked her with complete and reckless abandon. When it was over, he went out onto his terrace and fell asleep and Keshari came to him again in his dreams.

With her hands on her hips and that $40,000 sable coat swinging open, exposing the sheer perfection of her naked body, she whispered to him over and over again, "I'm still here...I'm still here...I love you."

Mars snapped awake and went into his bedroom. Ntozake was gone and he was glad. He hoped that he never saw her again. It was four in the morning and he sat in the middle of his living room floor, studying photographs of Keshari and him together, tracing the contours of her beautiful, smiling face with his finger. When he dozed off again, he was clutching a sterling silver-framed photograph of Keshari that usually sat on his cocktail table. He would love that woman forever.

♪ 🎧 ♪

One evening while going through his mail, more than one month after receiving the first postcard, Mars received a second one. This time, a scene of wealthy, Brazilian sunbathers was depicted on an ultra-exclusive beach area in Ipanema.

The postcard's message said, *"I'm still here. I love you."*

Mars located the first mysterious postcard that he'd received and studied it. Then he carefully studied the second one. The interesting thing about both of the postcards was that they had been typed. Postcards from vacationers were not typewritten. Someone who did not want their handwriting and possibly themselves identified had sent Mars these two postcards. However, Mars did not know if this "someone" was an individual or a group.

Both postcards had São Paulo postmarks. Mars studied every detail about the two postcards and thought of some of the conversations that he and Keshari had had prior to her death. There were times when she would get so philosophical and intense, telling him things that seemed almost locked inside a riddle. Then, out of nowhere, it all started to come together. Either that or he was truly losing his mind. The postcards had to have come from Keshari. As crazy as it sounded, Mars was certain of it. But he needed to try and get more confirmation.

♬ 🎧 ♬

Mars went to David Weisberg's office. Celeste, David Weisberg's legal secretary, was extremely pleased to see him. The last time that she'd seen Mars, he had been an emotional basket case, grieving over the loss of the woman he loved like the world had ended. He'd been unable to function on even the most basic level.

"You look really good," Celeste told Mars, "and I thank you for the orchid and the roses and the weekend at Canyon Ranch. It had been a really long time since I had gotten spoiled like that. I think you made my husband jealous."

"You deserve to be spoiled," Mars responded with a smile. "And I cannot thank you enough for all that you did for me."

"Just so you know, Mr. Weisberg is not in the office. He had a meeting with a client."

"If you don't mind," Mars told Celeste, taking a seat at her desk and winking at her flirtatiously. "I'd really like to wait. This is important."

"Well, I was just about to go out for lunch. Why don't I order something and have it delivered for both of us?"

"Sounds like a plan." Mars smiled. "My treat."

David Weisberg arrived back at his office a little over an hour later and Mars was still seated at Celeste's desk, enjoying their conversation and the pan-fried noodles and orange chicken that she'd ordered for lunch.

"Mars, what a surprise! What can I do for you?" David Weisberg asked.

The two men went into David Weisberg's office and closed the doors.

"Mr. Weisberg, what I'm going to ask you is probably going to leave you questioning my sanity. Even I am having to question my sanity every now and again these days. But, perhaps, if you look at this, you'll better understand why I felt so compelled to come and see you."

Mars placed the two postcards on David's desk squarely in front of him.

"Is Keshari still alive?" Mars asked without hesitation. David Weisberg stared down at the two, typewritten postcards from São Paulo, Brazil and was instantly pissed at Keshari for being so damned foolish.

"WHAT?!" he said distractedly, still staring down at the postcards. "Of course not. That's ridiculous. What exactly are you even suggesting?"

"I'm not suggesting anything," Mars answered. "I'm asking you directly...is Keshari still alive?"

"Of course not," David Weisberg said again. "What you're asking me clearly suggests that you believe I took part in a major impropriety and I can assure you that I would not jeopardize more than twenty-five years of legal practice to aid and abet a very serious illegality, no matter how much I cared for Keshari."

"So, who do you imagine sent me these postcards?"

"I know nothing about your personal life," David Weisberg said. "Therefore, I couldn't even hedge an educated guess to answer that question."

Mars slumped back in his chair and buried his head in his hands. His life was starting to come together again and a couple of postcards in the mail threatened to pull him back apart.

"I'm sorry," David said. "I'm so, so sorry. I know how much you loved her. I know that she loved you. But she's gone. She's dead. And it's time for you to let her go and move on with your life."

"Before Keshari's...passing," Mars said, "we talked a lot about so much and she repeatedly seemed to be trying to tell me something. She kept telling me how her whole life was changing. There was a strange sadness, like she knew that something was about to happen, but it was too dangerous to divulge even to me. My heart, my mind, my gut tell me that Keshari sent me these postcards. I saw the expression on your face when I placed them in front of you. It was shock from recognition, followed by what appeared to be anger. I know that you're not going to tell me the truth, but that expression on your face when you looked at those postcards said everything."

-48-

As if the entertainment newswire over the past several months had not already been a three-ring circus, Mars Buchanan stepped boldly and unapologetically back into the spotlight and promptly resigned from his position as West Coast general counsel at ASCAP. Some executives who knew him said that they had seen it coming. Mars hadn't been the same since his return to work following Keshari Mitchell's shocking suicide.

When Keshari and Mars were still together, Mars had talked candidly about his desire to one day take advantage of his many industry contacts and inside knowledge and start his own artist and athlete management firm. The level of autonomy that he would hold as owner of his own company had always been tempting and could definitely prove lucrative. Keshari was his inspiration, he'd told her. She was a shining example that it could be done.

In a press conference at ASCAP's Los Angeles offices, Mars was strategically evasive about his future business plans and he assured the media that he was not leaving ASCAP on bad blood. After the loss of someone truly significant to him, Mars said, he'd come to realize how precious time was and he believed that he needed to dedicate his time and energies to new endeavors that were more in tune with the current phase of his life.

Mars flew to New York and visited his family after the press conference. He had no desire to remain in L.A. and deal with the annoying harassment of the media pursuing him for a story. Mars's father was shocked at his son's completely unexpected resignation from his prestigious position, but he also knew how talented and determined his son had always been. He could do anything that he put his mind to and if he said that he intended to start his own company, he would, and it would, without a doubt, be a huge success.

Before Mars left his parents' home to return to Los Angeles, he told them that he was going to do some traveling for a few weeks before he actively proceeded to lay the groundwork for his new management firm.

Mars's sister asked him where he was going.

"I'm strongly leaning toward Brazil," Mars said.

♪ 🎧 ♪

The next absolutely mind-blowing news to hit the streets were the rumored, ultra-private nuptials that had taken place between the new CEO of Larger Than Lyfe

Entertainment, Misha Tierney, and real estate investor, Marcus Means, who the press said had links to the notorious and now-deceased Richard Lawrence Tresvant. Misha's New York Knicks fiancé rang every phone number that Misha had ever had and was unable to locate her anywhere. All that her assistant and the record label and her events planning firm could tell him was that she had taken a long weekend. All of it was a massive, "WHAT THE FUCK!" moment that sent Darian Boudreaux into tears when she read it online.

-49-

When one considers that the combined annual revenues from the production, distribution and sale of cocaine equate to approximately one trillion, tax-free dollars, it is patently ridiculous to dismiss the very real possibility that the United States has a direct involvement in this illicit trade and is profiting from said involvement...royally. The United States possesses a lengthy and sordid history of lies, unethical practices, corruption, and imperialist greed. There is no way that the U.S., like Mexico and other less-developed nations, would leave the level of wealth generated in the cocaine trade to the common Black and Brown criminal to amass without securing a substantial slice of the pie for themselves. In short, America's "war on drugs" is nothing more than one, huge FARCE, akin to leaving the fox in charge of the chicken coop.

America's "war on drugs" is a massive POLITICAL game more than anything. D.C. fat cats sit on Capitol Hill pontificating about the detrimental effects of illegal narcotics on the fabric of America, particularly on the public safety and American youth. They add insult to injury by referencing crime statistics and the ever-growing percentages of substance abusers, as if they are seriously engaged in a very real effort to destroy the problem when, in actuality, they either never do enough to get the problem solved or they fall prey to the corruption that pervades the entire system. They pound their fists vehemently and declare that we will win the war on drugs, no matter the cost. It's so much lip service, political figures telling their constituents exactly what they want to hear to keep the citizens in their comfort zones, politicians saying what they believe needs to be said in order to gain votes.

Bills are passed that look promising on the surface, but are thoroughly devoid of the ingredients required for positive and lasting change and are rife in just enough loopholes for the sophisticated, professional criminal to work right through and around.

Law enforcement is overrun with flaws as well. Men who are just men and have taken an oath to "protect and serve" are expected to invoke the powers of the crime-fighting superhero and avoid the temptation of skimming off the top some of the ill-gotten spoils confiscated from drug-dealing thugs that sometimes equates to more than these law enforcement officers will earn over the entire duration of their careers.

On salaries that are a gross disparity to the danger that most law enforcement officers confront daily, even the noblest officers of the law sometimes fall prey to the temptation of thousands of dollars in bribes offered by drug dealers asking them to just look the other way when a shipment arrives or overlook the sizeable "package" in the drug dealer's trunk while the average police officer's superiors make cozy bedfellows with the crooked mayors and other city and county officials to make their own dirty money on the side. Corruption in law enforcement is like a virulent disease, infecting every single area, no matter the rank, on police forces everywhere. And all accept it as par for the course, "everybody does it," until scandal breaks out and these dirty officers of the law are tossed unwittingly into a news camera lens with their pants down.

Politics absolutely comes into play when huge amounts of taxpayer dollars are allocated to law enforcement budgets and law enforcement is expected to satisfy citizens' and legislators' lofty expectations by bringing in major, drug-related convictions. When law enforcement drops the ball, then the blame game commences and someone must take the fall. The political game is never-ending.

Even though Richard Tresvant was dead, the game was far from over. Thomas Hencken knew this as he boarded his flight to Washington, D.C., headed to face his superiors. They'd demanded a meeting. He'd quickly complied. Words were not minced when he arrived.

"The agency would like you to firmly consider early

retirement," Robert Eickenberry, assistant director of the Western Division Organized Crime Unit, said carefully.

"What is this about?" Thomas Hencken said. "I know that you're not about to turn me into the fall guy for the Consortium mess."

"You overstepped the scope of your authority on more than one occasion in this nearly two-year, Consortium fiasco," Robert Eickenberry said. "Two federal agents lost their lives while working under your direction and the agency allocated well over ten million dollars to a special task force that was under your direct supervision without a single, major conviction, not even the convictions of the murderers of the two downed federal agents."

"I feel very, very strongly that Keshari Mitchell is still alive," Thomas Hencken said. "I've been working this thing on my own time, night and day. This case can still work in our favor."

"You see!" senior agent William Thorne snapped. "This is exactly what we're talking about! We have certified medical testimony confirming Keshari Mitchell's death and you're still determined to turn her into state's witness. It's OVER! Keshari Mitchell is dead! Richard Tresvant is dead! And you need to let this thing go and acknowledge the loss. A new task force is preparing to move forward on a top-ranking family in Los Angeles Yakuza. There is currently no firm leadership in place within The Consortium ranks. Therefore, they are not as great a threat and lower in priority now for the DEA. In a way, we have taken a small victory."

"You are a fifteen-year veteran with the agency," Robert Eickenberry said. "You have an impeccable record. That is why you're being offered the option of retirement in lieu of termination. Your pension shall be completely unaffected."

"I'm being made the fall guy for the failure of the Consortium case. I, ultimately, take my direction from YOU here in Washington, yet you're not assuming any culpability for the way that the Consortium case turned out. I will fight this, you know," Thomas Hencken said. "I'm contacting my attorney the moment our meeting wraps."

"Do what you think you have to do," Robert Eickenberry said calmly. "The offer is on the table for seven days. After that, unfortunately, the agency will have to proceed with your immediate termination."

Thomas Hencken angrily brushed out of the office and out of the doors of the Drug Enforcement Agency's Washington, D.C. headquarters. Politics had reared its ugly head once again. But he was as determined as ever that he would take down the remaining Consortium players, as well as expose their suppliers and client base, even as the DEA tried to oust him from the organization that he'd zealously dedicated himself to for years.

-50-

M ars smiled to himself as Northwest Airlines flight 8996 lifted off, departing Los Angeles International Airport for São Paulo, Brazil. He was scared. He didn't know what to expect. He didn't know if he would even be able to find Keshari...ahem... Darian...Boudreaux.

A week and a half before, Celeste, David Weisberg's legal secretary, had shown up at his condo.

"I will lose my job for this, Mars, if David ever finds out."

Celeste admitted that she had been nosily listening to snatches of Mars's conversation with David Weisberg earlier that day. She told Mars of a project that David had been working on single-handedly, not even using the assistance of his secretaries. She did not possess a large amount of details, but she felt certain that all of it had to do with Keshari Mitchell. David was being very secretive in terms of his movements with the project and very, very careful. However, he had made one slip recently that she'd caught. Celeste had come across an e-mail on David Weisberg's open, personal laptop. She read the transmission thread of the e-mail and it had come from an account that had been set up in Los Angeles, but had been sent from São Paulo, Brazil. The account was in the name of "Darian Boudreaux" and the communication from this person clearly indicated that he/she had a very familiar relationship with David because they closed their note to him by saying, "Love you." The person said that they had met with Dr. Claudio Henriqué and would commence the surgery in August.

"I did a bit of research online to find out who this Dr. Henriqué is and he is a plastic surgeon. The person said that they were still at Hotel Intercontinental, but would be leaving soon.

"I know it's not a lot," Celeste said, "but that's all I have...that and my female intuition. I guess that I, like so much of the public, got caught up in all of the speculation about Keshari Mitchell possibly faking her death to avoid prosecution. Since I work for her long-time attorney, I did what I do best...I started snooping."

Mars had sat up the rest of that night, thinking about the information that Celeste had imparted to him and he stared for hours at those two postcards. He thought about everything that Keshari had kept from him, the things that she had been involved in. He thought about their break-up...and he thought about her suicide. If she really was still alive, she had deceived him again in probably the worst way of all. But, still, he was so in love with her. Maybe he was a complete fool. But he was still so in love with her.

Two days later, Mars submitted his immediate resignation to ASCAP. Then he went to visit his family in New York. And now he was on a flight to Brazil, unsure what he would find, flying blind into the unknown with all of the hope in the world.

♪ 🎧 ♪

Mars arrived at the Hotel Intercontinental to check into his room and asked the front desk manager if Darian Boudreaux was still registered at the hotel. Mars said that Darian was a business associate of his.

"Miss Boudreaux checked out this morning," the desk manager said. "Lovely woman."

Mars's heart dropped. That was just his fucking luck.

"Did she...did she let on as to where she was going? Will she be coming back?" Mars asked, almost unable to control his frustration and disappointment.

"She took one of the large, luxury boats to travel up the coast. 'Guantanamera.' That's the name of the boat."

"Thank you," Mars said distractedly, taking his key and following the bellman to his room.

If it had still been daylight, Mars would have hired a driver right then and there to immediately begin the drive up Brazil's coast, hitting all of the open ports in search of "Guantanamera." Instead, he settled into his room for the evening, ordered dinner, and requested a wake-up call so that he could rise early and begin his search.

♫ 🎧 ♫

The concierge provided great assistance in helping Mars to secure a trustworthy, full-time driver for the rather arduous journey up the Brazilian coast. It had taken a full day to do it, which Mars felt was an enormous delay, but the following day, Mars was prepared to get started. Hector, the driver, was quite excited to be a part of Mars's little adventure once he finally comprehended why Mars was proceeding on such a strange mission that might render no positive result.

"You do this for love," Hector said in his thick, fragmented English. "A very special love."

Mars was glad that he'd had the presence of mind to purchase a dictionary of Portuguese words and phrases to bring with him. If he hadn't, his ride with Hector would have been a confusing one indeed.

The two men rode along, attempting conversation from time to time, but, most of the time, riding along in silence, each of them consumed by their own, private thoughts. The terrain of Brazil's eastern coast was beautiful and lush. Even the people that they spotted as Hector drove through the small communities and green hillside had features that were strong, distinct, sun-darkened, and very attractive. Brazil was well-known for its exotically beautiful women.

Their first stop was Porto Alegre. The port was small and lined with quaint, waterfront merchants and street vendors. Mars and Hector walked around the moderately crowded port filled mostly with people native to the area. Mars showed Keshari's photographs to as many of the merchants as he could who would actually talk with him. Hector acted as a translator. And all of the people he spoke to proclaimed that they had not seen the beautiful woman before.

The two men got back into their Jeep and drove a little farther north. Their next stop was Curitiba. The port was very similar to Porto Alegre, although slightly larger because it was closer to Rio de Janeiro. They headed through the crowded port, stopping to ask the vendors if they'd seen the woman in the photograph or if her yacht, "Guantanamera," had stopped there.

Finally, after hours of making their way through the bustling port with the sun beating down on them, they came upon a Brazilian produce vendor. The vendor said in Portuguese to Hector that Keshari's large boat had been at the port the day before. She did some shopping, and then re-boarded her boat and appeared to be headed for Rio.

Mars was both excited and disappointed at the news. He was excited that they were on the right track. He was disappointed that he had missed Keshari by an entire day and might wind up in pursuit of her, always several steps behind her, for an indefinite length of time.

The two men settled into a small, nondescript hotel

in Curitiba for the night. It was very clean, but very modest in comparison to the luxurious amenities that Mars was accustomed to. Mars lay down on his small bed, staring up at the ceiling fan that spun quietly in the moonlit room. He thought of words of encouragement that his mother used to say to him when he was growing up, when he was confronted with an obstacle that stood in the way of something that he really wanted. They were words that had stayed with him straight through law school and that he was sure had been used by his mother's mother and so many other Black mothers other than his own.

"Nothing really good comes to you easily, son. You typically have to fight and struggle for it and, if it's meant to be, it will be."

Mars was lulled to sleep by those words and the gentle, Brazilian breeze floating through the hotel room's open windows.

The next morning, Mars and Hector rode off to scour Rio de Janeiro, one of the most popular and most populous tourist destinations in the world. There were a multitude of wealthy travelers in Rio de Janeiro, so neither Keshari's yacht, nor Keshari, would stick out as prominently as she would have in one of the smaller port cities. Mars intended to dedicate an entire week, if necessary, to cover the entire area. And, this time, he did not intend to come away empty-handed.

Dressed in cool, white linen and looking like a male

model, Mars rode with Hector to Rio de Janeiro's Copacabana area. The beach area was one of Rio de Janeiro's most exclusive spots and it appeared to be dominated mostly by well-chiseled, homosexual men. Mars walked the beach, taking in the beautiful, swim-suited women slathered in suntan lotion, hoping to find Keshari somewhere in the crowd of amazing bodies. Mars and Hector spent the entire day in Copacabana, walking the beach and speaking to proprietors of upscale boutiques and jewelers where Keshari may have stopped. They even questioned workers at the docks, hoping to find out if "Guantanamera" had made a stop there.

Day turned to late evening and, with no sighting of Keshari, the two, exhausted men checked into a hotel for the night. Mars showered and lay in his bed and thought about Keshari. He thought about the woman that she was, her habits, and the kinds of things that she liked. Mars came to a realization. He had been searching for Keshari in all of the wrong places and at all of the wrong times. Keshari was an intensely private person and Mars knew that that fact had certainly not changed, particularly after having faked her own death. She loved luxurious surroundings and all of the accoutrements of wealth, but she also preferred seclusion.

Just before daybreak the next morning, Mars went to Hector's adjoining hotel room and the two men departed for Ipanema. Ipanema was one of the richest, chicest beaches in the world. With all that Mars had heard about

Ipanema right down to the song made about the "Girl from Ipanema," Mars somehow felt certain that, if Keshari had not been to Ipanema already, she was definitely going to be there. Hector assured Mars that, if his lady love was a wealthy woman, Ipanema was likely a place she would want to go.

The two men started off along Ipanema's waterfront shops. Because it was early morning, most of the shops were still closed. There was a small bistro at the end of the wharf and Hector suggested that they stop there for coffee. On the patio at a small table off to the side, the woman sitting there caught Mars's eye.

Mars had been on a fruitless scavenger hunt that was proving more and more mentally taxing, even though he had only been searching the densely populated region for a week...and there she was. As Mars stared at her, he felt almost as if he were staring at a mirage and that, if he approached her, said something to her, reached out to touch her, she would disappear, having never been there in the first place. She was as beautiful as she ever was. Deeply tanned, she wore a large sunhat and a white bikini with a short, almost transparent cover-up. She was reading a book and making notes on a legal pad.

Mars touched his pocket and felt the small lump of the five-carat, flawless, Asscher-cut, canary diamond that had cost him a quarter of a million dollars. He'd carried the very expensive ring in his pocket every single day since he and Hector had started out on their search and he had always hoped, believed, that he would be able to place the ring on the finger of its rightful owner.

"Excuse me," the six-foot-four, suave, former general counsel for ASCAP said smoothly, his heart racing a mile a minute.

Keshari...ahem...Darian Boudreaux looked up from her book and her eyes filled with tears. Words would not come.

Mars sat down beside her at the small table and, without saying a word, slipped the ring onto her finger and squeezed her hand. They stared at each other for what seemed like eons...time, history, secrets, mistakes, forgiveness and love passing between the two of them.

"My whole life is about to change," Mars said.

"Mine, too," Darian responded.

THE END

ABOUT THE AUTHOR

Cynthia Diane Thornton is the author of *Larger Than Lyfe* and *Rise of the Phoenix: Larger Than Lyfe II*. She divides her time between Los Angeles, CA and Memphis, TN. Cynthia is working on her third novel. Visit the author on Facebook.

RISE
of the
PHOENIX
LARGER than LYFE II

BY CYNTHIA DIANE THORNTON
AVAILABLE FROM STREBOR BOOKS

-1-

"Darian, baby, come on…wake up," Mars coaxed, gently stroking Darian's hair as he sat beside her hospital bed.

Claudio Henriqué, Darian's plastic surgeon, assured Mars that she would be fine. He and his staff had kept her under close observation since completion of the surgery. She would be extremely groggy from the anesthesia, but she was expected to make a full and relatively speedy recovery.

Keshari Mitchell, now "Darian Boudreaux," had been through a total of twelve very high-risk plastic surgeries in a massive physical transformation required for her to fully assume her new identity. A team of surgeons, over the span of a year and half, employed some of the most controversial, state-of-the-art medical techniques on the planet to deliver a clean slate to the former, internationally known record label mogul. She was now...physically... a completely different person. She'd undergone four levels of skin bleaching, taking her complexion from a deep cinnamon brown to a light honey color. A team of oral surgeons dramatically altered her dental profile by breaking and resetting her upper and lower jaws and implementing dental implants so that neither dental x-rays nor impressions would ever reveal the woman she used to be. Surgical contouring made slight but noticeable changes to Keshari's almond-shaped eyes and the rest of her distinctive facial features. Chocolate brown contacts concealed her natural, hazel-green eye color. An extremely risky surgical tweaking of her vocal cords changed her voice. Painful laser surgery permanently altered her fingerprints. Her trademark raven hair was professionally colored to a vibrant auburn hue that beautifully complemented her new skin tone. Keshari Mitchell ceased to exist, and Darian Boudreaux was born.

From the day Keshari Mitchell and David Weisberg, her longtime attorney and friend, sat down together and privately constructed, step-by-step, the intricate scheme to fake Keshari's demise, David had formed dummy corporations, a wealthy familial background, an inheritance fund, and a sizeable investment portfolio to legitimize both Darian Boudreaux and her more than $100 million net worth. It had taken years to pull it all together, but REAL gangsters always had a strong exit strategy...just in case.

-2-

Misha Tierney stared down at the seven-carat, flawless, radiant-cut, white diamond engagement ring with its matching platinum wedding band that Marcus Means had had custom-designed for her. The rings filled her with seething rage. She had no idea what had broken in her head to have caused her to wear them for as long as she had. She was clearly becoming as crazy as that motherfucker who called himself her husband. She took the rings off and hurled them across the dimly lit bedroom. They landed behind the tufted, cream-colored sectional, and she heard the clink as they hit the high-gloss bamboo floor. She truly hated that man. Today was officially their second wedding anniversary, and she would rather be dead than have to endure a third. The day before, Marcus had lovingly showed her that he had remembered their "anniversary" by having vases of premium, long-stemmed, white roses placed on every flat surface of the bedroom that Misha kept herself locked away in like a fortress. In every other room of the house that Misha walked through, there were more vases of the white roses to delight her eyes and nose. The gesture looked and felt to Misha as suffocating as a mausoleum. She quickly began organizing her affairs and making phone calls so that she could make a hasty departure from the house. She knew that if she stayed around for very much longer, Marcus would soon arrive with some other very expensive celebratory gesture for their second year of marriage, and Misha wanted to be nowhere around when he came. It was ridiculous that he even made the effort. There was no mistake whatsoever that she despised him.

Forced into a marriage to a man who made Satan appear to have some redeeming qualities, Misha Tierney's life had become a living hell. Marcus Means, her new husband, was in Larger Than Lyfe Entertainment's books, coercing her into paying The Consortium 10 points every month from Larger Than Lyfe's revenues. Marcus had even been peering into Misha's events planning firm, demanding to have his people take a look at the numbers there. Marcus and his people were following and watching Misha's every single move every day and she knew it. She also knew why. They were strategically surrounding her to make absolutely certain that no operatives of federal law enforcement came sniffing within fifty feet of her for information. They were also looking for someone, and they firmly believed that Misha knew exactly where this someone was; so they followed her, believing that, ultimately, she would slip and their target's hiding place would be revealed. Then they would eliminate this person who they had been looking for, and they would likely eliminate Misha too because she would have expended all of her usefulness.

Worst of all, Misha had been coerced out of her own home and was forced to live in the home that had previously belonged to her long-estranged biological brother, Richard Tresvant, founder and now-deceased head of The Consortium, one of the most powerful, Black organized crime rings on the West Coast and in the United States. Prior to his death, the blood had been extremely bad between Misha and Richard Tresvant for longer than she was interested in remembering and for reasons that were fairly obvious. Misha had changed her last name to ensure that no connection was ever made between her and her older gangster brother and now she was forced to suffer as a resident in the house where he'd once lived and run an extremely large criminal enterprise...with Marcus Means, no less. She was doing all of this, she believed, to protect someone she truly loved, but the cost for that protection required her to almost completely sacrifice herself, and she didn't know how much longer she was going to have the strength to do it.

Marcus Means, wealthy Los Angeles real estate investor, developer, entrepreneur, and all of the other formal, corporate-sounding business titles that he gave himself as a cover for all of the nefarious activities that he was really involved in, was America's newest nightmare, far worse, Misha believed, than her brother Richard Tresvant had ever been. Marcus Means didn't give a fuck about anything nor anyone that did not, in some way, benefit his own agenda. He took Gordon Gekko's mantra from the movie *Wall Street* and applied it on a whole different level of calculated ruthlessness to organized crime and cocaine. "GREED IS GOOD," he said with a smooth smile. "Greed is very, very good." And Misha Tierney had the grave misfortune of being married to the man for reasons, overall, in his grand scheme of psychotic plans that had yet to be revealed.

Los Angeles had no idea what they were in for in the coming months with Marcus Means. He was a whole different kind of monster, and everybody in the city had something to fear where he was concerned.